DIPLOMATIC SECRETS

She lay limply on her back, deep in her sensual daze and breathing softly through her open mouth, while Marcel put his hands between her knees and moved her legs apart on the bed. 'Lisette, *je t'adore*,' she heard him murmur while he unfastened her belt and opened her frock wide from neck to hem. His fingers traced delicately round the berry-hard tips of her breasts, then down across her belly with languourous anticipation, until they were gliding over the thin silk of her briefs, and then they rested directly above her secret place. She gasped when a fingertip pressed gently between her petals through the silk . . .

DIPLOMATIC SECRETS

Antoine Lelouche

A NEXUS BOOK
published by
the Paperback Division of
W H Allen & Co plc

A Nexus Book
Published in 1990
by the Paperback Division of
W. H. Allen & Co Plc
Unit 26, Grand Union Centre,
338 Ladbroke Grove,
London W10 5AH

Typeset by Medcalf Type Ltd, Bicester, Oxon

Printed and bound in Great Britain by
Cox & Wyman Ltd, Reading

ISBN 0 352 32748 0

Contents

Author's note 6
1 Business and Pleasure, Both Doubtful 7
2 The Endearing Elegance of Female Friendship 23
3 An Exchange of Favours is Negotiated 41
4 Salutations in the Market-Place 58
5 Sow the Wind and Reap the Whirlwind 77
6 The Worst is Yet to Come 95
7 Life, Liberty and the Pursuit of Happiness 111
8 Fortunate the Man who Knows the Countryside 128
9 Odd Figures Glimpsed Swimming, as Virgil Said 145
10 A Feast of Nectared Sweets 162
11 Confession is Often Good for the Soul 179
12 A Double Pleasure to Cheat the Cheat 197
13 Several Good Tunes Played on Old Fiddles 215
14 Appetite Grows by Feeding, Said Rabelais 233

The author makes no apology

In spite of careful anonymity, the first volume of the intimate memoirs of Marcel Lamont caused a loud outcry from those who thought they recognised their own disreputable activities. The only response to such people is mockery and disdain – and a strong determination to continue the account of my years in the Diplomatic Corps.

My desire to do so is not inspired by an intention to reveal any great secrets of State, for I never knew any and never wanted to. It is simply that my adventures abroad were unusual and amusing, and therefore worth telling for their own sake.

It has been objected that these events of thirty years ago show important persons, French and foreign, engaged not only in amorous intrigue but also in arrangements that might be described perhaps as discreditable, or even criminal. To that accusation I reply that I relate what I saw and recorded in my diary. It is for others to interpret these curious events – I make no judgments.

As in my first volume, *Diplomatic Pleasures*, these memoirs are presented as fiction in order to protect the reputation of certain ladies from whom I retain a warm affection.

Antoine Lelouche,
Paris 1989.

1

Business and Pleasure, Both Doubtful

In 1958, during Marcel Lamont's second year in the service of France at the Embassy in Santa Sabina, a lady who was a cousin of the Ambassador's wife visited the island as part of a world tour she and her daughter were making. The much-travelled Madame Coty was a widow who evidently was well provided-for, a light brunette of striking appearance, in her early forties, and very fashionably dressed. Naturally, from Marcel's point of view, Madame's twenty year old daughter Lisette was far more interesting.

Lisette Coty was small in stature; the top of her pretty head hardly rose higher than Marcel's shoulder. She smiled much of the time, making elegant little gestures with her hands, the left one weighed down with the largest diamond Marcel had ever seen. She talked incessantly, an inconsequential and humorous chatter that bubbled along with all the vivacity of a refreshing little stream. Her hair was the silvery blonde hair more often seen in Normandy than elsewhere in France and her eyes were a pale blue.

In short, Lisette was an agreeable sight to a man whose contact with women of his own country and culture was limited to a few Embassy wives. But there was more to it than that; the truth was that Lisette's most impressively appealing charms were her breasts. They were tantalisingly large, high-set and pointed; greatly in contrast with her otherwise young-girl figure. These bounties of Nature seemed to be only lightly restrained under her thin frock, so that they bobbed up and down in the most charming manner with every step she took.

It was a matter of considerable disappointment to Marcel

that Lisette's fiancé was travelling with mother and daughter on their tour of the entire world. His name was Olivier de Murville and, unless his appearance was deceptive, he was at least ten years older than Lisette. That made him several years older than Marcel. To look at, he was a thick-set and muscular man, with black hair cut very short and straight, much like a soldier's or a convict's. His eyes were grey and cold and he had too much hair on the backs of his hands. His manner was one which Marcel found excessively self-assured.

The occasion of Marcel's first meeting with Lisette, her fiancé and her mother was a formal one – lunch at the Embassy to welcome the travellers. When he received his invitation he assumed that it was to be a large function if it included him. He was, after all, on uneasy terms with the Ambassador, whose assessment of Marcel's value to France's diplomatic service was not at all flattering. For somewhat different reasons he was on ambiguous terms with the Ambassador's wife, whose assessment of his ability in another field of activity was too flattering.

To his surprise he found only six assembled for a glass of champagne before lunch – His Excellency and Madame Ducour, Madame Coty and her charming daughter, the bumptious fiancé and himself. At once he guessed that the occasion was more than merely social and he began to speculate a little on the reasons why he had been asked.

While the visitors were admiring the exotically gaudy blooms in the Embassy gardens from the shade of the verandah, Marcel made himself pleasant to Lisette. In the overbearing heat of Santa Sabina European women wore as little as was consistent with style and decency. Lisette was in an expensive little creation that hinted at safaris and tropical adventure, a short and sleeveless linen frock of pale lime-green. It was buttoned through from neck-line to hem, had pockets with flaps and, most attractively, was belted closely about her waist, to throw her oversized breasts into even greater prominence.

While he was talking to Lisette, Marcel glanced as often and as unobtrusively as he could at the long row of green

buttons that pleaded to be opened, one by one. Evidently, he reasoned, she must wearing some sort of brassiere, or the tips of her breasts would be pressed against the frock and show through the fine linen. But that said, whatever she wore by no means confined her treasures at all tightly. He found the thought so appealing that it became necessary to put his hand into his trouser pocket and rearrange matters more comfortably. 'Have you been stationed in Santa Sabina for long, Monsieur Lamont?' she enquired, turning the delicious gaze of her sky-blue eyes full at him.

'Almost two years,' he replied, breathing in deeply and silently to savour the expensive perfume she was wearing.

'And do you like it here?'

'I ask myself that question frequently,' he said with a charming smile, 'and it is extraordinarily difficult to find a satisfactory answer. To be rational, I am compelled to say yes and no and perhaps, all at the same time.'

She laughed, her breasts shaking gently inside her pale green frock, and asked him to explain this mystery to her.

'There are decisive reasons against being here,' he began, 'of which the most obvious is that nothing of significance has ever happened here or ever will. Santa Sabina is as lost in the onward march of history as a sailing-ship becalmed in the weed-banks of the Sargasso Sea. In short, this is where the careers of talented and promising young diplomats die.'

'I see. And you were one of the talented, of course,' she said with a grin and a little jig of her breasts that set his heart fluttering. 'But why, then, were you sent here?'

'It is a complicated story,' he answered evasively, 'and has much to do with malice and the envy of my superiors.'

What it really had to do with was the anger of a politician of importance who had returned to his Paris home one afternoon and found his elegant wife in bed with Marcel. By using his influence this ill-natured person had contrived to get Marcel posted overseas to the least well-regarded of all France's Embassies.

'So your objection to being here is that nothing happens to further your career prospects,' said Lisette. 'What then are the advantages to compensate for that?'

'The most obvious advantage of living here is exactly the same as the most obvious disadvantage – that nothing at all happens. This is Lotus-eating Land, where life is a sunlit dream of calm and pleasure. The Santa Sabinans eat and sleep and make love and sleep again – and we Europeans are soon seduced by the atmosphere into their manner of life.

'And are you content to exchange the uncertain glory that your career might have achieved for the tranquil pleasures of eating and sleeping and love-making?' and she grinned again.

'When I wake up at dawn, in the coolest moments of the day, and ask myself that question, I have to answer *Perhaps*. On some days that means *Yes perhaps* and on other days it means *No perhaps*. You understand the predicament, I am sure.'

'No doubt the shade of meaning depends on whose bed you wake in at dawn,' Lisette exclaimed with a little chuckle that set her bosom rolling again. 'To me your country sounds absolutely charming! I wish we could stay for six months or a year! But Olivier would never agree – he becomes restless very quickly.'

At lunch Marcel was pleased to find himself seated next to Lisette and able to glance frequently at her generous bosom without seeming too obvious. He hoped to profit by furthering his acquaintance with her. Her fiance was sitting across the table, on the other side of the Ambassador's wife, and Marcel had already come to an interesting conclusion.

In the course of their travels, the betrothed couple had spent some weeks in close daily proximity to each other, on board ships and in hotels. And naturally, de Murville would have passed a great many nights in Lisette's bed. To Marcel's expert eye the signs suggested that they were slightly bored with each other's company and would welcome a change. Of course, Lisette would be furiously indignant with anyone who suggested that she might be ready, given the right circumstances, to be unfaithful to her fiancé. But, if the circumstances could be arranged, Marcel believed that the

right man had a reasonable chance with her. And, without question, he was the right man.

'For how long are we to have the pleasure of your company here in Santa Sabina?' he asked, giving her his most charming and irresistible smile.

'There are no fixed plans,' she answered. 'It mainly depends on Olivier's business arrangements. We shall be here for two or three weeks, I suppose.'

'But what business could Monsieur de Murville possibly have here?' Marcel said in surprise, his eyebrows arching up his forehead. 'Imports here are severely restricted by a permanent shortage of hard currency. And that is brought about by the melancholy fact that Santa Sabina has nothing at all to sell to the world. Or to be precise, nothing that President da Cunha permits to be sold abroad.'

Lisette dabbed lightly with a lace-edged handkerchief at the open neck of her frock, where a gleam of perspiration showed on the delicate skin in the cleavage of her breasts. Marcel was so enchanted that he forgot what he was saying.

He had been about to inform her that, some years before, an expert survey had demonstrated the probability of a vast oil-field off the west coast of the island and massive deposits of gold and rare minerals, including uranium, in the Sierra Dorada mountains of the north. Until then no government in the world had thought it worth while to maintain any kind of diplomatic representation on so insignificant an island. But almost at the same time that the potential riches were revealed, it was also realised by the super-powers and nations aspiring to world influence that Santa Sabina was geographically ideally sited to be a base for long-range bombers, warships and submarines.

After that it was the most natural course of action imaginable for the French, the British, the West Germans, the Japanese, the USSR, the United States and others to set up full-scale diplomatic missions on the island, with generous offers of technical assistance, modern weapons, development loans, trade agreements, cultural exchanges and all the other manifold benefits of friendship.

But alas for friendship, the situation proved to be farcical

and there was nothing for the diplomats to do but entertain each other. President da Cunha was a traditionalist who wished to remain independent and keep his people untainted by the benefits of modern civilisation. He accepted whatever was offered free, rejected attempts to involve him in pacts and agreements, and kept his small nation completely unaligned.

Marcel's heart leaped wildly to see Lisette dab with her tiny handkerchief down inside her frock, between her breasts. There sprang into his exceptionally active imagination images of how, under her frock, her smooth and flat belly must also be gleaming with perspiration. And, of course, the insides of her slender thighs! How delightful it must be to have the rare privilege of laying bare Lisette's soft body and, very gently, drying her thighs and belly with that lace-edged handkerchief of hers! What lay concealed in Marcel's trousers raised its head in sudden interest.

Lisette said that she had no understanding of her fiance's business initiatives and that, if Marcel were interested, he must ask Olivier direct. Marcel took the hint and changed the subject at once.

'If you are still here in three weeks,' he said, 'you will see the Festival of St Sabina. It lasts for five days and it is one of the great events of the year. There are processions and bands playing in the streets, fancy dress parties and dancing, masked balls and a great deal too much to drink.'

But how fantastic – it sounds like the famous Carnival at Rio de Janeiro!'

'I have never been there,' said Marcel cautiously, 'but I imagine that the spirit is much the same. Though the Santa Sabinans interpret it in their own uninhibited way.'

The reality was, though he thought it unnecessary to explain it to a well brought-up young lady, even one with breasts as magnificent as Lisette Coty's, that the annual Festival of St Sabina began as a colourful celebration that had the sanction of Church and State, but soon turned into days and nights of riotous Saturnalia and at last declined into a non-stop orgy.

Mama!' Lisette said across the table to Madame Coty.

'Monsieur Lamont has been telling me about a Festival that will be held here in three weeks. We must stay for it.'

Her mother smiled and nodded without interrupting what she was saying to the Ambassador.

'She thinks we should stay,' Lisette told Marcel. 'But who was this St Sabina? I have never heard of her before.'

'The cathedral that the Portuguese built here is dedicated to her as St Sabina the Younger, Virgin Martyr,' he replied, 'and her history is instructive, though a little confused. She was an aristocratic young lady of sixteen or seventeen who lived in either the second or third century – there are no written records. Her place of birth is also uncertain. It might have been Pergamum or Ephesus, or perhaps Alexandria – there are alternative versions.'

'Virgin Martyr! I suspect that the entire story is no more than a romance,' Lisette protested with a smile, 'a tale made up by long-forgotten priests to persuade girls that virginity was the only path to the salvation of their souls.'

'You must hear the rest of her story before you judge,' said Marcel. 'Sabina refused one day to offer incense to the statues of the gods in the local temple and this was a serious criminal offence. But because her father was extremely rich and important, she was not tortured and executed out of hand. The Roman governor despatched seventy-seven of the most learned teachers, writers, and philosophers in the province to explain to her why she was wrong and to change her opinions by rational argument and discussion.'

'But to be lectured by that many professors is in itself a of torture!' said Lisette. 'And perhaps even fatal – an execution in which the victim is bored to death.'

'By no means. Sabina was so beautiful that within three days she was able to seduce all seventy-seven of those sent to teach her, even the most ascetic of the philosophers. And to make love with her was so divine that all were persuaded instantly of the truth of the Christian faith.'

'She did it seventy-seven times in three days!' Lisette exclaimed, her pale blue eyes opening wide at the thought. 'How can such exertion be sustained by so young a girl?'

'There is more yet,' Marcel said with a smile. 'In due

course the pedagogues and philosophers reported back to the Roman governor. They were so transported by the memory of the delights they had enjoyed that they committed the stupidity of informing him that Sabina was right and that the worship of idols was nonsensical. He, of course, being a politician, had no particular interest in matters of right and wrong, only in protecting his own career. He had them all executed and sent for Sabina to threaten her.'

'And did she seduce him too?'

'Alas, the legend relates that he was attracted to boys, not girls, and remained therefore untouched by her charms. Since she refused to recant, he had her beheaded in the market-place. After this tragic event her father claimed her body for burial in the family vault and the women who laid her out for the funeral were astounded to find that a miracle had taken place. As a mark of Divine approval of Sabina's sacrifice of her chastity for the sake of her faith, the good God had restored her virginity.'

'A clever trick, that,' Lisette commented, 'to have seventy-seven lovers and remain a virgin. Many a woman today would like to know the secret of it.'

'Sabina was chosen to be patron saint of this island not because she died a martyr,' said Marcel, 'but because of her marvellously inexhaustible capacity for love. The people here hold her in high esteem for that and pray to her constantly.'

To catch the attention of her fiance, who was listening with his head tilted to one side to something Madame Ducour was telling him, Lisette called 'Olivier!' He smiled at her across the table. Monsieur Lamont has been telling me a most amusing history of the local saint,' she said 'Her Festival will be celebrated in three weeks – can we stay for it?'

'It might be interesting, perhaps, in a provincial sort of way,' he answered with a shrug.

She took that to mean that he had agreed they should stay and began to ask Marcel about the island and its people and their customs. Marcel gave a brief history, beginning with the Arab slavers in the Middle Ages, his gaze discreetly on

her breasts, jiggling each time she raised her arms to eat or drink the Ambassador's excellent Chablis.

Marcel continued his history lesson with the Portuguese conquest and colonisation, which brought Santa Sabina within the ambit of European civilisation. The Genoese also made their contribution by establishing a trading-post and refit station for their ships. He had the pleasure of seeing Lisette smile and nod her head with such approval that her treasures bounced under her thin green frock. To still the throbbing in his underwear Marcel slid a hand secretly under his table napkin and pressed his stiffness against his belly.

'And for this reason many of the people of Santa Sabina have Portuguese names?' Lisette asked.

'That is so, Mademoiselle,' he replied, 'though they enjoy the good fortune of speaking the French language, as you will discover during your stay here.'

'But how is that possible?' and she half-turned on her chair to face him as she asked the question.

With his eyes fixed in a stare of admiration on her swaying prominences he recounted the annexation of the island by France soon after the beginning of the eighteenth century and then the establishment of an independent Republic in the nineteenth century.

'Of course,' he continued, 'some remnants of an older language are still to be found, though it is not so much a true language as a dialect – it consists of words and expressions from Arabic and African languages, mingled with Portuguese and whatever primitive tongue the original inhabitants of the island spoke a thousand or more years ago. But I am sure that you, Mademoiselle, will not hear any of this.'

'And why not ?'

'Because,' he replied, lowering his voice in a confidential way, 'the expressions that have survived in everyday usage are, in fact, the intimate vocabulary of love-making.'

'Oh, how appropriate! It would be interesting to hear more of this tradition, if the opportunity serves.'

Before Marcel could take advantage of what he took to be a half-offer, the Ambassador's wife tapped his left

shoulder to gain his attention and he had no choice but to turn his appreciative gaze away from the bounteous delights of Lisette Coty's bosom. He smiled with polite familiarity at Madame Ducour and she returned his smile briefly and carefully. For a moment her long and sensitive fingers with their red-painted nails and gold and diamond rings touched the back of his hand before she began to explain to him why he had been invited to lunch with the visitors.

Behind the exchange of smiles and the touch lay a wealth of significance and a secret. Shortly after his arrival on Santa Sabina, Jacqueline Ducour had seduced him into becoming her lover for a month or two. She was an experienced and skilful devourer of handsome young men and, even at fifty, still took infinite pains to remain attractive. The finger-tips which now brushed so very delicately over his hand had often enough in the past caressed his stiff and twitching part with a light and sure touch. She had spent many an afternoon in the hotel room where he lived, enticing him to let her make love to him in her own way.

In those days Marcel was exploring the exotic pleasures and the frustrating limitations of the olive-skinned and mop-headed girls of Santa Sabina. Jacqueline represented a link with Paris and the life he had enjoyed there, and for this reason he let her have her own way. She would remove her clothes, all except for fragile knickers of silk and lace, and lie on his bed, propped up on the pillows to display her slack but still attractive breasts and her slender thighs. 'Ah, *mon cheri*, kiss me, kiss me,' she would murmur, 'I can stay for only a few moments.'

Eventually she would murmur that he might remove her final little garment and say softly, 'Come to me, Marcel,' her knees drawn up and wide apart for him to kiss the thin pink lips between her thighs. Even at this point she would not relinquish her control. She would take his throbbing pride between her fingers and guide it slowly to the brown-curled slit she had exposed for him ' Show me how you love me – but very slowly,' she would sigh as he slid into her. But her words were cruel joke at his expense, for by then she had excited him so skilfully that the act of sliding into

her was enough to bring on his climax at once and he would writhe helplessly on her warm belly while his passion squirted into her.

Their strange meetings had ended when Marcel began to assert his masculinity by taking her forcefully, instead of permitting her to use him for her languid pleasures. The liaison was now long past, and Jacqueline had amused herself with many other handsome young men in the meantime, but she still retained a proprietorial attitude towards Marcel which sometimes seemed to him to be not unlike jealousy.

'She is charming, this little Lisette?' Jacqueline murmured confidentially. 'You are unable to resist staring at her bosom, I see. You must stop this at once or her fiancé will become angry with you. Monsieur de Murville is a very distinguished man and must not be annoyed. You understand me?'

Under cover of the table-cloth Jacqueline's hand found its way into Marcel's lap and rested lightly for a moment on the bulge in his trousers.

'As I thought,' she said with a dismissive shrug of her shoulders. 'you find her exciting as well as charming. Remember where you are, Marcel, and moderate this ridiculous display.'

'How well you know me, Madame,' he answered pointedly.

'All too well, I fear,' she said with a grimace. 'It is fortunate that Mademoiselle Coty will be well chaperoned during her stay here by either her fiancé or her mother. That being so, I feel that I can entrust you with the task of showing them the pleasures our little island has to offer – the restaurants, the dances – all the things young people enjoy.'

'Certainly, if you wish it. But why me?'

'You are the most suitable member of the Embassy, because of your youth. It would be absurd to ask dried-up fifty-year olds like Monsieur Bonamy or Monsieur Lafargue to take our visitors to the local night-clubs, even if they knew where they are to be found. And besides, it amuses me to

compel you to suffer a little. When you observe Lisette dancing in the arms of her fiancé your deplorably active imagination will torment you. You will picture his hands on those much too large breasts of hers, and envy him bitterly. You will imagine him kissing her breasts – ah, what pangs of excruciating jealousy that will cause you! I wish I could be there to see your face!'

'You are cruel,' Marcel murmured.

'You were cruel to me,' she retaliated. 'I adored you, but you deliberately spoiled a most beautiful and romantic love-affair by attempting to dominate me. I have not forgiven you, Marcel. Now it is your turn to suffer.'

After lunch the Ambassador asked Marcel to join him for a business discussion with Monsieur de Murville, while Madame Coty and her daughter returned to their hotel to rest through the heat of the afternoon. The three men sat in the spacious office of the Ambassador, a servant bringing them little glasses of excellent cognac to assist their deliberations.

'I am sure you are aware,' the Ambassador began, addressing himself to Marcel, 'that Monsieur de Murville is a person of importance in the financial and commercial affairs of our nation. He has a particular project in mind for Santa Sabina. It will bring distinct advantages to the local people, and great prestige to France for assisting an under-developed country.'

Marcel had never heard of de Murville before and, in consequence, had no awareness of his distinguished position in life. To look at the man, he thought, studying the heavy jaw and the white silk suit, he might easily be a big-time pimp in the tourist industry of Montmartre.

'It goes without saying, Monsieur, that we shall all do our utmost to be of assistance to you during your stay,' he said politely to de Murville, 'but as to my own part in this, I must admit to being a little bewildered. I regret to say that I have no knowledge of commerce or finance. Monsieur Lafargue is our commercial attache Have you spoken to him?'

'He's no use to me,' Olivier de Murville answered briskly,

'he's asleep on his feet. But you might be useful. I understand from my sources that you have plenty of unofficial contacts with the locals. That's what I need.'

'I don't understand,' said Marcel, shaking his dark head in apprehension of what he might be involved in. 'What is this business project of yours?'

De Murville's cold grey eyes fixed him with a hard stare, as if assessing his level of intelligence.

'It is one you will approve of,' he replied, 'I propose to offer the Santa Sabinan government a fleet of new buses. What do you think of that?'

It struck Marcel as an extremely good idea. The so-called buses that rattled and groaned round Santa Sabina were in fact used army trucks bought cheaply from abroad at the end of the war. They had tarpaulin tops and were open at the back, with wooden steps for passengers to climb in and out. Inside, a slatted wooden bench ran along each side and passenger's belongings were stowed in what space was left between the rows of opposed knees.

'An excellent plan, Monsieur,' said Marcel. 'I am sure that the Santa Sabina government will be extremely grateful to you and to France for so magnificent a gift.'

'Gift?' de Murville exclaimed, 'I said nothing about gifts! I intend to be paid for what I deliver.'

'Ah, I see,' said Marcel thoughtfully. 'Your business is the manufacture of buses and you have come here to obtain an order for them.'

'I am not a manufacturer of buses or anything else,' said de Murville firmly. 'I make arrangements for others to supply whatever is wanted. Do you understand?'

'I assume that you charge a percentage of the price for your expert services,' said Marcel, not liking what he heard.

'Of course. Do you suppose I work for nothing?'

'Well, in that case there are problems to be confronted, Monsieur. The first is a shortage of hard currency. But if you are very persuasive, the President may permit the Minister of Transport and Maritime Affairs to purchase a bus or two from you, if they are not too expensive.'

'A bus or two!' said de Murville in derision. 'I intend to

sell them a fleet of a hundred. Nothing less is worth my time and trouble.'

Marcel looked enquiringly at the Ambassador for a lead in this nonsensical conversation. Jean-Jacques Ducour averted his eyes and glanced at his watch.

'But Monsieur, there are no more than about fifty buses on the whole of Santa Sabina at present,' Marcel objected. 'There is no possible use for a hundred.'

The Ambassador distanced himself from whatever he suspected was in de Murville's mind by announcing that he was expecting an important telephone call from the Belgian Ambassador. He suggested that Marcel take their honoured guest to his own office and continue the discussion there.

As soon as they were on their own, de Murville gave Marcel a smile that was as false as it was hearty and proposed that they should leave the Embassy and go to some quiet place where they could talk over a drink.

'By all means,' Marcel agreed. 'There are some matters that are better discussed away from official surroundings.'

'I see that you understand me perfectly, Marcel. May I call you that? I'm sure you know a pleasant bar somewhere.'

Marcel took him to the Gran'Caffe Camille, which by local standards was regarded as fashionable. It was situated opposite the church of the Four Crowned Martyrs and its terrace took up almost half of the cobbled square. In the heat of mid-afternoon the only Santa Sabinan in sight was a waiter dozing on his feet with his back against the café wall. There were three European women sipping iced mint-tea and two Japanese men at another table drinking grotesquely expensive imported Coca-Cola. Marcel roused the waiter by clapping his hands together and ordered cognac and water for de Murville and himself.

'Before leaving Paris I cleared things with the Santa Sabina Embassy,' said Olivier. 'When the authorities here make enquiries they will be informed that I represent very important financial interests. Protocol requires that I make a formal call at the Ministry of Transport tomorrow, accompanied by your useless commercial attaché. From past experience, I have no doubt that I shall be introduced to

senior officials who have no power to make decisions. I am sure you understand that important affairs of business are not negotiated with subordinates, or at meetings where notes are taken.'

Marcel understood perfectly well that Olivier had paid the appropriate Santa Sabina representatives in Paris to speak well of him when asked and now wanted an opportunity to agree a suitable bribe with the Minister of Transports in person.

I can arrange for you to meet the Minister in circumstances as relaxed and agreeable as you could possibly wish,' he said, 'but I cannot involve myself in negotiations between you and him, for obvious reasons.'

'I have no intention of letting you be present,' Olivier said with almost insulting firmness. 'Arrange the meeting as soon as possible. I can be very generous, you will find, when all goes well.'

When they had finished their drinks Marcel offered to guide Olivier back to his hotel, and learned that the visitors were staying at the Grand Hotel Orient. To be sure, the choice was limited. Apart from the Orient, only the New Excelsior Palace and the Splendide-Ritz were thought suitable for important visitors, and all of them were fourth-rate. The Versailles Majestic had been a possible until the previous year, but an invasion of the upper floors by large and noisy fruit-bats, which neither dogs nor shot-guns had dislodged, had removed it from the list of tourist hotels.

'I have a room in the Grand Hotel Orient myself,' Marcel told Olivier. 'I find it more convenient to live there than to rent an apartment and have the trouble of servants to clean and cook for me.'

'But to live in a hotel must restrict you. Your social life, I mean,' Olivier said, gesturing tactfully.

Marcel shook his head and grinned.

'In this country there are no restrictions on any type of *social* activity,' he answered. 'Santa Sabinans, boys and girls, become interested in such matters at very early age. Between eight and eleven, it is said, though I have no direct knowledge of that. They *socialise* fully together from the

age of twelve onwards, and this I have confirmed from personal observation.'

'Really?' said Olivier in disbelief.

'Ah, you are sceptical, of course, exactly as I was myself when I came first to this island. But you will very soon find out for yourself that the women of Santa Sabina are remarkably obliging, married or unmarried. It is not an exaggeration to say that you have only to smile in passing at some of them to find yourself dragged into a doorway and your trousers round your ankles before you have time to as much as exchange names.'

'You forget that my fiancée is here with me' said Olivier, though the indignation in his tone was obviously a pretence.

'My apologies,' Marcel said casually. 'Naturally, there can be no question of unfaithfulness to the charming Mademoiselle Coty. It is unthinkable!'

'Naturally,' Olivier agreed. 'Though at the same time, it is well understood that a certain intellectual responsibility exists among men of influence like ourselves to achieve a sympathetic awareness of the culture of other nations. I am convinced that your guidance will be of very great value in these matters. And, it goes without saying, your discretion will be essential.'

'You may rely on me,' Marcel assured him.

As they strolled back to the hotel in San Feliz Square, the very obvious thought was in his mind that it should not prove too difficult to direct Olivier's attention towards a lengthy investigation of the pleasures of the local women. That would surely create for himself many opportunities to promote his own interests with the charmingly well-endowed Lisette, it being his ambition to get his hands on those superb breasts of hers at the earliest possible moment.

2

The Endearing Elegance of Female Friendship

An opportunity to make the closer acquaintance of Lisette Coty presented itself to Marcel much sooner than he had any right to hope or expect. After the somewhat disturbing talk with Olivier de Murville about his doubtful business plans for the passenger transport system of Santa Sabina, they returned together to the Grand Hotel Orient. De Murville suggested that they sat on the terrace and order more drinks, but Marcel wanted to hear no more that afternoon of the scheme to foist a hundred buses on to the government of Santa Sabina. He retired to his room in a thoughtful mood, stripped to his underwear and stretched himself out on his bed for a welcome hour of siesta.

There was hardly time to close his eyes before there came a discreet tap at his door. Thinking that it was the familiar chambermaid bringing clean towels or returning his laundry, he opened the door as he was and there, to his surprise stood Lisette. The expression on her pretty face was one of amusement as she gazed at his dark-haired chest and then down at the front of his grey and green striped under-shorts.

'Oh, a thousand apologies!' he exclaimed, dodging back into the room to reach for his silk dressing-gown.

By the time he had it on and the belt tied round his waist, Lisette was inside the room and had closed the door.

'It is I who must apologise for disturbing you,' she said with another little smile, 'but they told me at the reception desk that you live here. Did I wake you? I am so sorry.'

Marcel assured her that she was not disturbing him in the least. He offered her the only chair in his room, a straight-

backed and cane-seated affair of inferior local craftsmanship. Lisette glanced at it doubtfully and decided to sit more comfortably on the bed. Marcel decided to suspend judgment on where he should sit until Lisette clarified her motives just a little more. He stood against the long window opening on to his balcony, leaning gracefully against the frame.

'I came to ask your advice,' Lisette said, 'I hope I'm not being a nuisance.'

'Not in the least,' he assured her with a charming smile, 'I am entirely at your service. In what way can I assist you'

'It's the heat,' she said, her pale blue eyes staring at him with a gleam that could be interpreted as either interest or anticipation. 'Is it always as oppressive as today? All the windows are open but there is no breeze at all and the cold water in my bathroom is lukewarm. How does one survive?'

Indeed, her cheeks were flushed a delicate pink, but whether that was the effect of the climate or the sight of Marcel near-naked at the door, who can say?

'It will become a little cooler after sunset,' he said in an encouraging tone of voice. As casually as he could he seated himself beside her on the side of the bed. 'Not that you can see the sun today, of course,' he went on. 'The whole island is covered by thick white cloud for most of the year. But after night-fall the temperature falls to about 30%,which by our local standards is tolerable.'

'Olivier was mad to bring us here in the summer,' she said, 'we could have waited a few months.'

'But it would have made no difference,' Marcel explained. 'Santa Sabina is too near the equator to have summer and inter – it stays like this right through the year.'

'My God,' Lisette breathed, 'but it is totally exhausting. How do you find the energy to do anything at all?'

The specific aspect of human exertion she had in mind seen reasonably clear.

'You will make an interesting discovery within the next few days,' Marcel informed her. Far from being exhausting, the heat here stimulates the human organism to astonishing feats.'

'I find that impossible to believe,' she murmured .

'So did I when I first came here, but you will see that I am speaking no more than the truth. At present you feel the effect of Santa Sabina's climate as enervating. Lie down comfortably and rest a little while we talk. I am sure there are many other things you wish to ask me about.'

Lisette swung her legs up on the bed and stretched herself out. She had removed her silk stockings since returning to the hotel, Marcel noticed.

'What you told me at lunch about survivals of the old language was extremely interesting,' she said drowsily, her eye-lids drooping. 'At school I was good at languages. I did very well in Spanish and Italian.'

'The patois here has no resemblance to either,' Marcel informed her. 'It has a non-European base.'

'Even though this was a French colony and the Portuguese were here for so long before that? I am sure you must be mistaken. What, for example, is the word for making love'

'*Zeqq*,' he answered, pronouncing the word with the hard sibilant and guttural consonants of Santa Sabina.'A man *zeqqs* a woman here. Sometimes they say *zeqq-zeqq,* to indicate a very vigorous or a more than usually satisfactory encounter. The two things are much the same in an unsophisticated society.'

'*Zeqq*?' Lisette said slowly. 'An impossible expression!'

The afternoon heat came in through the wide open window in heavy waves that induced a total lethargy of the mind, an acquiescence in whatever required least effort and, at the same time, a fervour of the body to be appeased. As Marcel had long ago discovered, the air of Santa Sabna had an aphrodisiac effect. Europeans were astonished at first by the unending, shameless and uninhibited love-making of the locals, and then, not long afterwards, by their own constant, though much more secret activities.

As Lisette lay on his bed, her eyes closed and her pointed breasts rising and falling to the rhythm of her slow breathing, Marcel could with great ease guess at her feelings. Her mind was half-asleep and enjoying the fantasies of wish-fulfilment. Her mouth was a little open and she was sighing,

as if she felt an imaginary and loving hand caressing those superb breasts of hers. That he had guessed accurately was proved when he touched them through her clothes and she sighed in pleasure. She made no murmur of protest when her frock was unbuttoned and a real hand slipped inside.

'These are your *gublas*,' Marcel told her softly, freeing them from the transparent nylon brassiere that contained their plenitude.

A charming discovery awaited him. From past experience he had reason to know that, when large-breasted women lie down, their fleshy delights usually sag sideways towards their armpits, so losing their shapely fullness and spoiling the effect. But Lisette's were young enough and firm enough to remain proudly upright, pointing towards the bedroom ceiling. They were so beautiful that Marcel found himself blinking a tear or two of pure joy from his eyes

'My *gublas*,' she whispered, and her lips curved in a little smile, 'what a strange and primitive word!'

Her eyes remained closed while his fingers moved over their very warm flesh and touched the crimson buds as gently as a butterfly settling on a flower. She was mesmerised by the heat, drugged by the spice-laden air, so that it seemed the most natural thing in the world to lie on her back on the bed while gentle fingers and then a smooth wet tongue caressed her *gublas*. It was, after all, no more than an erotic reverie, a shadowy imagining that delighted the sleeping mind and vanished with the coming of morning; the sort of dream she had enjoyed many, many times.

'Say it again for me,' she whispered.

All her sensations were concentrated in her breasts as she thrust them upward towards Marcel leaning over her, their buds firm under his teasing fingers.

'Dear Lisette – your *gublas* are the most beautiful I have ever seen,' he responded, seeing no necessity to limit himself to strict truth in his desire to please her.

'Ah!' she sighed at the slow-rippling sensations of pleasure from his tender ministrations. The quality of her sigh indicated that she would surely reach a climax of delight before long, if he continued. Although she was not aware

of what she was doing, her bottom was squirming slowly against the bed cover and her legs had drifted a little apart. But Marcel was watching for these signs of her growing arousal before he went any further.

His hand moved lightly upwards under her pale green frock, along the warm bare flesh of her thigh. She sighed again,gently and appreciatively, when she felt him unbutton her frock to the waist-belt and reveal her underwear. In the climate of Santa Sabina it would be too much to say the uncovering brought any sensation of coolness, but there was a very slight lessening of the heat that enveloped her and for that she was grateful. Marcel's hands were very warm, of course, but he was caressing her with great sensitivity, to avoid causing her any feeling of oppression.

He had uncovered her to the waist, exposing her sun-golden thighs and the tiniest of ivory-white silk briefs. He paused to enjoy to the utmost these moments of exquisite anticipation, his finger tips resting lightly on her slender thigh without moving. Even with her eyes almost closed, Lisette was conscious of the fervent admiration in his long gaze and it aroused her further. She was ready and receptive, half sighing in tranquil eagerness for his touch, when he began to stroke her smooth bare belly in a slow and circular motion. A little moan of delight escaped her as he kissed her bellybutton.

She lay limply on her back, deep in her sensual daze and breathing softly through her open mouth, while Marcel put his hands between her knees and moved her legs apart on the bed. 'Lisette, *je t'adore*', she heard him murmur while he unfastened her belt and opened her frock wide from neck to hem. His fingers traced delicately round the berry-hard tips of her breasts, then down across her belly with languorous anticipation, until they were gliding over the thin silk of her briefs, and then they rested directly above her secret place. She gasped when a fingertip pressed gently between her petals through the silk.

'This is called your *kuft* in the patois of Santa Sabina,' he said, teaching her the word he had found most useful to him.

He hooked his fingers into the top of her briefs, to peel them down her thighs and strip her to her ultimate nakedness. My *kuft*, she thought sleepily, *'he's going to kiss me there!* There was a slow and wholly delightful throbbing deep in her belly that she knew would grow to delirious ecstasy the moment his wet tongue touched the pouting lips of her *kuft*.

Her legs slid apart on the bed,opening her thighs to him, her belly beginning to strain upwards to meet his kiss. And then, as she felt her underwear starting to glide down her legs, she woke from her reverie with a start and opened her eyes. She saw Marcel's handsome face poised over her, his dark brown eyes aglow with passion. With loud gasp of dismay, she clapped her legs together and sat up quickly.

'No, no!' she exclaimed. 'What am I doing here! I dreamed that I was with Olivier. This is impossible!'

And while Marcel was still numb with shock, she slid off the bed and stood to pull up her knickers and button her frock, her face blushing bright red with embarrassment. The stiffness in Marcel's underwear was pushing out the front of his dressing-gown in a far from polite manner, but he recovered his self-possession and gave her time to recover herself before resuming his advances.

'Between friends there can be no need for apologies,' he said, breathing deeply to calm himself. 'You see now what I mean by the effect of the climate here. We have to accept that we are not entirely in control of ourselves. And that being so, we cannot be held responsible for what may happen.'

'How fortunate that you warned me,' said Lisette, her blush faded from fiery red to pretty pink now that her underwear was readjusted and her frock smoothed down to cover her bare knees, 'for a while I felt as if I had been drugged. How atrociously you must suffer, living all the time in this climate.'

'But for the kindness of pretty women we poor men would live our lives in anguished frustration and quickly become insane,' he said, his smile as charming as he knew how to make it.

'I understand perfectly, Marcel, and I feel a warm sympathy for you,' she said, using his name for the first time.

He stood up so that she could see that his dressing-gown was bulging out below his waist. She glanced quickly down and then up at his face again.

'It would be so very simple for you to make me the happiest man in the whole of Santa Sabina,' he said, his voice vibrant with respectful desire for her unrivalled charms – that, at least, was what he intended it to sound like.

'What gives you the right to make demands of me in this way?' Lisette demanded, her cheeks still slightly flushed.

'Only you can give me that right,' he said, sounding very sincere. 'When you came to my room – that gave me some small reason to hope that you might take pity on me.'

When she glanced down, her attention caught by a slight movement of his hand, she gasped to see that he had drawn aside his dressing-gown and his distended shaft had escaped through the slit of his underpants and was pointing fiercely up at her.

'No, no,' she murmured under her breath, appearing to be fascinated by the sight of it.

'How can you be so unkind?' he asked softly, reaching out to put a hand on her waist.

He drew her towards him and, to his delight, she raised herself on tip-toe to kiss his cheek. He put his arms round her waist and held her to him, pressing his throbbing stiffness into the softness of her belly to make her aware of its strength.

'Oh Marcel!' she murmured, a note of sympathy in her voice, 'you must see that it is out of the question for one who is engaged to be married shortly to offer you the relief you need. I am sure you have women friends here to take care of you.'

Her eyelids drooped for a moment, encouraging him to slide his hands down her back until he had a firm grasp on the taut cheeks of her bottom. But his hopes were deceiving him; Lisette smiled up regretfully into his face and freed herself gently from his arms. 'You know it is impossible,'

she murmured, turning away from him. A moment later, she was gone.

His passions inflamed by her semi-acquiescence, it was out of the question for Marcel to swallow the disappointment and wait for his excitement to subside by itself. And, of course, there was no necessity to do so in so free-and-easy a place as Santa Sabina. And especially not in the Grand Hotel Orient. After five minutes, when he was compelled to conclude that Lisette would not return, he rang for the chamber-maid and asked her to convey to Mademoiselle Costa on the reception desk that he had a matter of urgency to discuss with her, if she could spare him a few moments of her time.

Concepcion Costa was the eldest of the eight children of the proprietor of the Grand Orient, a man whose marital problems were widely known and gossiped about freely. Blessed with an unbroken run of five daughters, most husbands would have accepted the verdict of Providence and fathered no more children. But Baltazar Costa's wife was determined to produce a son before her child-bearing days were over. She was a woman of character, and she was well fortified by traditional herbal potions, charms, amulets and folk-tale advice on the best position for love-making to conceive a male child.The upshot was that her sixth as indeed a boy.

After that, willy-nilly, Baltazar spent every afternoon in bed with his plump but very energetic wife, attempting to repeat the success. But the seventh, to his and his wife's chagrin, proved to be yet another girl. Undaunted, Madame Costa doubled her doses of herbal mixes, had her crucifixes, rosary, charms and amulets reblessed by her parish priest, went to the cathedral every day to light a candle before the statue of St Sabina, and consulted the nearest wise old village crone for any additional lore on the topic of conceiving sons.

Thus prepared, physically and spiritually, she kept Baltazar at his conjugal task until he had impregnated her again – with, as the passage of time triumphantly revealed, another boy. After that success, the exertions of the Costas continued daily and unabated. But two years had passed

with no result at all and the local betting was against another child being born, male or female.

Concepcion Costa was eighteen and a pleasant enough girl to look at. To Marcel's eye she resembled the majority of the city girls of Santa Sabina, her exoticism of appearance being the result of a passionate intermingling of races over ten or more centuries. She was broad-cheeked and dark-eyed, her skin a charming pale coffee colour, her mop of hair so dark as to be almost black, the Arab and the African as well as the Portuguese blood delightfully apparent in her. She had the obsessive attitude towards love-making of all the islanders, but working for long hours in her father's hotel limited her opportunities.

She and Marcel had been occasional lovers for about a year. It had begun almost by chance, though on her initiative rather than his, on an occasion when the infidelity of a woman he was half in love with had desolated him. Concepcion had offered him much needed consolation exactly at the right moment and in her enthusiastic embrace he had sought oblivion. After *zeqqing* her five times during an unforgettable afternoon and evening, he had forgotten about his broken heart.

After all, he told himself, shrugging his shoulders, it was foolish to pine over an unfaithful woman when the charms of so many other pretty women were at his disposal. After that useful debut, Concepcion would have come to his room every day, afternoon, evening or night, if he had allowed it. But he deliberately kept their friendship on as casual a level as was possible, not wishing to become too closely involved. She was, after all, her mother's daughter and Madame Costa's reputation for keeping her husband's nose to the grindstone, if one might put it thus, was formidable. For himself, Marcel had no intention of being compelled to devote his energies exclusively to one woman.

'You wish to see me, Monsieur Marcel?' she asked, smiling, when he let her into his room.

She was wearing a high-necked yellow blouse with a frilly ruffle down the front from throat to waist, and a plain grey skirt that fitted closely over her well-rounded hips. But for

the ruffle, Marcel knew, the buds of her breasts would have shown darkly through the thin cotton.

'My dear Concepcion,' he answered, 'I am so pleased you were able to spare a few minutes away from your duties on reception. You find me in a condition of desperation.'

With a dramatic flourish almost worthy of a leading tenor in a Grand Opera performance, he threw open his dressing-gown. He had taken off his striped underpants before her arrival and presented to her a view of the entire front of his body, from dark-curled chest down to the tuft of equally dark hair from which his dearest possession jutted strongly upwards. She was the second young woman to whom he had exposed the pride and joy of his manhood that afternoon; this time he hoped for a more positive reaction. And he got it.

Not hesitating for an instant, Concepcion sank to her knees on the polished wooden floor, wound her thin arms round his loins and took into her hot mouth his stiff *zimbriq*, as a man's part was known in the local patois.'Ah cherie' he murmured, his hands stroking her thick mane of black hair. Tremors of delight ran through his belly, growing so rapidly under the vigorous flickering of her wet tongue that his legs shook under him.

If only Lisette had been content to stay with him! With his eyes closed tightly, he pictured the French girl on her knees before him, ministering to his desires as exquisitely as dear Concepcion was dong. He blocked from his mind the awareness that the hair under his hands was so thick and strong as to be virtually coarse and pretended that it was fine silver-blonde hair. He could feel Concepcion's soft breasts pressed against his legs, and he made believe that they were the impressive beauties he had freed from Lisette's transparent brassiere. And very soon he realised that the moment of truth was almost upon him – and so, just in time, did Concepcion.

She pulled away from him and stood up, smiling and running her red tongue round her lips. Marcel discarded his dressing-gown and lay on the bed, staring eagerly at her while she unbuttoned her yellow blouse. To Santa Sabinans

underwear was unknown, except to the very rich. Off came the yellow blouse and he sighed in pleasure to see her bare breasts. At eighteen they were deliciously round and firm, the skin an attractive *cafe au lait* shade and their buds neither the pink or russet of European women, but a rich copper brown. She kicked off her shoes, dropped her skirt to the floor and stepped out of it.

'But how charming you are, my dear Concepcion,' Marcel told her,lost in admiration of her youthful body as was every time she stripped for him. Her belly was smooth and just slightly curved, its round button deep-set, but what never failed to hold his gaze and seize his imagination was the thick black fleece between her thighs, the curls so luxuriant that her *kuft* was completely hidden.

She smiled at his heart-felt compliment and got on to the bed with him. She lay on her side facing him, to let him feel her soft breasts and lick their firm little buds, her hand tugging impatiently at his stiff *zimbriq*. And all too soon for him, she whispered, 'Enough lie back now,' and twisted away from him. The sad truth was that, however often he had tried to introduce her to the refinements of love-making, like all Santa Sabinans she was convinced that foreplay was a pointless waste of time. She smiled at him once more as she smacked his bottom to make him turn on to his back.

A moment later she was perched over his loins, her knees up and wide apart, in true Santa Sabina style. In his enthusiastic exploration of local sexual customs, this had been the most surprising of Marcel's many interesting discoveries – that here it was the men who lay on their backs and the women who *zeqqed* them. Why this reversal of the usual European way was regarded as normal here, no one had been able to explain.

In fact, as he had learned, no one thought that there was anything to explain. The women he had asked after being *zeqqed* by them looked at him as if he were simple-minded and said that it had always been like that. Anything else, they implied, was evidently unnatural. The few men he knew well enough to ask shrugged and said it was better like that.

Not that Marcel had the least objection in the world to

this transposition of what he had grown up to believe was usual. Far from it; after the initial cultural shock had subsided, he concluded that the Santa Sabinan way had an indefinable appeal to something deep in his nature. He felt that there was a trace of highly exciting perversity about lying on his back to be *zeqqed* by a girl. There was a certain sensation of being used for her pleasure, a thrilling touch of masochism, almost an acknowledgment of being violated by her.

He watched in open-mouthed delight Concepcion's long fingers combing up through her thick black fleece to make a central parting and reveal the plump brown lips of her *kuft* And then, as she pulled them apart, he glimpsed its pink and moist interior. She held herself open with two fingers while she grasped his *zimbriq* and guided it where she wanted it to go. Then, with a deep breath, she lifted herself up a little and sank down again, pushing him hard and deep into her.

'Good, good, good,' she murmured, starting to ride briskly up and down on him.

It had been very soon after his arrival in Santa Sabina that Marcel had been led to the highly unsatisfactory conclusion that making love with its hot-blooded women was almost always disappointing. Their eagerness, which seemed to make the country a paradise for a sensual young man, had a very serious drawback. It caused them to race through the experience, as if the world was about to end. With few exceptions, when a Santa Sabina woman impaled herself on a *zimbriq* she was transformed, as if by some malign sorcery, in a throbbing machine that lacked a device for regulating the speed.

The natural outcome of such violent up and down bouncing was that the woman concerned and her partner reached their climax of pleasure in an astonishingly short time. At first Marcel had been unable to believe how very quickly what ought to have been a tender encounter could be consummated. On the one occasion he had, out of curiosity, kept count of the lunges of a pretty young married woman who was squatting above him, her love-making had

been so very frantic that her seventeenth stroke had drained his passion from him.

On previous occasions he had tried to persuade Concepcion to slow down. But not this time. Lisette's coquetry had lit a consuming blaze in him and he wanted it quenched, so that he could sleep a little and refresh himself in preparation for what might be a long outing that evening with the visitors. And how very efficient Concepcion was at putting out fires! She straddled his belly and rode him fast and hard, her pale brown gublas leaping joyously to the rhythm of her movements. Marcel cried out and jetted his rapture into her slippery *kuft*.

'Again, again!' she exhorted him in a shrill voice, then her head jerked backwards and she shook in a frenzy of release.

After that they lay in each other's arms, each enjoying the feel of their hot flesh pressed together. Marcel stroked the cheeks of Concepcion's bottom slowly, knowing she liked that, and she, with the tip of her tongue, licked gently at the skin of his neck.

'Concepcion my dear, what a delight you are,' he said lazily, 'a true friend upon whose good-nature I can always rely in times of difficulty.'

'For you I have a lot of good-nature, Monsieur Marcel,' she murmured, and wriggled her smooth bottom under his caressing hand. 'I would prefer it if you relied on it far more often.'

'Ah, if there were the time!' he answered with regret. 'But for those of us who serve our country in the Diplomatic Corps the working day never ends. During the day there are papers to be read in the office, reports to be written, meetings to attend. In the evening there are the functions – the cocktail parties and the dinners.'

'But there is time now,' said Concepcion with a chuckle, her fingers tickling his belly.

'Alas no, *cherie*. Important visitors have arrived from France and my Ambassador has instructed me to look after them. For the next week or two I fear that I shall have no time for myself at all.'

'Do you mean the new people who have arrived to stay in the hotel?' she asked.

'They are the ones. Monsieur de Murville has come for trade negotiations with your government. Madame and Mademoiselle Coty are enjoying a world tour in his company. This evening I am taking the three of them to dinner and afterwards perhaps they will want to dance.'

Then you must dance with the mother and flirt a little with her, while the gentleman occupies himself with the pretty daughter with the big *gublas*,' said Concepcion, grinning at the thought. 'It is your duty.'

'Alas, yes. Where in the hotel has your father put them?'

'Madame Coty and her daughter are sharing the Versailles Suite. Monsieur is in the large room next to it. Between them they brought so much luggage that it took poor Jorge an hour to carry it up to their rooms. They must be extremely rich.'

'Undoubtedly,' Marcel said absent-mindedly.

But he had already given a little thought to this matter and doubted if extremely rich people would bother to visit so out-of-the-way and unpromising a place as Santa Sabina. The tale of a world-tour was patently no more than a cover-story. The cruise-ships of the idle rich did not call at an island so totally lacking in natural beauty, interesting historical sites or colourful folk-customs. To arrive by sea the visitors had disembarked at Djbouti or Madagascar or perhaps even at Goa, to wait for a ship to bring them here.

'It is always prudent to know as much as possible about the people one has to do with,' he said, his fingers tracing gently down the deep crease between the cheeks of Concepcion's bottom.

'Ah,' she sighed in pleasure.

'You are my dear friend, Concepcion. I am sure you will keep me informed of anything unusual that occurs.'

She bent her mop-haired head to lick his flat nipples.

'What does *unusual* mean she enquired. 'Mademoiselle is in the room of her fiance at this moment and he is making love to her. But that can hardly be called unusual.'

'How do you know that?'

'Because I came past Monsieur's room to get here and when I put my ear to the door I could hear them panting and moaning.'

Evidently Lisette had been as aroused by having her breasts played with on Marcel's bed as he had been himself. And she had lost as little time as he had in getting her fires quenched. *But such an imbecility,* he thought, *I wanted to make love and she wanted to make love and here we lay on the bed together – but she ran away*! It was exasperating beyond belief to picture her spread naked on Olivier de Murville's bed, those superb breasts under his hairy-backed hands and her slender thighs spread for him to slither into her and take his pleasure.

With little conscious direction of what he was doing, Marcel let his hands roam in frustration over the soft cheeks of Concepcion's bottom. His thoughts were at once recalled to his actual situation, rather than the one he would have preferred, when he heard Concepcion's sigh of pleasure as his finger-tips found the tight little knot of muscle there between the cheeks.

In the super-heated climate of Santa Sabina, meteorological, cultural and moral, little boys and girls were playing the age-old game of *snakes and turtles* together at the age of six or seven at the latest – *I'll let you feel my snake if you let me feel your turtle.* By the time they were eleven the boys had made the exciting discovery that they could ejaculate and, from then on, they and the girls were *zeqqing* with more enthusiasm than skill, several times a day. In general the girls could conceive at twelve, but they chewed *qagga* leaves for the contraceptive qualities of the sap.

Concepcion Costa had ceased to be a virgin only a month or two past her twelfth birthday, Marcel knew, because she had satisfied his curiosity as liberally as she had his desires. But, of course, the infinity of times she had enjoyed the feel of fingers in her hairless little *kuft* in the years before that meant that the loss of virginity to a stiff *zimbriq* was no more than a technicality. Since then she had been insatiable, like all Santa Sabina females, who thought that five or six

times every day was normal and anything less indicated ill-health.

In fact, Marcel thought, struggling with calculations in his head while he enjoyed feeling Concepcion, the simple arithmetic proved that this charming eighteen year old with the soft round *gublás* and *cafe-au-lait* skin had already been *zeqqed* more times than the average woman would be during the course of her entire lifetime An astounding thought – one which brought into question, he considered, the basis and validity of centuries of Western sexual morality.

The realisation of the incredible extent of Concepcion's experience reawoke Marcel's interest. He pressed his fingers more closely into the warm crease of her bottom and tickled her until she squirmed against him. 'are you hard again?' she whispered, reaching down between their bodies. On ascertaining that he was satisfactorily so, she tried to sit up and squat over him. But Marcel grinned and threw his arms round her and rolled her over and flung himself across her. She giggled and squealed and struggled to break free, wanting to get him on his back so that she could zeqq him.

For some minutes they wrestled body to body, skin on skin, an encounter that was wildly exhilarating. Naturally, Marcel was the stronger of the two. Before long, he succeeded in turning Concepcion on to her back, her legs bent up and pinned by his left arm across the backs of her thighs, her knees up to her *gublas*, her bare round bottom and her hairy *kuft* exposed. This time his fingertips, not hers, made a parting through the luxuriant curls to reveal the fleshy lips they hid. They were wet and loosely open, and his joined fingers slid easily inside, into her slippery warmth, to find her engorged bud and caress it.

'I have you now, my black-furred kitten,' he said, a broad grin on his face. 'Before there is time to count to ten you will do it for me.'

'But not like this!' Concepcion exclaimed, her back arching with pleasure. 'Let me get up so that we can do it properly.'

'Now what possible meaning can *properly* have, in these circumstances?' Marcel asked with a chuckle, pressing down against the backs of her knees to hold her still while he

excited her secret bud with the ball of his thumb. 'The result will be the same for you, whether it is my thumb or my *zimbriq* that brings it about.'

'The other way is better!' she exclaimed, her voice shaky as her crucial moments came swiftly closer.

'The sensations you feel will be exactly the same,' he said, his fingers penetrating deep into her while his thumb moved in a fast rhythm. 'You are going to *zboca*, which is the entire purpose of what you and I do together.'

From where he half-sat, half-sprawled beside the up-ended girl, he could see her face, between her bare ankles. Her dark-brown, almost black, eyes were wide open, staring at him in an unfocused glare. Her mouth was open, showing her ivory-white teeth and her lolling tongue.

'Ah, ah, ah!' Concepcion shrilled as the promised delights overtook her.

Her bottom jerked up off the bed, ramming her wet *kuft* at Marcel's hand, forcing his fingers harder against her bud. He counted the number of her convulsions, amused by the ease with which he had vanquished her. After the fifth they weakened markedly, and after the seventh they stopped, to be followed by a nervous trembling of her legs. With a smile, he smacked her bottom very lightly and released her, so that she could stretch out her legs straight and lie sighing in the afterglow of her pleasure.

She recovered with astonishing rapidity, sat up, rolled him on to his back and straddled him without a word. Marcel stared in fascination down the length of his own body, at the thick bush of black curls between Concepcion's parted thighs. He found it almost impossible to believe that she could ever have been a young girl with a smooth and hairless slit.

'Now I have you where I want you,' she told him with a grin, 'but I shall not make you do it in my hand – that's foolish.'

How widely it opened, her thick-lipped and black-haired *kuft,* like a wet pink maw yawning lazily to take his twitching *zimbri* into its depths and swallow it down and squeeze it and suck at it until he was persuaded to reward its services by squirting his hot desire into it!

'Oh yes Concepcion he said when she lowered herself to drive him in her to the hilt.

'Yes,' she agreed, grinning down at him. 'Now I am going to *zeqq* you!' She slid her slippery *kuft* up and down his shaft with sudden energy. Her face was turned up towards the ceiling and her hands were grasping her own plump brown breasts. '*Yes*!' she repeated, her voice frantic 'do it for me!' Her *zeqqing* became so vigorous that Marcel had no choice but to comply with her request. A marvellous sensation deep in his belly informed him that his moment of crisis had arrived; he stabbed upwards into Concepcion's gripping *kuft* and spurted tumultuously.

Her folded knees dug hard into his ribs and her fast moaning signalled the coming of her own crisis. All through it she rode him in climactic frenzy, galloping flat-out and not sparing her mount. Drops of sweat ran down between her flopping breasts and across her belly, her black-haired head jerked up and down almost as if her neck were broken. Then at last her nervous energy ran out and she sagged forward, to lie on top of him, her breasts squashed against his perspiring chest.

3

An Exchange of Favours is Negotiated

Madame da Silva's well-known establishment on the Avenue of the Constitution was by no means the only house of pleasure in Santa Sabina, but all agreed that it was the best. Madame accepted only the prettiest and most good-natured of the girls who applied for employment and she stipulated that they must not be over the age of eighteen. After about two years in her service, she passed them on, for an appropriate fee, to other houses, where her training made them welcome for the remaining years of their professional career.

Naturally, with unrivalled standards of excellence, it went without saying that Maison da Silva was the most expensive in Santa Sabina. This had the effect of restricting its clientele to the well-to-do; land-owners who had inherited their wealth and the business entrepreneurs of the capital who had amassed their own. It was patronised by high-ranking members of the government and the civil service, who augmented their salaries by the acceptance of *douceurs* and bribes.

It was because persons of this level of influence were to be found taking their relaxation there that Madame da Silva's was in favour with the Diplomatic Corps. Because Olivier did not perfectly understand this, he raised irrelevant objections when Marcel informed him where he had arranged a meeting with the Minister of Transport and Maritime Affairs. It became necessary to explain that, in the sexual anarchy of Santa Sabina, no possible blame attached to visiting a house of pleasure. Where could be better to approach the delicate topic of cash for Ministerial

complicity than in the very place where money bought any kind of carnal favour a man could desire?

Reassured, Olivier accompanied him after dinner one evening to the big old house on the Avenue of the Constitution. No sooner were they inside the door than they were surrounded by half a dozen naked girls, chattering greetings and presenting soft breasts and bottoms to be fondled. Santa Sabinans insisted on seeing what they were paying for, Marcel explained to Olivier, and therefore uncompromising nakedness for the girls was the rule of the house. Olivier nodded his approval of the arrangement as two of the girls led them into the *salon* and settled them comfortably with a bottle of chilled champagne.

Olivier glanced carefully round the well-furnished room, where four men in white suits sat in discreet discussion about a low table. Their attention was seemingly undisturbed by the naked girl each had on his lap. And before he could convey his first impressions of the establishment to Marcel, there was a round bare bottom on his own lap and two arms round his neck to press his face gently between two soft breasts.

'The young lady who is honouring you by sitting on your lap is called Aretusa,' said Marcel, 'and this delightful creature on mine is Vitoria. There are about a dozen girls available.'

'Really' Olivier exclaimed, his enthusiasm apparent in his voice. 'Are they all as pretty as these two?'

Aretusa said *No* and Marcel said *But yes* at the same moment, they both laughed and Olivier's hands went roaming freely over Aretusa's light-brown skin, savouring its smoothness of texture, and paying particular attention to her bare breasts. Vitoria clasped one of Marcel's hands between her warm thighs and put her wet tongue into his ear.

'How charming they are!' Marcel said with a little sigh of pleasure, 'how skilled they are at making a man forget all about the inconveniences and annoyances of daily life.'

Olivier murmured his assent. No doubt he was remembering what he told Marcel when they first met, that for influential men like himself there was an intellectual

responsibility to achieve an understanding of other nations' culture. Certainly he was not about to let devotion to the fiancée waiting for him in the Grand Hotel Orient impede his progress towards this sympathetic grasp of the significant features of life in Santa Sabina. Aretusa had unbuttoned his jacket and her hand was down the front of his trousers.

Vitoria took Marcel's glass from his hand, dipped her fore-finger in the champagne and moistened the coffee-brown buds of her breasts with it.

'Come upstairs with me, Monsieur Marcel,' she suggested with an enchanting smile. 'You know very well that I am marvellous at *zeqqing*.'

'You are unsurpassed, *cherie*,' he agreed, 'but first there is a little matter of business to be attended to. Later on perhaps, we can together explore your delightful capacity for love-making.'

Olivier's face had turned pink and he was trembling at the attentions Aretusa was lavishing on the plaything she had discovered down inside his underwear.

'Aretusa, or Vitoria, or both together, are entirely at your service, it goes without saying,' Marcel informed him with a smile, 'but may I suggest that you postpone becoming more intimately acquainted with them until after your interview with the person we have come to meet.'

'Naturally,' said Olivier. 'Do you take me for a fool? At what time is he supposed to get here?'

He shrugged his thick-set shoulders in regret and with the utmost reluctance pulled Aretusa's hand out of his trousers.

'Most evenings he arrives about ten,' said Marcel. 'He chats to friends over a bottle or two of wine for an hour or so, then either chooses a girl to take upstairs or goes home to his wife, according to his mood. But this evening, because you are waiting for him, it will be his privilege to be late, as a little demonstration that he has the upper hand.'

'I understand. When I am the buyer I do the same to those who want to sell to me. But I am interested to hear you say that the Minister comes here most evenings. How do you reconcile that with what you told me the other day about the obliging nature of Santa Sabina women ? As I recall your

words, no more is needed than to smile at a woman in passing to be dragged into a doorway without the time even to exchange names. No such adventure has befallen me in the three days I have been in this city. Admit it, Marcel, it was all nonsense, what you said, a tale to impress a traveller.'

Aretusa was sitting up straight, her back arched, pushing the tip of a soft breast into Olivier's ear.

'The reason you have not yet sampled the local delights,' said Marcel, 'is soon explained. Whenever you leave the hotel you are accompanied by Mademoiselle Coty and her mother. Come for a stroll with me at about midday tomorrow and I promise you all the adventure you could wish for.'

'Agreed,' Olivier said at once and ran a hand over his short black hair. 'I expect you to prove your assertions.'

'As to why the Minister comes to Madame da Silva's in the evenings, so do most of the important men. Their interest is not in the girls, except casually. They use this place as an exclusive club for gentlemen. Over there, for example, the three men talking together – there were four when we came in, but one has gone upstairs with a girl. Do you know who they are – no, of course not. The completely bald one is the Minister of Finance, the one to his left wearing the blue-spotted bow-tie is the editor of the daily newspaper, and the third, the one with the bandit moustache, is the Governor of the National Bank of Santa Sabina.

'It was Teodora that Monsieur Sanches went up with,' Vitoria announced pleasantly. 'You like her a lot yourself, don't you, Monsieur Marcel – you *zeqq* her often when you are here.'

'Good God!' said Olivier in surprise, evidently impressed by the status of the men chuckling together over their drinks across the other side of the room. 'Then who is the one who went upstairs – an off-duty General in civilian clothes?'

'He is never off-duty,' Marcel answered with a smile, 'The man upstairs pleasuring himself with Teodora is Emilio Sanches, the head of the Bureau of Public Information.'

'And what is that, a government department, I suppose?'

'It is the name under which the secret police operate.'

'Secret police? But this is more of your nonsense! How can a torpid little provincial backwater like this require such an organisation?'

'It is better not to enquire too closely into the doings of the Bureau of Public Information, I assure you. Its reputation for ruthlessness terrifies most people.'

The stately entrance of Madame da Silva saved Marcel from further explanation. He rose to his feet, bowed and kissed her hand, before introducing Olivier de Murville to her. Madame was twice the age of her girls, a woman in her forties, and she alone wore clothes during working-hours, to signify her position. This evening she had chosen to wear dramatic black, a long evening gown of velvet cut low at the front, to display her long pale breasts almost in their entirety. If it had been cut only two centimetres lower, her buds would have been on show. The unsupported breasts inside her black gown were not her only long feature. She was long-faced, long-nosed, and had a thin mouth and thin black eyebrows that arched in permanent surprise. She was tall for a Santa Sabinan, and being without hips, bottom or *embonpoint*, her bosom was made to seem more prominent than its flattish shape warranted. And when the gown and her underwear came off, as Marcel knew from practical experience, she had a long thin-lipped slit between her long thin thighs.

With a flick of her beringed hand she dismissed Vitoria and Aretusa, seated her self between Marcel and Olivier and ordered the waiter to bring another bottle of champagne. In due course Olivier discovered, without surprise, that it had been charged to him.

'This is the first time you have visited me since I returned from my little vacation,' she said, her finger-tips touching Marcel's cheek for a moment, 'and you bring with you a friend straight from France – how very charming! What do you think of Santa Sabina, Monsieur de Murville?'

'I find it enchanting,' he said with total insincerity. 'But tell me – where did you go for your vacation, Madame?'

'I've been to Goa for a month,' she said.

They chatted for a while, Serafina da Silva probing for information about Olivier's background and business, while he deflected her questions by claiming to be a casual sightseer on a world-tour with his fiancée and her mother.

'Mademoiselle's mother accompanies you?' said Madame with a wry grin. 'Then that explains why you are here with my good friend Monsieur Marcel. Your fiancée is so closely chaperoned that you are unable to give full expression to your adoration for her. Am I right?'

'But of course,' Olivier lied with a straight face.

'It never fails to strike me as strange that foreigners are so different from us in this matter of love-making,' Madame da Silva said to him, refilling their glasses. 'You, Monsieur, I judge to be at least thirty years of age. Yet only now have you engaged yourself to marry. And here you are in my house, in search of pretty girls to play with, because your fiancée is not sufficiently available to you. This to me is most astonishing. If you were a Santa Sabinan, you would no longer have any interest in *zeqqing*.'

'And why is that, Madame?'

With her hand resting lightly on his thigh, she explained to Olivier that her compatriots entered upon the serious devotions of love at an early age, but the vigour of the youths was of correspondingly short duration. They were at their best at fifteen, she said, and of necessity were married before they were twenty, since by then they were so far past their peak that they were incapable of pleasuring a woman more than once a day. At twenty-five their powers had declined to the point where a great deal of stimulation was necessary to stiffen their resolve.

'And at thirty?' Olivier enquired in consternation.

'Finished,' she answered with a sad smile. 'Their poor wives refuse to have anything to do with them in bed, because it is too frustrating. And so they come here, once a week perhaps, to try to recapture some faint memories of their past pleasures.'

'But what of the wives whose husbands have become of no use to them? Are they doomed to frustration also, or do they turn to each other for consolation?'

'Of course not!' Madame da Silva exclaimed, amazed by the suggestion. 'They take young boys as lovers. A sixteen year old is easily enticed with presents and can *zeqq* a woman five or six times straight off.

'Ah, here is another of your good friends come to pay his respects,' said Marcel, gesturing towards the door.

Madame excused herself and went to greet the newcomer, who was being ushered into the salon by Vitoria and Aretusa, their arms through his and their naked *cafe-au-lait* bodies in pretty contrast with his steel-grey silk suit.

'That's him,' Marcel told Olivier. 'His Excellency Salvador Bonavista, Minister of Transport and Maritime Affairs.'

Olivier watched closely while the Minister disengaged himself gently from the two girls who were clinging to his arms and trying to get him to feel them between the legs. He patted their bottoms as a sign of dismissal and kissed Madame da Silva's hand. After an exchange of courtesies with her he glanced around, recognised Marcel and came across the room towards him. Marcel greeted him with elaborate politeness and introduced Olivier de Murville as the French financier of international repute he had the honour to mention to His Excellency when he called upon him the previous day.

The Minister bowed slightly to Olivier but did not offer his hand. When he condescended to sit down with them at the low bamboo table, the waiter appeared instantly at his elbow with a fresh bottle of champagne and clean glasses. In most other countries he would perhaps have been thought very young for a Ministerial post, this Salvador Bonavist. He was a man in his middle thirties, only a year or two older than Olivier. The handsome olive tint of his skin marked him out as a member of the so-called Hundred Families, the old land-owning and ruling élite of Santa Sabina.

He owed his office partly to his descent and wholly to his good fortune in being a nephew of the President. The politics of Santa Sabina were not always the simplest to explain to visitors from Europe, Marcel knew, and he had taken great care in his briefing of Olivier. Constitutionally,

Santa Sabina had been a Republic since achieving independence from France in the nineteenth century, being governed, on paper at least, by an elected President and an elected Chamber of Deputies.

The law required that these elections were held every seven years and punctiliously and democratically held – even women had been permitted to vote since 1952. But during the previous century and a half, it had been found expedient to introduce certain modifications into the way things were done. Only those who owned a minimum of one hundred hectares of land could qualify as candidates for election to the Chamber of Deputies. To buy or sell land it was necessary to obtain the permission of the President, a simple device that ensured the Chamber was constituted entirely of his supporters.

Since the law expressly forbade any kind of bar or discrimination on grounds of race, colour, religion, literacy, social class, occupation or financial standing, it followed that any citizen of the Republic over the age of thirty, women included, could stand as for election as President. The first President after Independence in 1815 had been the country's richest land-owner, Augusto da Cunha, and he had stamped his personality so forcefully on the office that every President since then had been a direct descendant of his, da Cunha sons following da Cunha fathers in unbroken succession. In effect, the office of President might be said to have become hereditary in the da Cunha family, which had been blessed through the years with ever-increasing wealth. No one could guess what might happen to a citizen bold enough, or even foolhardy enough – or perhaps insane enough – to run for election against a theoretically outgoing da Cunha President. The prospect never came up for discussion. But all knew that a stroke of misfortune would alight on the hapless person before polling day. Death in some unsightly form, for instance.

After a glass of champagne and a pleasant exchange of small talk with Salvador Bonavista, Olivier evidently thought he had the man's measure. His cold grey eyes stared briefly at Marcel and he reinforced his message with an almost imperceptible nod.

'If you will excuse me, Excellency,' said Marcel at once, 'I will leave you alone to discuss matters of mutual interest with Monsieur de Murville.'

'Certainly, my dear Lamont,' the Minister answered, 'but I hope that your intention is to amuse yourself with one of Madame da Silva's charming girls, not to leave.'

In truth, Marcel's intention was to return swiftly to the Grand Hotel Orient to find Lisette and make a second attempt to subvert her fidelity to her fiancé.

'But we shall not need him again,' said Olivier, scowling slightly. 'We are capable of reaching our own agreement. And surely, this concerns matters of State that should be kept very confidential.'

'Doubtless,' Bonavista agreed. 'But in case there arises a need for, how shall I say it, *conciliation*, between us, it would be most useful to have the services of a skilled diplomat like Monsieur Lamont at hand. Choose a pretty girl, my friend, and I will tell Madame to put her on my account.'

Marcel thanked him and left him to his negotiations with Olivier. To be asked to stay indefinitely displeased him. Not that Bonavista had any authority to command him, of course, but his instructions from the Ambassador were to do everything possible to help Olivier conclude a successful business deal. And to ignore a request from Bonavista was certain to annoy the man. All the same, Marcel had not the least intention of letting the Santa Sabinan think that his compliance could be bought for the price of a girl.

As he strolled across the room Vitoria rose to fling her arms round his waist and squeeze her bare breasts against him. Marcel smiled at her and disengaged himself courteously, asking where Madame could be found, as he had important matters to discuss with her. Vitoria pouted and informed him that she was in her office and it was impossible to disturb her. But seeing that Marcel would not be put off, she insisted on leading him there, though he knew the way perfectly well. On their short walk to the rear of the house she held his hand between hers and rubbed it against her curly-haired *kuft*.

Still trying to persuade him to accompany her upstairs, she even knocked on the office door for him. She was smiling to feel his fingers tickling her, and her warm palm slid firmly up and down the front of his thin trousers, in a final attempt to arouse his interest in her. It was only when he opened the door and entered, in response to a voice from inside, that she let him go.

The office was not a large room, but it was comfortably, if idiosyncratically furnished. An inlaid rosewood desk, with a green leather top and a dozen little drawers, stood against one wall. Near it were two matching chairs, made in a half-hearted imitation of a late eighteenth century style. In front of the tall window was a *chaise-longe* of indecipherable ancestry, upholstered in emerald green brocade. On the wall above the desk hung a crucifix of polished brass, long as a man's arm. On the opposite wall, what else but a nineteenth century oil painting of St Sabina herself? The artist had chosen to depict her moment of triumph as she displayed her unanswerable case to the seventy-seven philosophers. There they sat on tiered benches, old and young, good-looking, wrinkled, strong, grey-bearded, their attention caught by the saint. She was sideways on to the viewer of the painting, in the very act of letting her white robe slip to the marble floor, stripping herself naked to present her argument for the truth of her beliefs.

Madame da Silva was sitting on one of the chairs before the desk, a half-empty bottle and a well-filled glass to hand. She was studying a lengthy document and had put on tortoise-shell spectacles to read it, a sight Marcel had not seen before. And, to afford herself some little relief from the heat of the evening, she sat with her black velvet gown hoisted up on her slender thighs, and her knees well apart. She gave Marcel a look of enquiry as he made his way towards her, then instantly removed her spectacles and hid them away in one of the little drawers of her writing-desk.

'Are you very busy, Serafina? Do I interrupt?' he asked.

'I am never too occupied to talk to you, my dear friend,' she answered with a friendly smile. She gestured towards

the other chair and poured a drink for him. He raised his glass in salutation to her and restricted himself to no more than a small sip. She was drinking *araq*, a liquor distilled by the Santa Sabinans from the sugary sap of palm-trees. In those unused to the potion it quickly produced spectacular drunkenness and atrocious hangovers.

'You seem uneasy – is something wrong?' Serafina asked.

'No, no, it is merely my bad humour.'

Though vanity had caused her to hide her spectacles, it had not prompted her to adjust her evening-gown to cover her legs. From where he sat opposite her, Marcel had an unimpeded view of her thighs and the pale flesh above her black silk stockings.

'I hope that your vacation was enjoyable,' he said. 'Do you have many friends in Goa?'

'Oh yes, many. And some of my family are in business there.'

She caught the direction of his stare and parted her knees a little wider.

'I have something to show you,' she said with a little grin, 'something I brought back with me as a souvenir. I am sure you will be interested.'

She hooked two fingers in the oval *décolletage* of her gown and pulled it down just far enough to uncover the tip of her right breast. Marcel gasped, as well he might! The brown bud of Serafina's long and dangling breast had been pierced, as if it were an earlobe, and an ornamental ring inserted. It was a hoop of shiny gold, with a diameter of about three centimetres.

'But this is enchanting!' he said with a happy smile. 'And the other?'

She obliged him by pulling down the other side of her gown, to let him see that she was wearing a golden ring on each of her pale breasts. She even wiggled her shoulders to make the rings sway about for him. Marcel was so enraptured by her adornments that he rose from his chair to approach close enough to reach out and touch them gently.

'Then you approve of my little souvenirs?' Serafina asked, smiling up knowingly at his rapt expression.

'They are utterly charming!' he murmured.

'Ah, but that's not all,' she said. 'Go and sit over there on the *chaise-longe* and I will show you something else you've never seen before.'

The natural effect of her enticements was to stiffen his *zimbriq* so strongly that it was necessary to rearrange it in his underwear before he could in comfort take the few steps across to the *chaise-longe*. He threw off his jacket and tie in preparation for what he believed was about to happen, and waited in happy anticipation. Serafina pulled open a little drawer of her desk and took out something small which made a tinkling sound in her hand. She stood up to remove her long velvet frock, then walked slowly towards Marcel, still dressed all in black, though now only in her stockings and her silk and lace knickers.

With each step she took towards him a tinkling and melodious little chime reached his ears. He was struck wordless with delight to see that she had attached a tiny golden bell to each of her hoops. She stood close to him and bent forward to put her hands on his shoulders, her long pale breasts with their decorations hanging and swaying for him to reach up and feel. He sounded her chimes with hands that trembled with excitement, while she smiled and smiled to see his pleasure.

Before long he put his forefingers through her hoops and very gently pulled her down to sit beside him on the *chaise-lounge*. They sat half-facing each other while he played with her until she became so aroused that she took his face in her hands to pull his head down towards her bosom. He pressed his face between her soft and dangling playthings, but Serafina had other ideas and put first one and then the other breast into his mouth, to let him suck their buds. The unfamiliar taste of the gold thrilled him as her little bells rolled over his wet tongue.

Marcel's motives for wanting to make love to Serafina da Silva had always been mysterious, even to himself. That he had been more than half drunk the first time it occurred

explained nothing and to say that she excited him was no kind of answer. After all, he was not a prematurely exhausted Santa Sabinan. He was young, strong, good-looking, attractive to women and widely experienced. How was it possible that this woman of forty-something with her drooping breasts and thin thighs had the power to arouse him? Since his logical mind demanded an answer, he had decided that his motive for *zeqqing* her occasionally was that she was the repository of all the important political, economic, social and domestic secrets of Santa Sabina.

His chain of reasoning for this astonishing conclusion was that the influential clients of her establishment divulged whatever they knew to the girls, after they had been pleasured. The girls passed on the information to Serafina and this made her a most useful friend for a foreign diplomat. And what more convincing a way to persuade her that he was a true friend than to demonstrate that he preferred her to her girls by *zeqqing* her from time to time. The fact that she had never yet told him anything about the affairs of the Republic's government that he did not already know had not diminished his confidence in her value to him as a *contact*.

As to why Serafina welcomed his advances, he was in no doubt. She was Santa Sabinan born and bred and had therefore never refused a man or boy since she turned eleven, or thereabouts. And besides, after owning a successful house for fifteen years and working on her back for another ten before that, to have as interesting and attractive a man as Marcel show a sexual interest in her was immensely flattering to her female vanity. The question of payment for services rendered did not arise between them – they were *friends*. Or so Marcel told himself.

While he was deriving an intense pleasure from sucking her gold-ringed breasts, Serafina opened his trousers and pulled out his upright *zimbriq*. She stroked it with affection, making it shake and jump with eagerness. And then, with little cries of pleasure, she slipped the wet end of her right breast out of his mouth and stood up, her grasp on his fleshy handle tugging him to his feet with her. His undone trousers

slid down his legs to his ankles as they stood facing each other, very close together, she massaging his *zimbriq* briskly, while he brought his hand up between her legs to feel the smooth flesh of her thighs above the top of her silk stockings.

How she sighed and murmured and pecked at his lips with warm little kisses! With what ardent zeal she rubbed her soft breasts against his chest! Her dark brown eyes were staring at him with such hungry passion that it was as if she wanted to eat him whole! Marcel gasped in delight as his hand found its way up inside the lace-edged leg of her loose knickers. Feeling her confirmed what he already suspected; that Serafina improved upon nature by taming its wilder excesses. The fleece of black hair between her legs was clipped to within a centimetre of her smooth skin and trimmed back to an area his palm could cover.

His fingers were shaking slightly as he caressed her warm *kuft* with deft little strokes that soon opened it wide exposing her sensitive bud. In her excitement she climbed him as if he were a tree and she a vine, her arms round his neck to support herself while she stood on one foot and raised herself on tiptoe, her other leg twined round his waist.

Marcel swayed and sighed in delight. He felt under her bottom, inside her knickers, and between her legs, until he could slide two fingers into the long moist slit that her stance had drawn gaping wide. But she wanted the feel of more than his fingers and reached down to grip his *zimbriq* in fierce desire and guide its distended head up inside the leg of her loose knickers and into her slippery *kuft*.

'*Amasta na zeqq-zeqq*,' she murmured over and over again. The only word Marcel understood was the last one, but there could be not the least doubt in the world as to the meaning of her exclamation.

The position in which they found themselves could in no way be described as comfortable; in fact, it might even be thought to be slightly ridiculous, and certainly it was precarious, the trousers round Marcel's ankles hobbling him so effectively that he dare not take a step either forward or backward. But all such mundane objections notwith-

standing, his eyes were half-closed in pleasure and there was a broad smile on his face as he pushed upwards into her welcoming depths and began to *zeqq* her strongly.

Serafina leaned outwards from him, supported by his arms around her waist and his hands under the small of her back. Her belly was tight against his, but her breasts were free to bounce and jolt to his vigorous stabbing, so that her golden bells rang and chimed in the staccato music of love.

'Serafina, Serafina, *je t'adore*,' he gasped. She was babbling incoherently, her belly smacking against his in unison with the urgent rhythm of his thrusting. They clung together, only a few heart-beats away from the moment of release, and suddenly there was a discreet tapping at the office door.

'Madame,' a girl's voice called softly, 'are you there?'

Serafina was much too far gone to call back. She hung twitching in Marcel's arms, her eyes closed and her belly jerking. There were footsteps outside the door and man's voice could be heard, asking something of the girl, before the discreet tapping was repeated. Marcel remembered, through a daze of pleasure, that in the heat of their desire for each other, when he had sucked Serafina's gold-ringed breasts, they had not given themselves the trouble of locking the door. In another moment, he thought frantically, the door will be opened and one of Serafina's clients will see us like this! It would be a joke throughout the entire foreign Diplomatic Corps, not to mention Santa Sabina governmental circles – the young Frenchman caught with his trousers down, pleasuring the Madame of the house!

'Madame, are you there?' the girl called again, a little more loudly, and Marcel recognised Teodora's voice, 'Monsieur Sanches wishes to speak to you before he goes.'

Marcel stopped his hard and fast pumping into Serafina's slithery *kuft*. He pulled her closer to him and tried to stand motionless and also hold her absolutely still, to silence the telltale ringing of her little bells. But his outraged *zimbriq* refused to be brought to so cruel a standstill and of its own volition vibrated strongly in Serafina. And she too was out of control, jerking convulsively to the movement inside her.

She was moaning under her breath; in a second when her critical moment arrived, Marcel thought feverishly, she would surely scream and give the game away. Already her breathing was loud enough and harsh enough to be heard through the office door!

'Let me try,' the man said, and the discreet tapping gave way to the brisk rat-a-tat-tat of knuckles on wood and he asked loudly, 'Serafina, are you in there? It's me, Emilio.'

Serafina was staring glassily over her shoulder at the door, her eyes bulging and showing Marcel their gleaming whites. But even then, she was unable to prevent her hot belly rotating on Marcel's, her *kuft* massaging him like a clasping hand and threatening to precipitate his crisis in another instant.

'Come away, Monsieur,' Teodora's voice could be heard saying, and there was the sound of a throaty male chuckle, as if she were touching him up, 'Madame is not in the office.'

'Very well,' Sanches conceded. 'But if she is in there, she is doing something she doesn't want me to know about. I shall talk to her at some other time.'

Still locked together in their intimate embrace, Marcel and Serafina listened intently, hardly daring to breath. They heard footsteps retreating away from the door and Serafina heaved a long, shuddering sigh of relief. Unable to do any other, Marcel thrust fast and at once climactic sensations burst inside his belly with all the force of a grenade. He clamped his lower lip between his teeth to stop himself crying out in wild ecstasy while he gushed into Serafina. Her mouth opened wide, but she made no sound at all, flopping in his arms like a rag-doll to the throes of her passion. After the nerve-twisting delay in reaching this point, the spasms were long and intense for both of them. But eventually Serafina disengaged herself, and Marcel pulled up his trousers and sat down on the *chaise-longe* to rest the aching muscles of his back and legs. Serafina slipped her black velvet evening gown over her head and came to sit beside him, bringing two full glasses of *araq* from the bottle standing on her desk.

'A fortunate escape!' she said, raising her glass.

Marcel swallowed down half his ardent drink.

'To be truthful, my dear Serafina,' he said, 'the threat of discovery and element of danger made our little encounter even more exciting than usual. Don't you agree?'

'You are a strange one,' she replied. 'No one else would find Monsieur Sanches at the door amusing. But perhaps it is true what they say, that you are all mad, you foreigners.'

'Perhaps,' Marcel agreed readily.

Even while he said it, he put his hand into her low neckline and flipped out a long pale breast, to dangle in full view, so that he could admire the gold hoop through its dark bud. The sight was so inspiring, even after his recent exertions, that he emptied his glass and set it on the floor out of the way, to have both hands free.

'If you permit . . . , he murmured politely, groping up under the hem of her long frock. She sat smiling at him, her slender thighs offering no resistance, but parting to let his finger-tips reach the close-clipped curls between them. 'It was delightful, standing up,' he told her, pressing his middle finger delicately into her very wet *kuft*, 'but not precisely as either of us would have wished, I think.'

Serafina leaned forward to press her lips to his and breath into his mouth a long voluptuous sigh of appreciation of the pleasure of being felt.

'Then we shall do it again,' she said. 'This time I shall lock the door and we will lie on the *chaise-longe*.'

'Oh yes!' he said fervently, 'I want you to sit over me, so that I can listen to the music of your little bells.'

4

Salutations in the Market-place

After his meeting with Salvador Bonavista at Madame da Silva's, it was two days before Olivier reminded Marcel of his promise to show him proof of the obliging nature of Santa Sabina women. They set off together from the Grand Hotel Orient sometime after eleven in the morning, Olivier first explaining to Lisette that he was going with Marcel to the Ministry of Transport for further discussion, which might take the entire afternoon. It was possible that he might not return much before dinner, he told her, and Marcel nodded in support of the lie.

The two men strolled across San Feliz Square in the formidable heat, Olivier wearing a handsome Panama hat of the first quality to give his head more protection than that afforded by his brutally short black hair. And Marcel learned the reason why there had been a delay before Olivier accepted his offer to see the sights. On the conclusion of his talk with Bonavista, Olivier said, he had gone upstairs to celebrate. When Marcel enquired which of the girls he had taken, Olivier confessed that he had celebrated with three of them.

'Three girls straight after each other!' Marcel exclaimed, his voice tinged with admiration, 'my sincere congratulations, Olivier! I am not surprised that you gave yourself a day off after that to recover from your exertions. I myself have never taken more than two of Madame's charming girls upstairs in the course of an evening.'

'It was not one after the other – I had all three together,' said Olivier.

Marcel halted and stared in fascination at his companion.

'Three at the same time! What a fantastic thing to do. Do you prefer to make love in a group?'

'I've never done anything like it,' Olivier admitted, 'but it seemed to me that an opportunity was there for me that had never presented itself before. Throughout my business life I have been accustomed to making immediate decisions – it is the reason for my success. I ordered the three girls sitting round me after Bonavista left to accompany me upstairs.

'Extraordinary – my felicitations!' said Marcel. 'Which girls were they?'

Olivier shrugged his muscular shoulders. 'I didn't bother to ask their names,' he said. 'After all, I was paying them – it did not seem to me an occasion for formal introductions. One was the girl who sat on my lap when we first arrived there. I hadn't seen the others before.'

'How, if I may ask, did you arrange matters?' Marcel asked, his curiosity keenly aroused. 'Did you have them on their back on the bed, one after the other? Or did you choose the Santa Sabina way and lie on your back for them to mount you in turn – or were you more adventurous?'

'This local native custom of the man lying underneath seems to me effete and lacking in manly virtue,' Olivier replied. 'I hugged all three girls together in my arms and rolled them under me, my mouth and hands occupied with their breasts, until I felt myself entering a slit at random. When I had made full use of it, I pulled out and continued to roll around with the girls until I was ready again, whereupon another of them spread her legs for me. And then the third.'

'It sounds both unusual and enjoyable,' Marcel commented, by no means certain that it was either. 'In a word, what was the most exciting feature of the encounter?'

'The sheer amount of soft female flesh at my disposal,' said Olivier, a faint smile of reminiscence on his face, 'the quantity – all those mouths and breasts and bellies and slits being pushed at me! You cannot imagine how stimulating it was to make love to three different girls, instead of three times to the same girl.'

'You have made me determined to find out for myself,' said Marcel, letting his imagination roam freely. *But why restrict oneself to three*, he asked himself, *why not have five girls, or eight, or twelve, at the same time and explore the outer limits of one's desire*?

'The truth of the matter is,' Olivier continued with a smile of superiority, 'it was so stimulating that I'm sure I could have carried on with another three girls as well, except that I'd drunk so much cognac with Bonavista I fell asleep.'

'You are going to enjoy your visit to Santa Sabina,' Marcel promised him with an engaging smile. 'There are so many pretty women to be had for the asking that you can enjoy five or six different ones every day of the week – for just as long as your strength endures.'

'You need have no anxiety on that score,' Olivier retorted, 'Without being arrogant, I can assure you that my strength is greater than most men's.'

'Of course,' said Marcel in a conciliatory tone, 'and if, when you have enjoyed twenty or thirty of our local beauties, a certain mild lassitude makes itself felt, there is a herbal product the men of Santa Sabina make great use of to raise flagging spirits and reinforce natural vigour.'

'Really? And what is that?'

'They call it *datra* and it is made from the dried sap of a species of wild shrub. You can buy it at any apothecary in the form of yellowish pills. It contains natural alkaloids of some kind which have an aphrodisiac effect on the nervous system.'

'It sounds very interesting,' Olivier conceded. 'It surprises me that so useful an addition to the pharmacopoeia of the world is not being shipped to Europe. If it does what you say, it could be extremely profitable to import it. The demand in Paris alone would be tremendous. Have you tried it on yourself?'

'I've never yet had need to, but those who use it regularly claim that it gives rise almost immediately to a rock-hard stiffness that maintains itself through several encounters.'

'The difference between you and me is very obvious,' said Olivier, shaking his head at this evidence of Marcel's lack

of commercial acumen. 'You learn by chance of this aphrodisiac and you do nothing about it, not even test the claims made for it. But with my background in finance, I recognise the potential instantly. *Datra*, you said it's called? I shall buy some and try it out.'

Fifteen minutes easy stroll brought them to the market-place. It was one of the larger of the city squares, flanked on all four sides by old and ill-maintained tenement houses, with a long dried-up fountain and basin in the centre. Every day except Sunday, from eight in the morning until midday, faded awnings protected rows of ramshackle stalls. Here were heaped for sale the luxuriant fruits of the island; purple-fleshed figs, cucumbers as thick as a wrist, black olives, bright-skinned oranges, pumpkins the size of a mule's head, pistachio nuts and cashew nuts, melons of all shapes and sizes, from small yellow-skinned ones up to gigantic mottled green water-melons, blonde-fuzzed peaches so tender that to pick them up clumsily was to risk bruising them, palm-tree kernels, golden apricots, big oval lemons, hairy brown coconuts full of sweet milk, all the abundance of Santa Sabina.

And here too was to be found in profusion the other natural delights of Santa Sabina. They were everywhere, dark-haired and olive-skinned, round-bosomed and big-bottomed, young girls, adolescents, women of twenty and twenty-five. Some of them were behind the stalls in aprons, to sell their produce; most were walking about in front of the stalls, with shopping-bags of woven straw, looking for bargains. Olivier's eyes were starting from his head as Marcel led him slowly through the market, easing their way between the crowds of chattering women.

For a man who declared that his pleasure was in quantity, this was the nearest approach to Paradise on earth that he would ever be privileged to see. Everywhere Olivier looked there were women in colourful frocks of cotton thin enough to show that they were without underwear. His mouth hung open as he stared at women clad in emerald-green, vermilion, amethyst, tangerine, cornflower-blue that did

almost nothing to disguise smooth bellies, round thighs and plump breasts that rolled loosely as they walked.

'But this is astounding!' he murmured, clutching at Marcel's arm. 'Not one of them is wearing a brassiere! And I don't think that many are wearing knickers!'

'That is true,' said Marcel. 'Brassieres are unknown here and only the very rich women have learned the European custom of wearing knickers. The ordinary women of the island wear the thinnest and simplest of clothes and no underwear of any kind. There are several reasons for this.'

'Several reasons? What do you mean?'

'First, underwear costs money, and the average Santa Sabinan is poor,' said Marcel, counting off his reasons on his fingers. 'But what young woman ever let a lack of money stop her buying clothes? No, in my opinion, poverty is the least important reason. Second, and more convincing, these children of nature delight in showing off their beautiful bodies. Third, to go without knickers keeps them cool, while making the men hot. And fourth and last and best reason of all in my view, the absence of restraining knickers means that quick and casual love-making is not hindered in any way.'

'Ah, that again!' said Olivier, a certain scepticism in his voice. 'Well, now is the time to prove the truth of your claim that the women here are more than usually obliging.'

'But certainly,' Marcel replied at once. 'Stand here for a moment and watch. They were not the only men in the market-place, although it was notable that women outnumbered by at least ten to one the few men who were there. 'Over there to the right,' said Marcel, bending a finger in that direction, 'you see that open doorway – the fifth door from here.'

'Well, well!' Olivier breathed.

A little inside the open doorway a couple were standing close to each other, neither of them older than seventeen or eighteen. What had caught Marcel's eye was a swift movement by the girl as she flicked her mustard-yellow frock up to her waist. And what had caused Olivier's sigh was to see put her hand over her dark-haired *kuft* and rub it to

excite her friend. After a moment to the boy pushed her hand away and replaced it with his own. He moved even closer to her and though his body was hiding hers, it seemed very obvious to the two men watching that the girl's hands were in his trousers and she was feeling him with as much enthusiasm as he was feeling her.

But then, over his shoulder, she caught sight of Olivier's face turned towards her. Her face split in a grin of white teeth and she pulled her companion further inside the house, to escape being seen.

'And they're still so young!' said Olivier. 'How fortunate you or I would have thought ourselves if we had been able to persuade girls to collaborate as freely as that!'

'Let us walk slowly past the doorway,' Marcel suggested. 'A quick glance inside will be enough to confirm what we believe is taking place. But without disturbing the pretty pair.'

'Why do they not go somewhere private where there is no fear of interruption?' Olivier asked.

'Why should they waste time doing that? The Santa Sabinans *zeqq* each other so frequently that it is the most natural thing in the world for them to slip into a doorway or alley together for a few minutes and then go their separate ways. Look into any blind corner or concealed entrance round the market square and you will see the same activity taking place.'

They walked slowly past the house entrance in which they had seen the young couple. The door was two-thirds open and partly concealed the busy pair. The girl had her back to the wall, her frock round her waist and the boy stood between her legs and *zeqqed* her rapidly.

'They call this standing position the 'belly-to-belly,' said Marcel helpfully. 'As you know, it is more usual for the women to ride the men, a position they dignify with the name of 'mule-ride'. The upper partner, the woman, controls the mule, and the ride is deliberately wild and boisterous. From that, no doubt, it would be possible for sexologists, theologians, psychologists and other learned persons to formulate theories about the relations between

Olivier, delighted to think that he had found this tropical Utopia.

Marcel shrugged lightly and ignored the remark. There was a time, soon after his arrival on the island, when he had thought the same way. Longer acquaintance with the people had caused him to change his mind completely. 'Before we sample the charms on offer here today,' he said, 'I must explain that there are two methods employed for the 'belly-to-belly,' according to the temperament and mood of the participants. The women do not stand idly with their legs apart and leave all the work to the man, as perhaps would be the case if you were having a stand-up with a Frenchwoman under a tree in the Bois de Boulogne.'

'I am utterly without experience of these low-class delights you describe,' said Olivier with heavy sarcasm. 'Be so good as to inform me of the correct etiquette to be observed on an occasion of this type.'

'With pleasure. In one method the partners butt their loins at each other like two goats fighting. This is for those who prefer their pleasure to be short and sharp. The other method is somewhat slower; in this the partners hold each other round the waist and see-saw backwards and forwards together.'

'And how is it decided ?'

'The woman chooses, of course! Everything of importance is decided by the women here. Family concerns, politics, social affairs, finance, business, the arts, economics – everything! Even the government is run secretly by the President's sister.'

'That's nonsense!' said Olivier heartily. 'I was introduced to Madame da Souza by the Ambassador's wife yesterday at lunch. She is a charming and elegant woman, not a schemer or an *eminence grise*. She has invited us, Lisette and myself, to the Presidential palace for cocktails tomorrow.'

'As you wish,' said Marcel with indifference. He knew many things about Mariantonetta da Souza, none of which he had any intention of telling Olivier. 'What about the two delightful creatures haggling over the price of apricots on

that stall?' he asked, nodding towards them. 'Do they please you?'

'Why not?' said Olivier. His tone made it obvious that he was sceptical of Marcel's ability to make good his promise of instant availability. But he walked beside him until they stood next to the two women who were chattering to stall-keeper. 'Delightful' was perhaps too emphatic a word to describe them, but it was Marcel's custom to err on the side of optimism. 'Pleasant' was perhaps nearer the truth. They were a pair of young married women, cleanly dressed and in their mid-twenties, to judge by appearances. They had the characteristic Santa Sabina mop of dark hair and *cafe-au-lait* complexions. And, of greater significance to the male eye, both had good-sized bosoms swinging loosely inside their clothes.

No doubt Olivier expected that Marcel would raise his hat and introduce himself. That being so, he was startled enough to gasp aloud when, without a word said, Marcel put his hand on the bottom of the woman nearest him and thrust a couple of fingers into the deep crease between the cheeks. Her reaction was what Marcel had come to expect but which to Olivier was not yet familiar; she wriggled her bottom against the intruding fingers and smiled over her shoulder at whoever was responsible. And seeing a good-looking and well-dressed man, her smile grew broader. To Santa Sabinans all foreigners were rich.

'You are very pretty,' said Marcel, responding to her smile with his own most charming smile 'I would like to *zeqq* you.'

'Come on then,' she answered, 'I know where we can go. Does your friend want to go with Asuncion?'

The question was unnecessary and had already been answered. The approach to her friend had raised the hopes of Asuncion, and she had put her hand inside Olivier's trouser-pocket. A foolish grin spread over his heavy face, indicating that his expectations too were being raised. The woman whose soft bottom had been the point of attack led Marcel out of the market, his arm held firmly under hers. Her name was Luisa, she told him, hurrying along impatiently. In one of the narrow streets leading into the

market square there was a covered alley and, as they turned into it, Marcel glanced back to see that Olivier and the other woman were following.

The alley led to a courtyard entirely surrounded by tall tenement buildings. It seemed to be something of a dump for the discarded possessions of the inhabitants, for it was littered with several broken and empty cardboard boxes, two collapsed wickerwork chairs, a splintered wooden bedframe, a rusty old bicycle with only one wheel, and other less easily identifiable items of rubbish. The high buildings cut off the sun, so that even at midday the yard was in heavy shadow and not a place in which anyone would loiter without very good cause.

With one practised look Luisa assured herself that the courtyard was deserted and that there were no faces at windows around it. She tugged Marcel by the arm into a corner where a heavy door set back half a metre in the wall created a little niche. And he smiled in genuine amusement to see the speed with which she positioned herself up on the worn stone step, her back wedged for support in the corner made by door and wall. He was looking over his shoulder to see where Olivier had got to when he felt Luisa open his trousers with hasty fingers and grasp his *zimbriq* to pull him up on the step close to her.

'But it's soft!' she complained. 'You are useless!'

'Be patient for only a moment,' he answered, smiling at her, 'and all will be well.'

Standing with well-parted thighs, she lifted her pea-green frock to confirm what Marcel had been sure of since he first set eyes on her in the market – that she wore no underwear. He took hold of her by her bare hips while she rubbed the head of his *zimbriq* against the warm lips between her legs.

'Ah, that's better!' she said after a moment or two.

She held herself open with her other hand, just enough to guide his fast-stiffening shaft to her entrance and insert it a little way. She retained her tight grip and rubbed it up and down between the moist lips of her *kuft*. He sighed pleasurably, his hands clenching on the bare cheek of her bottom. Only when she was satisfied that he was iron-hard

did she tell him to push. He shuffled his feet inside hers, bent his knees and then straightened them again, completely penetrating her. After her earlier complaints, she had the grace to acknowledge that it was the longest and thickest she had ever felt inside her.

Perhaps what she said was true, more probably it was not, but that was of no importance. Her words flattered Marcel's male pride and made him eager to demonstrate what he could do with it. He rammed hard into her, well aware that was how the women of Santa Sabina liked to be *zeqqed*, and he felt her belly thumping back at him – *like goats butting heads*, as he had told Olivier. She was soon gripping his shoulders hard and moaning, her head rolling from side to side on her short neck, flicking her thick black hair against his face.

'Harder, harder' she gasped, her belly beating against him so frantically that, to keep from being pushed over, Marcel tightened his grip on her bottom until his fingers sank deep into the soft flesh.

The onset of her ecstasy was announced by a wailing cry that reverberated round the silent courtyard. It seemed that the sensations Luisa experienced at her moment of climax were so strong that she almost lost her senses; her legs trembled so violently that, without Marcel's hands under her bottom to take her weight, she would surely have sagged to the ground. The effect on Marcel of this tremendous response to his *zeqqing* was to make his own desire erupt instantly in hot throbs. Luisa gurgled and gasped and clung tightly to him, shuddering uncontrollably long after he had finished. When her tremors at last were concluded, she giggled and kissed his cheek.

With his clothes arranged decently again, Marcel turned to look for Olivier. He was immediately to the right of where the alley debouched into the courtyard, and only his back was visible. His trousers were round his ankles and it was obvious from the way his broad bottom rocked steadily back and forth that Asuncion was pressed between him and the stone wall and that he was still climbing the slope towards the summit of his pleasure. Marcel slipped an arm round Luisa's waist and they stood side by side in the doorway,

waiting patiently for the other couple to complete their endeavours.

'He is very slow, your friend,' Luisa observed, 'but he's over thirty, by the look of him, so that's to be expected.'

Marcel thought it his patriotic duty to defend a fellow Frenchman. 'It is true that he may be a little slower that you are used to with young boys, but I can assure you that his staying-power is prodigious.'

'Oh yes?' said Luisa, with a certain scepticism.

'Only the evening before last he *zeqqed* three girls, one after the other, within the space of half an hour.'

The half hour time limit was pure conjecture, of course, but it sounded impressive and it was for the honour of France.

'For a man of his age three times in a row isn't bad,' Luisa conceded, 'if it's true. Did you see him do it?'

Marcel was compelled to admit that he had not observed the feat himself, but insisted that Olivier was a man of his word, in whom every confidence could be placed. Luisa snorted in derision.

'In the affairs of love,' she said, 'no man in the world can be trusted to tell the truth. Lies and exaggerations and half-truths are what men deal in when they talk about going with women. You all pretend you can do more than you really can – and you boast to each other that you've done more than you are capable of. It is only the woman whose *kuft* was used at the time who knows the truth of the matter. Oh good, your friend's finished at last!'

Across the yard Olivier's bottom had stopped its thumping and in another moment or two he stooped to pull up his trousers. Luisa and Marcel strolled across towards them, arriving as Olivier stepped backwards to reveal Asuncion with her back limp against the wall, her eyes closed and her mouth wide open. Her red and white striped frock was still tucked up round her waist, exposing the bushy tuft of black hair between her parted thighs and trickles of perspiration down her belly.

'You've been *zeqqed* deep and hard, girl!' said Luisa with a grin. 'No mistake about that!'

Asuncion opened her eyes and straightened her back against the wall. She grinned at her friend and pulled the hem of her frock out of her belt and let it descend to cover her thighs. 'This man has a *zeqqing* machine in here,' she announced, tapping the front of Olivier's trousers. 'He goes on and on and on – it's incredible! I tell you, Luisa, he made me *zboca* four times before he finished! I've been *zeqqed* bow-legged!'

Marcel glanced at Olivier in mild surprise. Olivier's costly Panama hat had been pushed to the back of his head during his exertions, showing his brow wet with perspiration and the short black hair on the front of his head standing up like bristles.

'My congratulations,' said Marcel with a nod of his head to represent a bow. 'I've never heard a Santa Sabina woman compliment a man like that before.'

Luisa took her arm away from Marcel's waist and stared hard at Olivier, her brown eyes shining with a new interest.

'I hear from your friend that you're a man who likes to *zeqq* more than one girl,' she said to him. 'Why don't we go along to my house? It's not far away, we can walk there in ten minutes. All four of us, I mean. You can show me what you just did to my friend, while those two amuse each other.'

'Yes, let's do that,' Asuncion agreed, 'I want some more of him myself. I want to see if he can *zeqq* me into a faint.'

Olivier raised his eyebrows in an enquiring look at Marcel.

'It would give me infinite pleasure to accept your most kind invitation,' Marcel said to Luisa, 'but unfortunately I am expected in my office shortly. However, there is no reason to prevent my friend from accompanying you, if he wishes. I have every reason to believe that he is strong enough to give both of you every satisfaction.'

'Of course I am,' said Olivier, taking the bait. 'I shall be delighted to entertain you two and two more like you, if you have any other friends near where you live.'

'No, no more!' Asuncion said at once. 'Two of us are enough for you – you will see!'

And so it was arranged. Olivier set off happily down the

street, a pretty woman on each arm chattering away about the diverse pleasures in store for him when they reached Luisa's apartment. Marcel went in the other direction, ostensibly on his way to the French Embassy, but in reality to find a cab to take him to the Reserved Beach, where there was a good chance of finding Lisette.

The Reserved Beach was in the western outskirts of the city, well away from the harbour and docks. The proprietor, that is, the local entrepreneur who rented the strip of fine white sand from the city authorities, had chosen the grandiose name of Reserved Beach to give it an undeserved air of exclusivity. It was divided from the main road to Selvas by a long line of seaward-leaning palm-trees and a woven straw fence no more than a metre tall. Far from being exclusive, the beach was open to any and all who could afford to pay the modest entrance fee.

The patrons were entitled to disport themselves in the sea or lie and bake on the sand to their heart's content. They could have cold drinks and other refreshments brought to them by attentive beach-boys from a little hut thatched with palm-leaves. Inside it the proprietor dozed all day in a hammock and his wife prepared whatever the sun-bathers required. No Santa Sabinan would ever behave so eccentrically as to sit willingly in the sun, even though the sun rarely broke through the cloud cover and, in consequence, the Reserved Beach was used almost exclusively by the foreign Diplomatic Corps and their wives.

An unstated attraction of the Beach was the row of twenty changing huts that stood under the boundary palmtrees. In effect, these huts were little more than cubicles, without any roof and ramshackle in construction. Nevertheless, they were a major facility and, needless to say, the principal use to which they were put was not changing clothes. Bored wives passing their empty afternoons on the beach took note of whatever males were there and entered into casual conversation with them. If matters went well and stirrings of mutual attraction were felt, a withdrawal to the nearest changing hut made it possible for acquaintances to develop, in privacy, to a pleasant intimacy.

In this respect, Marcel often thought, there was but little difference between local women so easily picked up in the shops and streets and European or American women found on the beach. They all did it. But the Santa Sabinans were open about their casual adventures and the foreigners went to some lengths to pretend that nothing had happened. Indeed, some of the married women that Marcel had pleasured in the huts affected not to know him the next time they met and required him to introduce himself, as if he were a complete stranger.

The entrance to the Reserved Beach was through a wooden arch painted with its name in fading black letters. One of the proprietor's children squatted on the sand, a boy of nine or ten, a small metal cash-box with a slot in the top beside him. Marcel greeted him as an old friend and, before he paid to go in, prudently enquired whether the young lady with silver blonde hair was on the beach. The child asked if she was the one with the big *gublas* and when Marcel confirmed that was so, grinned and nodded. Marcel paid the small sum demanded and went through the arch, to stand just inside while he scanned the beach carefully from left to right.

There were perhaps thirty swimsuited people lying about or sitting on the sand, the majority of them women, and another ten or twelve splashing about in the sea. He spotted Lisette to his left, recognising her by the colour of her hair, for she was face-down on a raffia beachmat and her outstanding charms were thereby concealed. He sat down for a moment to remove his shoes and socks, to avoid getting the fine white sand in them, rolled his trousers half-way up to his knees, took off his tie and jacket and set off barefoot towards his quarry.

As he approached more closely to her, his heart started to beat faster. His reason told him that it must be a trick of the perspective, but Lisette appeared to be naked. He could see her flat shoulder-blades and all of her back – and the bare round cheeks of her bottom! But of course it was an illusion; when he was at last within a step or two of her he saw that she was wearing a poppy-red bikini. Whatever

contained her breasts was joined across her back by a mere string and the lower part of the bikini was so small that it left her cheeks bare, another string of material cutting up between them to join that about her slender waist.

He stood over her for some moments, revelling in the sight of her exposed flesh. Was she asleep, he wondered; dare he sit down quietly beside her and let his hand flit as lightly as a butterfly over those smooth cheeks? He called her name softly and she rolled over slowly and stared up at him through her white-framed sunglasses. The top half of her bikini consisted of two triangles of red nylon that gave only a minimum of cover to her pointed breasts and left very little to the imagination. He sat down beside her on the sand his knees up to accommodate the evidence of his fast-growing interest.

Her smile was welcoming, but her question was disappointing. 'The meeting at the Ministry is over already?' she asked. 'Is Olivier with you?'

'No, it is possible that the meeting may go on for most of the day,' he answered. 'But my presence was only a formality and after the preliminaries I was able to slip away and leave Olivier to it.'

Even if Marcel had not been staring with such admiration at her, she would have know what was in his mind, of course, for women always know that. Fortunately, her spectacular figure had brought her so much admiration, spoken and unspoken, since she was seventeen that she was no longer in the least embarrassed by men's desire. She chatted casually to Marcel and accepted a refreshing glass of iced mint tea when he suggested it. He used all his considerable charm to amuse and interest her and, after an hour or so, had brought matters to the point where Lisette agreed it would be pleasant to take a stroll along the beach.

It was a slow stroll, for Marcel paused to speak to his many acquaintances along the way and to introduce Lisette to them. In the main, they were women that he knew, and they regarded nearly-naked Lisette in her poppy-red bikini with expressive eyes. She responded to their greetings with an innocent charm that delighted Marcel, though she could

hardly fail to be aware that some of the smiles she received were wry, some knowing, some cynical, some jealous.

At the far end of the beach the dusty Selvas road came swinging in to pinch off the open sandy foreshore and run alongside the sea. The low fence followed the curve of the road almost to the water, and here they stood while Marcel pointed out the distant off-shore rocks that were used, according to local legend, as a dumping place for unwanted and sick slaves in the bad old days. Lisette expressed appropriate indignation at the inhumanity of man to man and, since they had walked almost half a kilometre along the sand and the day was hot and sultry she agreed that they rest for a while before starting back towards the safety of her beachmat.

They sat under the last of the palm trees, sheltered by the fence from the eyes of passers-by along the road and far enough away from the closest sunbathers on the beach not to be aware of them. Marcel put his arm round Lisette's golden-skinned bare waist and she turned her face towards him and let him kiss her. What began as a light embrace grew passionate after a time, and Marcel pulled her down until they lay facing each other on the sand. She resisted at first, protesting that they were in full view of everyone on the beach, but when she glanced over his shoulder she saw that an upturned rowing-boat a few metres away effectively concealed them.

At that, her tense body relaxed and, with a little sigh, she turned to lie more comfortably on her back, her legs together. Marcel's *zimbriq* twitched continuously and impetuously in his underwear at the sight of her superbly pointed breasts, so close to him and only half-covered by the thin nylon triangles of her bikini top. He sat up to slide his hands under her and, holding his breath in suppressed excitement, he unfastened the string below her shoulderblades. There was a little gleam in her pale blue eyes as she stared up at him; she was savouring the expression on his face as he bared her fleshy delights.

He stared at them for some time without moving, as if he were mesmerised by their sumptuous shape. He breathed

out, a long sigh of pleasure, and bent over her to kiss their red-brown tips. He lay down beside her again to play with them. Lisette murmured, 'We shouldn't be doing this,' but her voice was drowsy and content, just as it had been when she visited his room in the hotel and he felt her, the first day they met. 'But why, Marcel?' she asked softly.

He gave her the answer she wanted to hear: 'Because you are so very beautiful.'

His palm moved at last over the edge of her ribs and down to her belly, to circle round the shallow dimple of its button. He caressed her in the most soothing manner he could devise, but her submissiveness was starting to vanish now that his hands were at her waist-line. When his finger-tips reached the top edge of her bikini, she exclaimed, 'No, it's impossible!' and grabbed at his hands. She pulled them away from the threatened area and back up to her naked breasts.

'Do not think badly of me,' Marcel murmured, his mouth close enough to her ear for her to feel his warm breath inside it. 'You are so exceptionally beautiful that only to be near you overwhelms me completely.'

His half-apology sounded less than convincing to himself, but proved perfectly acceptable to Lisette. 'If you cannot control your emotions, then I must move further away from you,' she said, but her words were teasing, not to be taken seriously. It was obvious to Marcel that she greatly enjoyed having her breasts played with. He resumed his skilful stimulation of them and continued until she began to sigh loudly and her body was trembling. At this point, judging that her resistance would be diminished, he unzipped his trousers and guided her hand inside. She gasped when she touched his hard *zimbriq* and her hand closed round it. He was leaning half over her, using his tongue on her breasts, and her breathing was fast and ragged.

Though her hand in his underwear was clenched tightly about his *zimbriq*, it remained motionless, doing nothing to arouse his sensations further. But that was hardly necessary now – his self-willed stiffness was leaping in her hot grasp.

'Marcel!' she gasped, her thighs trembling. 'You must stop now before I do something I shall regret!'

He understood what that meant; his attentions to her breasts were bringing on her critical moments. If he quickly peeled off her bikini bottom and threw himself on her belly, perhaps her legs would open wide to let him plunge into her!

'Oh Marcel!' she exclaimed, more urgently. 'Don't force me to go too far!'

'Lisette, *je t'adore*,' he murmured evasively, rolling her buds expertly between his fingers.

'Oh my God, it's too late!' she wailed.

Though Marcel too was shaking with wild desire, he knew that if he forced her now it would be the first and only time – she would never forgive him for taking advantage of her exquisite moments of vulnerability. Not that she relied on his good sense or forbearance; while her body shook in climactic spasms, she rolled on to her side away from him, her thighs pressed tightly together, to protect her virtue.

'Too late!' she gasped out. 'I've done it!'

In turning away from him she had released her hold on his throbbing *zimbriq*, but not before it had been pulled out of his open trousers. Marcel gave voice to a long cry of dismay and squeezed himself against her, jabbing furiously against the smooth flesh of her bottom. Even through her ecstatic shaking Lisette was aware of what he was doing. 'Ah no, Marcel!' she moaned. 'I beg you!'

By then it was too late, of course. Marcel's desire came surging out in furious jets, wetting the bare cheek of her bottom up as far as her hip. He held her tightly to stop her getting away from him, listening in great satisfaction to her diminuendo whimper of 'Ah, ah, ah . . .'

5

Sow the Wind and Reap the Whirlwind

According to the experts in such matters, the mountains of the Sierra Dorada range across the north of Santa Sabina were responsible for the thick white cloud that hung so often over the island and made its climate oppressive beyond belief. But there were days when a breeze sprang up from the south and dispersed the clouds, letting the sun shine through. This was very much to the gratification of those who enjoyed lying unclothed on the Reserved Beach. But there were also other days when a hot wind blew fro the north-west, the *Suruq*, born in the sand-storms of Arabia Deserta.

The *Suruq* reached Santa Sabina with a ferocity undiminished by the thousands of miles of ocean it had crossed to arrive there. It cleared away the cloud in minutes and sent the temperature soaring to unbearable heights – never less than 40C, and it had been known to go to 50C on occasion. This relentless blast-furnace wind made almost everyone short-tempered and quarrelsome, provoked uncharacteristic violence, and drove some almost to the edge of madness.

For some inexplicable meteorological reason the *Suruq* always started just before dawn. Marcel, like everyone else in the city, was awakened in the half-light by the wind's rising moan. In exasperation he got out of bed to close the long windows to his balcony, though he knew the sound and heat could not be shut out. The next two days were going be uncomfortable in the extreme; and then, as suddenly as it came, the murderous *Suruq* would vanish.

It was impossible to take breakfast on the hotel terrace

that morning, of course. The strength of the wind would have stripped the table-cloth from the table, complete with coffee cup and plates, and sent the lot skittering across San Feliz Square. Nor was the walk to the Embassy the usual entertaining stroll, with smiles at pretty young women and polite regrets at having to decline their invitations. In fact, the journey was a struggle against the elements, head down and body leaning into the hot wind. And no sooner had Marcel arrived there, somewhat later than his usual time, than he was informed that Lafargue, the Commercial Attaché, was asking to see him. It was Mademoiselle Delacoste who brought the message and the little grimace with which she delivered it warned him that the discussion was not likely to be a friendly one. Marcel looked at her with raised eyebrows, hoping she could be tempted to say ore about Lafargue's state of mind, but she shook her head, even though she returned his smile.

Gabrielle Delacoste was a well-fleshed woman in her thirties; indeed, unkind persons might have called her decidedly plump. And plain, of course, for she was of a certain type. She wore her dark hair parted in the middle and pulled back to cover her ears. There was never a trace of make-up on her face, her finger nails were short and bereft of colour, her eyebrows thick and untrimmed. She wore no rings, no necklace; in fact, the only jewellery she ever displayed were small gold studs in her ear-lobes, and they were almost hidden by her hair.

The best that could be said for her clothes was that they were neat. Usually for work she wore a crisp white cotton blouse and a black skirt, dark stockings and well-polished flat-heeled shoes. In short, she presented the perfect picture of a woman who lived entirely for her job. Yet as Marcel had discovered one memorable day, she was not entirely impervious to the stronger emotions although, in her secret heart, she despised the pleasures that others sought so eagerly.

'It is the day of the *Suruq*, Mademoiselle Delacoste,' said Marcel, smiling at her again.

His smile was charming, of course, but it was much more

than that; it deliberately reminded her of a secret they shared. She lowered her eyes modestly and blushed a faint but pretty pink 'Monsieur Lamont!' she murmured, as if in reproof.

The gross discomfort of the *Suruq* had first brought them together. Because of her plumpness she felt the heat greatly. Her cotton blouse, ironed with loving care before she left her apartment that morning, was already limp and showed large dark patches under the arms. A wisp of hair had escaped from her coiffure and was plastered to her perspiring forehead.

'You look very hot,' Marcel said. 'You would find it helpful to bathe your wrists and dab cold water under your chin.'

'Monsieur Lamont!' she exclaimed once more.

The colour of her cheeks deepened, while her small pudgy hands fidgeted together.

It was almost a year ago, on a day like this, when the *Suruq* was making the office intolerable, that Marcel had gone for a walk in the Embassy grounds. He knew it was no cooler outside, but all the windows had been closed to keep out the wind and the office was stuffy enough to give him the beginnings of a headache. The trees in the Embassy garden were whipping about in the hot gale, and so he turned away from them and strolled along the blank side of the building, intending to go all the way round it and back inside.

One window was open on the ground floor, or partly open; an oblong glass that hinged upward and outward at eye-level. Through it came a refreshing sound of running water. In his mind Marcel tried to picture the floor plan of the Embassy, to identify what lay beyond the window, and not sure that he had got it right, he glanced casually in as he went past. And at once he stopped and looked again. It was a cloakroom, of course, that had been obvious from the frosted glass, and there at a wash-basin stood Mademoiselle Delacoste, stripped to the waist and splashing cold water on her breasts.

To spy on a woman at her private ablutions was

despicable, of course, but the sight was too enchanting to walk away from. Marcel pressed himself close to the wall while he studied the size and shape of Mademoiselle Delacoste's *gublas*. She had removed her white blouse and the brassiere which reason said she must wear to contain such weighty treasures and was sideways on to Marcel, bending forward so that they swung loosely over the wash-basin. With hands cupped together, she was taking cold water from the tap and splashing it over them.

There was something about her posture, perhaps the curved line of her broad back, or in the dark hair pulled back into a knot on the nape of her neck, that brought a faint smile of recognition to Marcel's lips, something that stirred a distant memory, a feeling almost of *deja-vu*. And then it came to him. It was a painting he had seen somewhere. Mademoiselle Delacoste was, unconsciously, recreating the model's pose – but who was the painter? Marcel thought furiously, while he studied her breasts with a connoisseur's eye.

He could recall several paintings in the Louvre by Degas, of women washing themselves. But on second thoughts, was the scene reminding him of Toulouse-Lautrec's pictures of whores washing in a brothel he visited in the Rue des Moulins? After a careful consideration of the question Marcel exclaimed aloud 'But of course, Edgar Degas!' The victory of memory brought disaster. Alerted by Marcel's voice, Mademoiselle Delacoste glanced over her shoulder and saw his face at the open window. She blushed dark red and reached for a towel to cover her breasts. 'Oh, excuse me, Mademoiselle,' said Marcel, trying to sound nonchalant, 'I had no idea anyone was there.'

But he was not to be let off lightly. The darkening of her face, he was to discover, was due to anger, not shyness, and she gave him in outspoken and wounding detail her opinion of men who peer through windows at undressed women and the steps that ought to be taken to discourage the from repeating the offence. He tried to calm her by claiming that she had wholly misunderstood a casual glance, and when that failed, he said it was impossible to continue the

discussion through a cloakroom window and a more private place was necessary.

With that she agreed, and by the time he returned to his desk, she was there and waiting for him, fully clothed and with her white blouse well-buttoned. Her anger had developed by then beyond the level of red-hot rage into a cold white malevolence of an intensity that alarmed him. She would accept none of his apologies, however often repeated. The sexual molestation of women by delinquents like him had been allowed to continue for far too long by a male-dominated society, she announced, and she, Gabrielle Marie-Madeleine Delacoste, intended to make a stand against it here and now. With sinking heart, Marcel recognised in her voice the authentic call to the barricades!

The best he could persuade her to agree to was to postpone any further official action until they had time to discuss very fully the disagreement between them. But she refused with scorn his invitation to have the discussion over dinner, declined to meet him at the Gran'Caffe Camille to settle matters over a glass of cognac . . . in short, there was nothing he could suggest that was acceptable to her. When he threw up his hands in a gesture of capitulation and asked her to select the place for their discussion, she instructed him, in a voice that reminded him of a blizzard blowing straight off a glacier, to be at her apartment at nine that evening.

He went armed with a thousand reasons why she should be gracious and accept his humble apology for his thoughtlessness in glancing through an open window. She did not offer him a chair; she stood facing him in her sitting-room, glaring at him stonily. The windows and shutters were closed to keep out the *Suruq* and the apartment was stifling. She had changed into a knee-length house-coat of pastel pink cotton for this ominous meeting. It was impossible to guess what she might be wearing under it, but her legs were bare.

Marcel asked himself, not for the first time, what strange processes went on in a woman's mind. How could Mademoiselle Delacoste's accusation of visual rape be reconciled with the opportunities presented by this casual

style of clothing? Or did she entertain the hope that he might put his hand up her skirt? That thought had not previously crossed his mind, but it merited serious consideration. What would be her reaction to a manual invasion of her privacy – would she sigh and dissolve into pleasure, or would she scream in noisy horror? Had she invited him to her apartment as part of a ruse to compromise him further?

Before he could begin the rigmarole of apology he planned, she held up a hand to silence him. She said that she had given a great deal of thought to the unfortunate occurrence of that afternoon, and to his explanation of it. She had reached the conclusion that his misbehaviour was that of a naughty child, not a deliberate act of harassment. While Marcel considered the implications of that, she astounded him by saying that he must be punished like a naughty child. Without knowing what she had in mind, he agreed at once. Anything was better than being reported for peeping through the ladies' cloakroom window.

She told him to remove his jacket, lean over the table and grip the far edge with both hands. Marcel was amused by her presumption and did as she said. In truth, his limitless sexual curiosity was aroused by the ambiguity of her proposals and he felt a keen pang of pleasure when her loins pressed against his bottom and her hands reached under his waist. She unbuckled his belt and pulled it right out of the trouser loops. By then his *zimbriq* was growing longer, and it jerked up hard when she unzipped his trousers.

It had all been make-believe, he concluded with a grin that she did not see. She had been playing an elaborate game, of which the object was to get him to make love to her – a woman he would not in the ordinary course of events consider appropriate for his advances. Being good-hearted, he let her continue, fairly sure that her serious demeanour and her severity of appearance ensured that there had been very few lovers in her life. Or perhaps it was the other way round; she made herself look drab in order to conceal her inability to attract men.

While these thoughts were running through his mind, she had pulled his trousers halfway down his thighs, followed

by his underpants. He guessed that she was staring at his pompoms and he began to tremble a little in delicious anticipation of what was to come. And then he gasped in pain as she laid into his bare bottom with his own belt. She told him to keep his hands on the table and hold still, for he was squirming under her lashing. How many times she struck him he did not know, but eventually she was satisfied and told him that he had learned a lesson she hoped he wouldn't forget in a hurry.

Marcel straightened up, rubbing his smarting bottom with both hands. Mademoiselle Delacoste told him to get down on his knees and kiss her feet as a token of humility. With a grin on his face he turned to face her, his stiff *zimbriq* jutting out impudently from under his shirt. She seemed not to notice it. In fact, the shamefaced way in which she ignored it was a naive insult that made him grin inwardly once more.

'It is better not to keep Monsieur Lafargue waiting today,' she said from across his desk, destroying his reminiscences. Marcel sighed and shrugged to indicate his lack of interest in anything the Commercial Attaché might have to say. But he put on his jacket on and went to knock on the door of Lafargue's office on the upper floor.

Henri Lafargue had been Commercial Attaché for twelve years and did not enjoy his job. A posting to Santa Sabina was, so to speak, the French Diplomatic Corps equivalent of service in the Foreign Legion. There was no chance of a transfer; the choice was to march or die! Marcel was young enough to retain some hope that there would come a day when he would be recalled and sent elsewhere, but for Lafargue the only release he could look for was his eventual retirement on pension.

At the lunch party where Marcel met the Cotys and Olivier de Murville, the Ambassador's wife had described poor Lafargue as a dried-up fifty-year old, and as a description of his appearance this was entirely correct. He was as thin as a stick, with a long wrinkled face and the remnants of sandy-coloured hair strewn in wisps about his narrow head. He sat behind his desk in a dark suit of old-fashioned pre-war cut, his spectacles pushed up his forehead, bad temper

evident in his stare, as Marcel entered his office and took a chair unbidden.

'Why am I not consulted on matters which concern the proper execution of my function as Commercial Attaché to this Embassy of the Republic of France?' Lafargue demanded in his most officious manner, a finger stabbing the air in the direction of Marcel's face.

'I take your question to be rhetorical, my dear colleague,' Marcel responded calmly. 'No doubt you intend to explain to me what lies behind it.'

'You may curb your insolence, young man,' Lafargue shot back at him. 'I am your senior and I insist on being treated with the respect due to me.'

The windows were tightly closed to keep out the hot wind. The temperature in Lafargue's office was intolerable. Marcel was sweating freely in his thin white suit; how much more must Lafargue be enduring in his dark woollen waistcoat and jacket. Perspiration was running freely down his face and a drop had fallen from his pointed chin to land on the coloured ribbon in his button-hole. For what service to France Lafargue had been awarded the Legion of Honour, Marcel had never enquired; perhaps for surviving twelve years in Santa Sabina.

'Monsieur Lafargue, I have a great deal of work to do,' he said untruthfully, 'there are files and dossiers stacked half a metre high on my desk. I shall be grateful if you will clarify the reason for this discussion.'

Lafargue controlled his rage and spoke coldly. 'You are aware that some days ago I took Monsieur de Murville to the Ministry of Transport and introduced him to the senior officials there. At his request, I may point out. He opened formal negotiations for the sale of a fleet of modern buses to the government of this country.' Marcel nodded, guessing what was coming next. 'It has been brought to my attention that you, without any official standing whatsoever in this matter, have subsequently intervened. Is that or is that not correct?'

'Certainly not,' Marcel replied, keeping his voice firm but calm. 'I have nothing to do with commercial affairs. You

are drawing the wrong conclusion from a chance social occasion.'

'Ha!' Lafargue snorted in disbelief.

'Madame Ducour asked me to show de Murville and his fiancée round the city. I took him with me one evening to call upon a friend. Among other guests in her drawing-room, we encountered Monsieur Bonavista. I introduced them to each other.'

'Drawing-room indeed!' Lafargue exclaimed angrily. 'It is a question of a brothel and a clandestine meeting set among a low class of person! Do not deny it – I have heard all about you and your underhand contacts!'

'Your words are insulting, Monsieur Lafargue,' said Marcel, 'but I fully realise that it is the *Suruq* that is causing you to behave in this outrageous way and so I refrain from taking offence.'

'You are very glib,' Lafargue said 'but do you know what you have done? It is my opinion that de Murville will attempt to persuade Bonavista to authorise the purchase of his wretched buses by corrupt means – in short, by offering him a large bribe.'

'You must forgive me, but I have no personal experience of business,' said Marcel, allowing a certain hauteur to creep into his tone. 'I have the impression that much of it is conducted in that way, especially overseas trading.'

'You are missing the point completely. I regret to have to say this, but de Murville's credentials are not of the best. I had enquiries made through Paris soon after he arrived here.'

'You are correct, Monsieur, I *am* missing the point,' Marcel agreed acidly, his forehead wrinkled in puzzlement. 'What can it possibly matter to any of us what sort of record de Murville has in business? Bonavista will either accept his offer or refuse it and that will be the end of the matter, either way. Who profits, and whether it is above-board or not, is hardly a question with which we need concern ourselves.'

'You are very eager to defend de Murville,' said Lafargue, his finger stabbing the air again, as if to pierce Marcel to the heart. 'Are you aware that he is wanted for questioning

in Gabon, Upper Volta, Martinique and French Guiana? And perhaps elsewhere too, for all I know.'

'Wanted?' Marcel repeated, sounding foolish as he said it. 'Wanted for what? What has he done?'

'To be blunt, Monsieur Lamont, your friend de Murville is a swindler. He persuaded the authorities of those countries to deposit large sums of money in bank accounts in Lichenstein and other ambiguous financial centres as payment for whatever he was pretending to sell them. Do you begin to understand the crisis into which your meddling has plunged us?'

'Good God!' Marcel exclaimed. 'He is operating here under the auspices of the Embassy! It will be thought that we are personally involved in his schemes!'

'Precisely!' said Lafargue, malicious satisfaction in his voice now that he had conveyed the awfulness of the situation.

'But what are we to do?' Marcel asked, dabbing at his brow with the silk handkerchief from his breast-pocket.

'*We*, Monsieur? What are *we* to do?' Lafargue said nastily. 'I have the satisfaction of knowing that I have acted exactly in accordance with protocol and good sense. My conscience is perfectly clear. I did no more than arrange an introduction between a visiting French businessman and the officials of the appropriate Ministry, as was my duty. I cannot accept responsibility for his actions or for theirs. But perhaps you should give consideration to your own position.'

'No, no – it is *you* who have the information about the man's previous activities,' Marcel riposted anxiously. 'It is up to you to issue warnings to those who ought to be told.'

'I? You are in error,' said Lafargue. 'I have received from Paris some details of a man calling himself de Murville who is in disfavour with a number of governments round the world. But names are easily changed, particularly for dishonest purposes. I find it impossible to believe that there is any connection between a swindler who travels the world under an assumed name and the distinguished person at present visiting this country.'

'This reluctance to connect the two – is it due to an excess of prudence?' Marcel asked. 'To a consideration that this de Murville is engaged to be married to the daughter of a lady who is related to the Ambassador's wife?'

'The suggestion is preposterous!' said Lafargue, trying his best to sound indignant. 'I have said all I wish to say to you and you may go now.'

'But how is de Murville to be stopped?' Marcel demanded.

'I have no idea,' said Lafargue sounding uninterested. 'You could perhaps raise your doubts with the Ambassador personally. But in view of the engagement, de Murville will shortly be a member of His Excellency's family and your intrusion might be resented. Especially as Madame Ducour appears to have become very fond of Madame Coty and her daughter. Mademoiselle Coty's engagement would surely be broken off if her fiancé were to be exposed as a wanted man, and you would be blamed.' Lafargue was enjoying himself. He pulled his spectacles down from his forehead and peered through the steamed-up lens at Marcel, a sly grin on his long face. 'On the other hand,' he went on, sounding very pleased with himself, 'suppose a day comes when the Santa Sabina government discovers that a large sum of money has disappeared through a foreign bank account. Bonavista would be punished severely, but it would be remembered that you took the missing financier to arrange the fraud with him. I would not want to be standing in your shoes on that day.'

'But this is absurd!' Marcel protested. 'I did nothing more than introduce them to each other at Madame da Silva's.'

'You enjoy diplomatic immunity, therefore no action can be taken against you here,' said Lafargue, his grin stretching wider and wider across his face, 'but the Ambassador would send you home at once. And in Paris a serious view might be taken of your implication in de Murville's conspiracy. Prosecution would await you, I have no doubt. And the sentence for so gross a breach of trust could only be a term of imprisonment.'

'Monsieur Lafargue, I appeal to you as a loyal and valued colleague to advise me on what action I can take to extricate

myself from this mess!' Marcel said hastily, hating himself for asking for the other man's help.

'I can do nothing for you,' said Lafargue, twisting the knife in the wound. 'I must protect my own position – after all, I shall be called as a witness against you at your trial. I trust you will be able to make it a long process, so that I can enjoy my stay in Paris at government expense.'

Marcel got up and walked out of Lafargue's office without another word. He slammed the door behind him, but he knew it to be futile, an act of irritation rather than of defiance. This threat of criminal proceedings was nonsense, of course; it was Lafargue's unpleasant way of getting his own back. But it was true that Oliver de Murville's plans must be thwarted, and how to achieve that without bringing down recrimination on his own head was by no means clear to Marcel. He sat with his jacket off and his feet up on his own desk, trying to devise a way.

As the morning advanced, the heat became too intense to permit rational thought for more than three consecutive minutes. His eyes half-closed, Marcel drifted back into the lulling half-dream of his first encounter with Mademoiselle Delacoste. Though it had taken place months before, its strangeness had impressed it so vividly on his memory that it might have taken place only a day before. He had let her whip him, and then she demanded that he kiss her foot. He went down on his knees, his trousers and underwear bundled round his ankles, and she steadied herself with a hand on his shoulder while she raised her left foot.

He removed her flat-heeled slipper to kiss her bare instep, and with her foot clasped in his hand, he lifted his eyes to her flushed face, to see how she intended the game to continue. At last, she seemed to notice that his *zimbriq* was hard and exposed. She reviled him for daring to insult her in this shameless way, her pudgy hands clenched into fists to pound on his shoulders.

All the same, she was swaying on her feet and there was a breathless catch in her voice that made him think that she had reached the limits of her imagination. The initiative had passed to him. He reached up to unbutton her pink

housecoat and unhook her brassiere, and for the second time that day her bare *gublas* were exposed to his gaze. She protested that she refused to be treated in this degrading way but did nothing to stop him using both hands on her breasts. He took their pink tips in his fingers and stretched them rhythmically, until she was sighing loudly. He sank his fingers into the abundance of soft flesh and she gripped his wrists to keep him at it.

Her sighing grew louder and heavier and her body shook against him like an earthquake. He parted her house-coat and kissed her broad belly above her pink nylon knickers. He was staring at her face and saw the deep blush that spread over her cheeks when he insinuated a hand down the front of her knickers and felt a broad expanse of thick curls. Before he could push his investigations any further, she seized him by the hair and dragged his head painfully away from her.

In a voice choked with emotion, her breasts heaving above him and her face crimson, she accused herself of depravity as deep and damnable as his in permitting him to touch her body. Worse even, for beastliness was to be expected from a man, but she had ignored the precepts of a moral upbringing in allowing herself to become, however momentarily, the object of his vile desires. She must be punished severely for her lapse. Before he had digested this strange information, she pressed the belt into his hand and spread-eagled herself face-down on the table.

The swollen head of his *zimbriq* stuck out from under his shirt and nodded up and down as he took three steps to place himself behind her. When he hesitated, she told him in a fierce voice to begin the punishment and he lifted her house-coat to her waist. Her bottom was a vision of sensuality he had not expected; bending over the table had stretched tight the pink and semi-transparent nylon of her knickers over a miracle of firm-fleshed cheeks. Marcel stared entranced, and again she ordered him to punish her. He held the leather belt double in his hand, swung it over his shoulder and brought it down across her knickers with a great crack. She winced and uttered a great sob, and he gave her four more hard slashes with it.

She did not arise immediately from her undignified position, but with her rump exposed, lay across the table, her arms outstretched to grip its far edge. In a subdued voice she informed Marcel that only her strong character, formed by a rigorous upbringing, had enabled her to protect herself from whatever bestialities he would have committed on her body by now. She begged him to purge his soul by openly confessing the guilty intentions he had harboured. Truth to tell, it was only while Marcel contemplated the fleshy rotundites of her bottom that he began to harbour ideas she would think guilty.

Much amused, he untruthfully confessed that he had arrived at her apartment determined to ravish her body. She called him a brute and demanded to know how he would have done it. He said that he had planned to drag her into the bed-room and fling her face-down on the bed, and hold her down with a hand on the nape of her neck while he stripped off her pink underwear. At this, she called him loathsome and demanded to be told what he would have done to her next.

Fanciful though his tale was, it had its effect on Marcel. His stiff *zimbriq* was twitching below his shirt and he reached out a trembling hand towards Mademoiselle Delacoste's rump. The reddening of her skin by the whipping showed through the transparent pink of her nylon knickers and he felt the heat he had induced in her cheeks while he explained how, if she had not stopped him, he would have thrown himself over her bottom while she lay helpless on her bed, and rammed his *zimbriq* into her. Even now, he told her, in his mind he could hear her squeals of terror as he defiled her soft body with it.

She moaned and shook and begged him most earnestly to punish her again, to quell the vicious urges of her animal nature. Marcel hooked his fingers in the waist-band of her knickers and pulled them halfway down her thighs. The flesh of her rump was pale, except for two red patches he had caused, and he ran his fingers up and down the deep furrow between the superb cheeks. She hardly seemed to know what he was doing, even when his probing fingers touched the

split in the fat and hairy mound below her exposed cheeks; she shuddered and moaned and pleaded with him to beat her.

Her urgent request presented him with an opportunity not to be missed – the opportunity of a lifetime. Marcel raised his arm and gave her five more hard cracks with the doubled belt on her bare backside, pausing between blows to permit her to experience the pain fully before the leather cut into her flesh again. At each cut she gave a wailing cry and, when he had finished, she lay limp and sobbed quietly. As if in a wonderful dream, he dropped the belt and moved close behind her, to caress with his finger-tips her red and smarting cheeks. Her sobbing continued while he rubbed his *zimbriq* against them.

Needless to say, his curiosity was not yet satisfied. With both hands he spread her cheeks apart to examine the small knot of muscle between them. He inserted his fore-finger a little way and she squealed and jerked so hard that he was afraid he might hurt her if he continued. He moved in closer between her splayed legs and pushed his hard *zimbriq* against the split of her *kuft*. She groaned deeply and he found that, though she was not a virgin, she was a tight fit. He reached under her bottom and used his thumbs to pull her open while he eased in gently, progressing a centimetre at a time.

When he was satisfactorily lodged in her and she was shaking under him as if gripped by a fever, he lay forward over her, flicking her open pink house-coat up over her head to hide it completely, while baring her sturdy back for him to lie on. He felt underneath her to grasp her plump breasts tightly while he rocked back and forth. What improbable mixture of overwhelming emotions she experienced while she was being *zeqqed* was beyond imagination, but no doubt disgust was overlaid by desire. She soon began to utter long heavy moans, her *gublas* shook in his hands and her body quaked beneath him.

And like her, he too was shaken by strong emotion and wild sensation and rode her fast, hearing the rhythmic slap-slap of his belly against her soft bare behind. In the grip of ecstatic convulsions, he gushed his triumphant pleasure

into her, at which she screamed aloud and writhed so frantically under him that he was almost rolled off, and only remained in possession by hanging on to her *gublas*. But at last she was still again and he withdrew from her and stood up to let his belly cool.

But the heat was unbearable and he freed his ankles from his underwear and trousers and took off his wet shirt, his chest heaving and his heart still racing. Mademoiselle Delacoste remained as she was, her head hidden under the upturned house-coat, her arms stretched out to grip the table-edge and her bare back shining with perspiration. For some moments Marcel was afraid that she might have passed out from the shock of what he had done to her, but then her legs twitched and she gave a gasp or two. He went round the table, naked, to uncover her head and unclench the grip of her fingers.

With his aid, she raised herself slowly from the table, all the time staring at his nakedness as if hypnotised, her breasts heaving to her agitated breathing. The explosive release of her strongest emotions had rendered her speechless. Marcel took her by the hand and led her into the bathroom, where he peeled off her housecoat and knickers, turned on the shower and pulled her under the cold water with him. In reality it could hardly be said to be cold at all, but it brought relief to hot flesh and troubled spirits.

Mademoiselle Delacoste was content to lean her back against the tiled wall while Marcel soaped her body from neck to hips. When he let the water wash the creamy lather from her breasts, their red-brown buds were standing up very prominently. He put his head down and sucked them in turn. She insisted he must not do that. And when he paid no attention, she complained that he had polluted her and that she regretted bitterly that she had not struggled harder to stop him. He assured her that she was allowing herself to become nervous for no reason at all and that he was only trying to cool her down a little.

His hand circled on her belly, so gently and soothingly that she moved her feet apart for him to soap her between the legs. Naturally, his *zimbriq* was iron-hard again by then,

but he kept it from brushing against her, not wanting to alarm her, while with great delicacy of touch he washed the soft lips between her thighs. Her forehead wrinkled in genuine puzzlement, as if she found it incredible that anyone would wish to repeat so utterly repulsive an act of debauchery.

But though she evidently had reservations about this second encounter, she made no objection when he pushed her feet further apart and moved in close. With a dip and a slow careful push, he slid up into her tight *kuft* and heard her half-moan.

He asked if she knew that the Santa Sabinans call what they were doing together a belly-to-belly. She replied with contempt that in her opinion the people there were all depraved beyond redemption and she chose to know nothing of their low ways. The tepid water of the shower splashed pleasantly down between them, over her plump *gublas* and between their bellies, while Marcel swayed backwards and forwards in an easy rhythm. But however steady his movements, however gentle the stimulus, however loathsome Mademoiselle Delacoste found the physical manifestations of desire, it quickly became apparent that being *zeqqed* in this shameless way had a considerable psychic effect on her. Her breathing became heavy and ragged and her breasts rose and fell against Marcel's chest. He winced when her finger-nails sank sharply into his bottom and she started to thump her belly against him furiously. But not once did she dare to look him in the eye; her gaze was fixed on a point in the distance somewhere over his right shoulder.

Soon her open-mouthed panting became a long racking moan of ecstasy and she shook uncontrollably. The experience of bringing on a woman's climax never failed to hurry Marcel over the brink and with short stabs he squirted his desire into her clinging *kuft*. She tried to pull away from him, but he held her pressed against the tiles, the water cascading down over them until his throbs of pleasure faded and his *zimbriq* became small and soft enough to slide out and dangle between his legs.

Later that evening, both fully clothed and on separate chairs placed well away from each other in her sitting-room, they discussed what had taken place, though in a roundabout way, for Mademoiselle Delacoste was unable to confront her repressions. Marcel knew without being told that a woman like her did not want a lover; the very idea made her blush and look away in horror. But, she explained in a faltering voice, when the *Suruq* blew, the effect on her nerves was to unleash the bestial side of her nature, unless she could crush it by force.

It was at such times, she informed him, that she was in dire need of a man of character, a person she could trust, to thrash the wickedness out of her. She had never found an entirely suitable man for this onerous task, but Marcel was better than no one at all. At that he grinned, and they made an agreement that he would come to her whenever the *Suruq* blew, which was perhaps five or six times a year, to render assistance in her struggle against the base promptings of her nature.

How pleasant it was, when the heat made work impossible, to sit with his feet up on his desk and dream about his visits to her apartment since then; to contemplate in his mind's eye the baring of her fleshy bottom to be abused with a leather strap he had bought for the purpose. Marcel opened his eyes and there she was, standing on the other side of his desk in her wrinkled skirt and white blouse with dark patches under the arms.

'This evening about nine, Mademoiselle Delacoste?' he asked and she blushed pink and nodded.

6

The Worst is Yet to Come

The second day of the *Suruq* was always worse than the first. Most shops remained closed and many people did not trouble to go to work. After an evening of chastisement for the wicked urges of the flesh, Mademoiselle Delacoste stayed at home the next day and, by ten in the morning, Marcel decided it had been a mistake to go to the Embassy and fled out into the wind that threatened to twitch him off his feet at each step. He strode through the almost deserted city streets with no particular destination in view, but he was a creature of habit and found himself, eventually, outside the Gran'Caffe Camille.

Naturally, the tables and chairs were not set out in the square that day; they were stacked together, close to the wall for shelter, with a rope lashed round the stack to keep it from being blown away. Inside, where large wooden fans on the ceiling served merely to stir hot air sluggishly about, three men stood at the high bar with tiny cups of black coffee. Olivier de Murville sat alone at a table with a glass of cognac and ice, smoking a long thin cheroot and reading the *Daily Chronicles*. 'Too hot to work?' he said glancing at Marcel over the top of his newspaper. 'Sit down and have a drink. Something to refresh you – you look as if you need it.'

But it was not the heat alone that was responsible for Marcel's flushed face. Knowing what he now knew about Olivier, he was unable to make up his mind what attitude to take towards him. Instinct urged him to confront Olivier and threaten to expose him, unless he dropped his plans and left Santa Sabina immediately. But expose him to whom?

That was the problem – Olivier might feel secure enough in his connection with the Ambassador's family to laugh at threats.

Expose him to Salvador Bonavista? To ask the question was to realise how catastrophic that might prove. The Minister would need to protect himself from suspicion of complicity, and the easiest way would be to denounce Olivier and have him deported. And if Bonavista felt that more protection was necessary, then he could claim that Marcel was an accomplice in Olivier's scheme and have him declared *persona non grata*. He would be sent back to France under a cloud and that would be the end of his career in the diplomatic service.

For the present the only course of action that Marcel could think of was to pretend he knew nothing and remain on friendly terms with Olivier, in the hope of finding some way to thwart his intentions before matters went too far. It was an absurdly feeble position to be in, but he could see no other practical choice. He sat down at Olivier's table and asked the waiter for a glass of iced mint tea.

'I am surprised to find you here,' he said, forcing himself to be pleasant. 'I thought you would stay safe inside the hotel until the *Suruq* blows itself out.'

'That's for the ladies,' said Olivier with a shrug, putting down his newspaper, 'I stayed with them yesterday, but I find it impossible to be confined in one place for long.'

'Leaving them to their own devices in the hotel?'

'Madame Coty is going to the Embassy to visit Madame Ducour. Women of their age enjoy nothing more than a good gossip together,' said Olivier dismissively.

The simmering annoyance in Marcel's mind was erased by the thought that Lisette was alone in the hotel – alone and bored, most probably. It seemed an ideal opportunity to resume his attentions towards her. There was the additional consideration now that, if he succeeded in his ambitions, he would be taking revenge on Olivier.

'What are your plans for the day?' he enquired mildly.

'I don't know. There's not much to see or do while this wind is blowing. The market is closed – I've been to see.

No little adventures today, more's the pity! Do you think that tomorrow will be any better?'

'Yes, the *Suruq* almost never blows for more than two days together. But cause the streets are deserted, it does not follow that all entertainment has come to a standstill. It is a question of knowing where to look.'

'Good man!' Olivier exclaimed, throwing his hairy-backed hands up in approval. 'I knew I could count on you!'

'Forgive me if I state the obvious,' said Marcel, 'but there is the possibility of returning to the hotel and inviting your charming fiancée to your room.'

'No, no, that won't do at all! I can have Lisette anytime I want,' Olivier replied with a lack of gallantry that was far from pleasing. 'But we are here for only a short visit and may never come back. I want to enjoy the pleasures of Santa Sabina to the full while I have the opportunity. As a man of the world you understand that, I'm sure.'

'Of course,' said Marcel, 'I understand you very well. Let me think for a moment or two where our local specialities are to be found. Several *rendezvous* are frequented by obliging women in this weather, when strolling is impossible. The Augusto da Cunha Memorial Library, for instance, and the National Museum, but certain rules are observed there. You would find it tedious and time-consuming. We need somewhere as uncomplicated as the Fruit Market . . . ah yes, I have it!'

'Tell me and I shall be on my way,' said Olivier.

'The church facing us across other side of the square – the Four Crowned Martyrs. You have only to walk across and attend Mass. There's one at eleven and another at twelve.'

'Go to Mass looking for a girl?' said Olivier, surprised if not offended. 'Is this more of your nonsense?'

'No, I am serious. Find yourself a seat near the back of the church so that you can observe everyone who goes in and out. And then wait. Santa Sabinans are deeply religious and many go to church every day.'

'Not the sort of woman I'm looking for!' Olivier said with a chuckle, and stubbed out his cheroot.

'But you are wrong, I assure you. Young women go there with a double purpose; to make their daily devotions and to look for a suitable partner for their other daily devotions's.

'But it is out of the question for me to approach a stranger in a church and put my hand up her skirt!' said Olivier.

'Nor is it necessary. Just sit quietly near the back of the church with your hands together in an attitude of prayer. When a woman comes in who arouses your interest, smile at her and let her see that your hands are like this . . .' Marcel demonstrated what he meant, the stiff forefinger of one hand thrust into the clasped palm of the other in a gesture of unmistakable significance. Olivier stared as if stupefied for a moment or two and then roared with laughter.

'But no!' he guffawed. 'It's that easy? What will the girl do in response to this immodest gesture of mine?'

'If she likes the look of you, she will kneel beside you while she says her prayers. And when she gets up to leave the church, wait a few seconds and then follow her. She will wait for you outside.'

'And she'll let me go home with her, like the two we met in the Fruit Market?'

'Oh yes, if you explain that's what you want. Otherwise she'll think you're after a quick belly-to-belly and take you up an alley somewhere.'

'I think you'd better come along with me until I've got the hang of it,' said Olivier. 'You're in no hurry, are you?'

'If it were any other day,' Marcel murmured, false regret in his voice, 'but I am on my way to the British Embassy, on official business.'

'Then I shall chance my luck alone,' Olivier declared. 'Is there anything else I should know before I go?'

'If you indicate your desire to a woman who doesn't find you acceptable, she will smile back at you but she will go further down the church to look for someone more to her liking. But in my experience, foreigners are almost never refused. You can afford to take your time over your choice; it is not necessary to go with the first woman you see.'

'This is an amazing country,' said Olivier. 'You are living in a real-life paradise. I envy you, my friend.'

Not for the first time Marcel concluded that de Murville was remarkably imperceptive to believe that. It was difficult to understand how a man of so little imagination had succeeded in cheating so many government officials. 'Ah yes, Luisa and Asuncion, with whom you went off on your own,' he said. 'Did you find their company rewarding?'

'They were delightful, both of them,' said Olivier, with a grin right across his heavy face. 'We went to Luisa's apartment and I *zeqqed* both of them two or three times each. They still wanted more and they massaged me all over with oil to rekindle my enthusiasm. Have you ever been massaged by two naked women at the same time? It is a delicious experience, I can assure you. But I'd had enough for then, whatever they did, and I took my leave. I was so tired that evening I went to bed straight after dinner.

'And your fiancée, did she not think it strange?'

'No, she thought the heat had exhausted me,' Olivier replied as he glanced at his wristwatch.

'The Mass will be starting now,' he said, and stood up quickly. 'I must hurry or the best bargains will be snapped up by others. Pay the bill for me, there's a good fellow. We'll have a drink after dinner and I'll tell you how I get on.'

Through the glass front of the café Marcel watched him cross windswept Martyrs' Square, walking briskly. *I mean to demolish you, my friend*, he thought, waiting to see Olivier to go into the church before putting the price of the drinks and a tip on the saucer under his tea-glass and leaving the café. The Grand Hotel Orient had all the appearance of withstanding a siege; the awning above the terrace had been removed before the *Suruq* ripped it away in tatters, the chairs and tables were stowed in a safe place, and the normally ever-open glass door was tightly closed.

Marcel exchanged friendly words with the Costa daughter on duty – it was not Concepcion that day – and collected his key. Whether the creaky old lift was still working despite the *Suruq*, he did not wait to find out. He loosened his tie and collar, took off his jacket and folded it over his arm,

and climbed a flight of stairs, heading not for his own room but for the floor where the Versailles Suite was to be found. There was no one in the corridor and, because of the overwhelming heat the door to the suite stood open. Marcel paused on the threshold to gaze at the unexpected spectacle within.

Lisette was at an open window in the corner of the sitting-room, leaning out. Marcel wondered what she was doing, until a moment's thought produced the reason. The main windows gave on to a long balcony overlooking San Feliz Square and were closed to keep out the hot wind, but the corner window faced east and would be sheltered from the gale. If there was any cooler air to be found, comparatively speaking, she would find it there. At least, it had to be better than the still and stifling air in the hotel.

Her arms lay flat on the window ledge, and she was leaning so far out that only her lower half was visible. She had not yet completed dressing; she was barefoot and wore a thin slip of peach-coloured silk. Marcel found her state of *deshabille* charming and he stood in silent admiration of the superbly rounded rump thrust towards him by the way she was standing. Under the silk, the cheeks of her bottom were clearly outlined, much as Mademoiselle Delacoste's had been the previous evening, when she bent over the table for him to whip her. Memory and reality combined to produce a vision of sensuality that stirred his blood and stiffened up his *zimbriq*.

With a quick glance up and down the corridor to make sure he was not observed, he stepped into the suite and closed the door noiselessly behind him. He lowered his jacket to the floor and crept across the room, intent on surprising Lisette. As to what precisely was in his mind, who can say? Perhaps he was not entirely certain himself; the *Suruq* affected everyone, even him and perhaps he deluded himself that surprise would be changed instantly into acquiescence and then into desire. Perhaps she could be persuaded to go with him to his room, where he could guarantee they would not be disturbed for an hour or two.

He moved very stealthily and the wind was moaning

outside; she heard nothing as he crossed the room. He hardly dared to breathe while he knelt down behind her and opened his trousers to let his stiff *zimbriq* leap out in joyful freedom. His hands were trembling in excitement as he lightly took hold of the hem of her slip and rased it to uncover her thighs and bottom. His mouth opened in a sigh of astonished delight as he observed how the oppressive heat had caused the peach-coloured silk of her knickers to become stuck in the cleft between the cheeks of her bottom. His twitching *zimbriq* bounded rock-hard.

He heard her long indrawn gasp of disbelief when his lips touched the bare flesh above the tops of her silk stockings, so tender and so vulnerable to his ardent kiss. This Mademoiselle Delacoste did not permit, and he had not forced the issue. But now, where no repressions denied him the pleasure, he kissed Lisette's thighs in a fervour of delight. For a moment or two her surprise held her immobile and in those precious instants Marcel had both hands under her slip to stroke her soft belly. By now she must have guessed who was taking advantage of her in this audacious manner, and before she could turn to confirm her guess, he had her knickers down to her knees and was pressing kisses on her bottom.

On the Reserved Beach, when they lay behind the rowing-boat, he had become so excited by playing with her breasts that he had flooded his hot desire against the warm flesh of her bottom – here on her smooth-skinned right cheek, on the very spot he was now kissing! She had pretended to be displeased with him, but there was an undercurrent of sexual interest in her voice while she scolded him. The memory of how close he had been then, and was again now, to having his way with her, inflamed his mind. His fingers delved down into her knickers, right into the join of her thighs, to stroke the fleshy lips of her *kuft*.

She completed her turn within the circle of his arms and struck him a tremendous blow in the face that rocked his head on his shoulders. He jerked backwards on his knees and let go of her, staring up in bewilderment as a second blow landed on the other side of his face.

'What do you think you are doing!' she screamed.

'*Bububububub*!' he stammered, when he saw what he had done. It was not Lisette. It was her mother. Marcel was trying to say *But you are out*, not that Madame Coty would have taken his meaning, even if words had not failed him. Her face scarlet with indignation and her hands clenched into fists, she stood gasping at the outrage. Her wild-eyed stare fell to his undone trousers and the foolishly-stiff *zimbriq* poking out. She stared in horror, made a choking sound in her throat, and fled across the sitting-room as if pursued by a fiend from Hell. Marcel heard a door slam and a key turn in the lock, while he fastened his gaping trousers and scrambled to his feet.

On either side of the sitting-room a door led to a bedroom. Madame Coty had retreated into the sanctuary of hers and secured the door firmly against her would-be ravager.

'Good God, what have I done!' Marcel exclaimed in anguish, smacking his palm against his forehead.

His mind was racing as a hideous sequence of events flashed through it. Madame Coty would run to Madame Ducour with a tale of how he had attempted to violate her in her own sitting-room. Between the two women the story would be elaborated by fantasy until it became shameful and monstrous beyond belief when they told it to the Ambassador! Marcel could expect to be sacked, at least, and that was assuming Madame Coty could be persuaded not to prosecute him, for the sake of avoiding scandal.

It was all too obvious to Marcel that the *Suruq* had brought gross injustice with it. He had endured a threat of disgrace and imprisonment because of Olivier de Murville's business affairs. Now a new threat came from Madame Coty! To be accused of fraud and rape was excessive, particularly when he was innocent on both counts. After all, it was to Lisette he wanted to pay his respects, not to her mother. And Lisette would have accepted his kiss of homage on her bare bottom in the spirit in which it was offered.

Between men of honour it was surely accepted that to mistake one woman's bottom for another, when her face was hidden, was an accident not to be taken too seriously.

In countries where women went veiled, it must frequently happen that a man found himself fondling a bottom or a pair of *gublas* in mistake for another. Where was the harm in that? To ruin a career for so trivial an error was injustice on cosmic scale!

Perhaps if he explained to Madame Coty that there had bee a most unfortunate misunderstanding and offered his profound apologies . . . but on reflection he realised that approach might only make matters worse. To any woman of spirit and principle, a deeper insult than to be the victim of unwelcome attentions was surely to be informed that the outrage to her modesty was not meant for her at all. There was also the complication of the fiancé. If Madame Coty learned that Lisette was on terms of the slightest affection with another man, after only a few day's acquaintance, paroxysms of rage would no doubt ensue.

Nevertheless, an effort must be made. To introduce a note of formality into the proceedings, and perhaps reduce the mistrust Madame Coty must be feeling, Marcel put on his tie properly and the jacket he had dropped on first entering the room. He assured himself that his trousers were properly fastened and tapped on the door through which the indignant lady had fled.

'Madame Coty,' he said, keeping his voice light and sincere, 'I beg you to accept my most heart-felt and humble apologies. There is little I can offer by way of excuse for my behaviour, except to plead that this dreadful gale is notorious for the insanity it provokes in otherwise honourable men.'

There was a long silence on the other side of the door, as if she were considering his words. And then the key turned in the lock, the door opened, and Madame Coty stood facing him. She had put on a dressing-gown.

'I guessed the reason for the dreadful thing you did,' she said, and Marcel was relieved by her calm and assured manner. 'The hotel staff explained at breakfast how this awful mistral affects people,' she added, 'but you are a civilised man and a diplomat – you must control yourself better.'

'Tell me that my discourtesy is forgiven,' Marcel pleaded, hardly able to believe his good fortune, 'I implore you.'

He took her hand gently and raised it to his lips to kiss it in token of his gratitude for her understanding.

'You shocked me beyond belief,' she said. 'I am not at all a violent person, but the fear aroused by being touched in that way when I thought I was alone . . . it caused an uncontrollable reaction. I hope I did not hurt you too much.'

'I deserved it,' he said, noting that he still held her hand and that she was making no attempt to free herself.

'I would not want you to think of me as a prude,' she said, smiling at him. 'I am a woman of strong emotions and you are a very attractive man . . .'

She let her sentence trail away into a silence that was more eloquent than words. Her smile took on a new significance and Marcel grasped that there was a course of action open to him that would eliminate all possibility of a complaint about him. How to account for this astonishing change of mood, from horrified repulsion to a scarcely disguised invitation to the most intimate of acts, was beyond Marcel. He assumed that, once Madame Coty had recovered from the tremendous shock of having her bare bottom kissed by a stranger, she had evidently found it not unpleasurable after all.

She was in a foreign country, alone in a hotel room, and she would perhaps allow herself to accept the thrill of the new more readily than if she were at home in Paris. And she was in her forties; it was not often that handsome men slipped their hands into her knickers . . . here was a heaven-sent opportunity for her to experience the delights a vigorous young man could provide. It sounded rational enough, put like that, but Marcel was firmly of the opinion that women were wholly irrational, and there was no point in attempting to understand why they did what they did. It was enough to adore them and enjoy them.

'I believe that the *Suruq* is driving you a little mad too,' he said softly. He reached up to stroke her face with his fingertips. Her eyes closed for an instant and she gave a long sigh.

'It is true – you have guessed it! The *Suruq* is burning through my body,' she said, with all the sultriness of a cinema actress on screen. 'I feel it in my bones and in my blood. My flesh is on fire!'

With this encouragement, Marcel reached forward to untie the sash round her waist and let her dressing-gown fall open. Her breasts were rising and falling under the peach-coloured slip to the rhythm of her suddenly heavy breathing.

'Are we safe from interruption?' he enquired as with both hands he squeezed her warm breasts through thin silk. 'Is your daughter likely to return soon?'

'Not for hours . . . Madame Ducour has taken her out of the city in the Ambassador's car to find somewhere cooler . . . I felt too exhausted from the heat to go with them.'

In another moment they were in her bedroom, the door closed and locked, sitting together on the side of the bed and clasped in each other's arms. Denise Coty was a slim and small woman, like her daughter, but with light brown hair rather than Lisette's silver-blonde. Marcel slipped his hand under her slip and up her bare thighs, while she pressed her hot mouth to his. He felt slowly upwards, spinning out these moments of dizzy anticipation, until his fingers touched the thin silk of her knickers and she opened her legs for him.

'Too exhausted to go riding round the countryside, but not too exhausted for love, I hope,' he murmured.

He slipped his hand down the front of her knickers and ran his finger-tips through her curls. Her thighs parted a little further and he felt the soft skin of her groins and then the moist lips of her *kuft*.

'I am never too exhausted for love, never!' she declared. 'Put your finger inside and tickle me, darling Marcel.'

What a perfectly damnable day this is turning out to be! he thought in exasperation while he plunged his fingers firmly into Denise. Instead of the tender passages he had hoped for with Lisette, he was committed through an act of folly to pleasuring her mother. And though he was bestowing a favour on a woman twenty years older than himself, she was trying to tell him how to go about it. That

had to be changed. He removed his hand from between her legs and she gasped in disappointment.

'But what are you doing, my darling?' she asked, anxiety in her voice, 'I want you to feel me – don't stop now!'

All the same, her blue eyes bulged when he unbuckled his belt and flicked his stiff *zimbriq* out of his trousers.

'You did not give yourself time to look at it before, when I was on my knees before you,' he said, giving her his charming smile. 'What do you think now, Denise – does it measure up to your expectations? Be frank with me – I would be desolated to fall short in any way of your standards.'

Denise's cheeks were blushing a bright pink, but this time it would be reasonable to assume that desire was the cause, not insulted modesty. 'It is very beautiful,' she said breathlessly.

'Indeed it is,' Marcel agreed with pride, 'and I treasure it highly. Feel how hard it is.'

She took hold of him and gripped him tightly with a shaking hand. Marcel felt down her knickers again, to caress the wet bud inside her open *kuft*. After only a few moments of that, her eyes closed and a shuddering climax overtook her. Marcel was astonished by the speed of it. She had warned him that she was a woman of strong emotions, but this seemed absurd. At the same time, however, he was pleased to think she could be dealt with quickly, allowing him to fulfil his obligations and be free of her.

She lay limp in his arms while he removed her dressing-gown and lowered her on to her back, her bottom on the edge of the bed and her feet still on the floor. He took off her knickers and pulled her slip up under her arm-pits, fully baring her body to his sight. From the waist down she was well made, with a gently-curving belly and a neat triangle of brown curls between slender thighs, but her breasts were flabby and lay slackly on her chest.

'And now, my dear Denise,' he said, smiling as he gazed down at her, 'your moment has come.'

He stood between her knees to position her legs widely apart in readiness for his entrance. Denise gazed up at him

with a look of adoration, her arms folded under her head, to show him how comfortable she was in this revealing position. Her mouth was open a little and set in a curve that could perhaps be a half-smile. Not that Marcel noticed, his attention was focused lower down her body. The separation of her thighs had opened her brown-haired *kuft*, the lips were drawn loosely apart to display the moist pink interior and her prominent little bud.

Never in his entire adult life had Marcel declined that sort of invitation, no matter who offered it. Without troubling to remove any of his clothes, not even his jacket and tie, he lay on Denise, she took hold of his jumping *zimbriq* and guided it into her. With his feet braced sideways against the floor as a solid base for his operations, he pushed in deep and rammed away to discharge his duty as quickly as possible. Denise did nothing at all to assist him, or even to show that she was enjoying what he was doing.

It is too soon to arouse her again, thought Marcel while he jolted up and down, *so much the worse for her*! After all, this was just a quick in-and-out, calling for no great exercise of skill, and his own excitement was racing towards its point of culmination in a most satisfactory manner. He had been sheathed in her for hardly more than a minute before he uttered a gasping cry and his desire released itself in throbbing bursts. Denise acknowledged his critical moments by arching her back and pushing her belly upwards, while she whispered, 'Oh yes, Marcel, yes, yes!' She was in the grip of another mild climax, he realised with surprise, yet she remained almost motionless.

Before Marcel was finished, she let her back descend to the bed again. Her arms were still under her head as she kissed him on both cheeks. 'That was delightful,' he murmured as he climbed off her not at all sure that he believed his own words. While he tucked away his softening *zimbriq* and fastened his trousers, Denise sat up to remove her slip.

'Yes,' he said, totally mistaking her intentions, 'a shower will refresh you and you can rest for an hour before lunch.'

But Denise had mounted the bed fully and spread herself

on her back, legs wide and arms lying loosely at her sides.

'Rest,' she said softly, her brown eyebrows curving up her forehead at the suggestion. 'But I told you, my darling, I am never too exhausted for love. To think of leaving so soon after doing so little is ridiculous. Take your clothes off – you must be very hot.'

He stared in stupefaction at the brown curls that lay wetly on her *kuft* and at the gaping lips extending their welcome to him. He'd no inclination to spend half the day in gratifying a woman who gave so very little sign of ecstasy. But before he could find words of excuse and polite refusal and take his leave, his treacherous *zimbriq* made the decision for him. From its limp position between his thighs it jerked upright. Denise noticed at once what had happened and slid her legs a little further apart on the bed.

'Come and play with me,' she said, 'I can see you want to.'

On her lips was the half-smile he had seen before. And between her thighs, her *kuft* also seemed in some inexplicable way to be smiling at him. The lure was too attractive to resist and Marcel's reluctance vanished while he was undressing. There was a challenge here too that he found impossible to resist; to compel Denise to announce her pleasure in the way other women did. With this in mind, he knelt naked on the bed between her parted legs and stared down at her with a smile, his stiff *zimbriq* swaying.

'I know that look,' she said softly.'I have seen it before. You believe that you can make me scream and kick my legs in the air. Well, we shall see.'

'Certainly we shall see,' he agreed. 'Before I let you up off this bed, my dear Denise, I intend to wring from you tears of pleasure and shrieks of joy.'

'It is strange, the first impressions we form,' she said. 'When we were introduced at Jacqueline's lunch, I couldn't help thinking that it would be very nice if you made love to me.'

'Yet now that we are here together,' said Marcel, staring at her, 'you are disappointed. I have pierced your body, but not your heart. Isn't that what you mean?'

'Perhaps,' she admitted. A glance showed him that she had folded her arms under her head again, in the nonchalant gesture that had astonished him before. This time he was annoyed by it; no woman in the world had the right to appear so composed when he was about to make love to her. He lurched forward between her legs to press his face to her warm belly and reached up with both hands to pinch the soft buds of her slack breasts. He treated them so cruelly that he wrung a gasp from her – of pain, perhaps, but at least it was a sign that he had made her feel something.

'You are so passive,' he accused her. 'Even a climax does no more than make you tremble a little. Why is this, Denise?'

She gripped his wrists to pull his hands away. Marcel held on and squeezed her buds harder, until she groaned. On either side of him her legs twitched – an indication, however small, that he had woken her body from the lethargy with which it accepted a lover. Unable to break his hold, she wriggled from under him to escape, progressing on her back until her head hung down over the side of the bed and she could go no further. She let go of his wrists and submitted to his cruel handling, groaning lightly as he tugged and tweaked and pinched her sensitive buds without remorse.

'For me the sensations of love are very gentle,' she gasped, answering his question at last. 'What else can I do but enjoy them calmly?'

Marcel ended her ordeal by transferring his hands down to her thighs. He pushed them further apart while he licked down her belly until the tip of his tongue touched her brown-haired lips, and for the first time her legs came up off the bed and velvety thighs closed around his head. He could feel their soft flesh against his ears as his tongue probed into her warm *kuft* to find her bud. He flicked his tongue over it again and again, pressing hard, giving Denise no choice but to react to the strong stimulus, and eventually he felt a throbbing begin inside her belly.

Her fingers were twined painfully in his hair, pulling his face tighter to her, until he could hardly breath, her legs locked so strongly round his head that it seemed she wanted

to break his neck. But the discomfort meant nothing – it went almost unnoticed in the excitement of what he was doing. An enormous feeling of triumph flooded through him as Denise's belly and loins bucked against him in wild abandon. He lapped faster at her and, at the instant her body was shaken by its crisis, her sharp cry was music in his ears. Such welcome music that he refused to let her throes fade; his determined tongue flung her into climax after climax. 'Enough, enough . . .' she gasped at length, 'let me breathe . . . darling Marcel, stop for a moment . . .'

By his feverish reckoning she had by then experienced the crisis twelve times, perhaps more. It was very difficult to tell where one ended and the next started, for what was happening to her was like the regular rise and fall of waves on the ocean. He was so aroused that he could stand no more. He freed his head from the grip of her legs and threw himself upon her palpitating belly. His *zimbriq* needed no guiding hand – it found its way to her open *kuft* and sank deep into it without the least effort.

In his delirium of pleasure it seemed to him that Denise was returning his compliment – her slippery depths were like a hot mouth sucking at him. For without question, letting her breathe had not stopped her continuous crises; her belly was quaking under his in the rhythmic spasms of delight. Her arms were no longer folded under her head – they were wrapped tightly round his waist, dragging him closer to her. In another moment she screamed wildly and pushed her pelvis up hard at him, to drive him in deeper. Marcel plunged with all his might, feeling her hot *kuft* sucking at him, and his essence came pouring out just as Denise locked her legs round his hips and sank her teeth into his shoulder. His persistence had at last aroused her deepest desires and it would take him the next three hours to quench them.

7

Life, Liberty and the Pursuit of Happiness

The party given by the Americans on the day in July when they celebrate their independence was always the largest and most generous of any diplomatic function in Santa Sabina. In theory, the guest list included government ministers and top senior civil servants; ambassadors of countries with which the Americans were on speaking terms, and their most senior staff; the leaders of Santa Sabina society, which meant the large landowners and their wives who comprised the Hundred Families; local businessmen of importance, and various others.

Naturally, in the wake of the war in Korea the Chinese were not invited. For other political reasons the representatives of several countries were left off the list. At any given time there would be a Santa Sabina official or two under house-arrest on suspicion of going beyond the acceptable level of corruption. Others who had lost the president's confidence for various reasons chose not to be seen in public, or were told to refuse the invitation. There were some businessmen whose presence would be an embarrassment and some whose dealings with Communist Embassies made them refuse to attend a US function.

All this had the effect of reducing the numbers accepting to three or four hundred, and the party could be accommodated in the grounds of the American Embassy. On the diplomatic scale, Marcel was not important enough to be asked to the function and in consequence he was surprised to receive an invitation. He consulted His Excellency Jean-Jacques Ducour, who displayed an unworthy suspicion.

'I can think of no reason in the world why the Americans have invited you to their party, Lamont,' he said. 'At least, no reason which reflects any credit on you. As I recall it, you were a friend of their military attaché who disgraced himself – what was his name – the secret gun-runner?'

'Colonel Errol Hochheimer,' said Marcel coolly, 'but we were never friends, only acquaintances.'

'Evidently someone in the US Embassy takes a different view,' Ducour observed. 'I must say that I am displeased with you. An invitation to you is highly irregular and there is a hint of something discreditable about it. It will be noted on your dossier. Have you been indiscreet?'

'Certainly not!' Marcel assured him. 'I shall decline the invitation.'

'No, you must accept. If it is a question of the CIA and a clandestine approach, we must know what they intend. You will report personally to me after the party.'

'I hardly think it is anything like that,' Marcel retorted. 'If the Americans were looking for an undercover approach, it would surely not be at a party in sight of hundreds of people. At a bar, perhaps, or the beach.'

'Who knows what diabolical ruses they employ, the spies of the CIA!' the Ambassador exclaimed in distaste. 'They are all masters of duplicity. I warn you to be on your guard.'

Marcel had never regarded His Excellency as particularly intelligent, though he was a man of distinguished appearance, well-bred, tall and slender, with luminous brown eyes and a long upper lip. His hair had retreated from his forehead, and this gave him a look of prodigious intellect which was not matched by either his words or his actions. After all, he would not have been sent into exile on Santa Sabina unless he had behaved foolishly at some moment in his career. His nonsense about the CIA served to confirm this dismal view of him.

'You may rely on me to defend the honour of France,' Marcel said dramatically, thinking nothing too ridiculous for Ducour.

'I demand nothing less!' said the Ambassador. 'If you are offered American soft drinks with ridiculous names, take

care that they are not laced with special drugs to make you tell all you know. These things are insidious, I have been informed.'

Marcel thanked him with a straight face for his warning and said he would drink nothing but champagne. His Excellency shook his head sadly.

'As a good Frenchman you will be scandalised to hear that there is no champagne served,' he said, 'only American whisky and a species of imitation wine from California.'

'Good God!' said Marcel, truly astonished. 'But why?'

'They wish us to appreciate their home products, I suppose, just as the Japanese serve their wretched warm *sake* and the Russians their barbarous vodka,' said Ducour. 'In the line of duty a diplomat must be prepared to suffer these hardships with equanimity, for his country. I shall be at this function with Madame Ducour, of course. My stomach churns when I contemplate the terrible food that will be pressed upon me.'

The interview had been totally unsatisfactory. Marcel would have left it at that and gone, but the Ambassador detained him. 'How are the affairs of Monsieur de Murville progressing?' he asked. 'Lafargue has informed me that he introduced him to the top men in the Ministry of Transport I cannot be burdened with details, of course, but I would appreciate an assurance from you that matters are proceeding well.'

Marcel understood perfectly what was required of him. Ducour had no wish to be told that de Murville had been taken to a brothel to offer a bribe to a member of the government. To an Ambassador, knowledge of that sort could be compromising and dangerous. It was only because of the engagement to Lisette that he had any interest in the affair of the buses. And even then he was being characteristically wary.

'I believe that Monsieur de Murville is satisfied with the progress of his plans so far,' Marcel answered with delicacy and the necessary tact. 'Naturally, you would not expect me to be acquainted with the technicalities of his arrangements.'

'Naturally,' His Excellency agreed, with a faint smile of understanding. 'But matters are in train, are they?'

'Without doubt,' said Marcel vaguely.

For a moment or two he hesitated while he wondered whether to take the risk of explaining that Olivier de Murville was a swindler. He reached the view that such dangerous accusations were best left to others. He returned to his own office, to sit and consider, for the twentieth time, how best he could ruin Olivier's plans.

The United States Embassy was large, if not architecturally distinguished, a modern concrete building standing in extensive gardens, not very far from the city centre. For the party the building and gardens were floodlit, with a great show of Stars and Stripes flags on masts everywhere. They would have made a much better show fluttering in a breeze, but after the *Suruq* had blown itself out the weather reverted to the usual oppressive stillness and the flags were dangling limply.

The heat of the day had eased a little after the sun went down, but it was still hot enough to make everyone pleased that the party was outdoors. Marcel made a point of arriving half an hour after the time on his invitation card and was greeted with a great show of cordiality by the new US Ambassador, whom he had never met before, and his wife. He was directed towards the gardens, which he found crowded with several hundred elegantly dressed men and women.

Long tables had been set up close to the back of the Embassy to dispense drinks and food. Further down the gardens there was the only swimming pool in Santa Sabina, installed presumably as an illustration of the American way of life. To Santa Sabinans, who never exposed themselves to the sun if they could avoid it, the swimming pool was proof of their settled belief that all foreigners were mad. And to foreigners like Marcel who were keenly appreciative of the pleasures of the Reserved Beach and its changing huts, the American pool had no purpose.

The guests were standing about in groups, drinking and talking to each other, the men mostly in white dinner jackets

and the women in evening frocks. Marcel presented himself at one of the tables arrayed with bottles and glasses and asked the servant in charge what was available. And it was as Ducour had warned him days before; the drinks were all of American origin. Rather than risk the disillusionment of wines grown in the suburbs of Sacramento, he chose Bourbon whisky with ice. At least the name was French.

Before long, as he moved about the gardens and mingled with the crowd, an amusing scene was played out in front of him. He found Jean-Jacques and Madame Ducour standing in a small group of people which included the Canadian Ambassador and his wife. He attached himself to the group briefly, to pay his respects, but Jean-Jacques seemed not to notice his presence, so busily did he address himself in French to the part-baffled Canadian. Inwardly Marcel shrugged. It was obvious that Ducour regarded him as out of place in this company. Jacqueline Ducour was more gracious to him, as well she might be, in view of the intimate dealings between them in the past.

But a gentle swirl of the crowd revealed Salvador Bonavista in another small group, almost within touching distance, talking to a grinning and bespectacled Japanese. As Ducour's eyes met Bonavista's, he hesitated for a moment and then bowed very slightly towards the Minister. Bonavista smiled and nodded back. While Marcel was considering the implications of this vague greeting, the two men half-turned, to face away from each other, while they resumed their conversations.

When the food was served, or rather when the guests were invited to serve themselves, Marcel found that the al fresco meal was primitive but not as terrible as Ducour had envisaged. The main dish consisted of gargantuan steaks barbecued over beds of charcoal, their exterior burnt almost black and the interior red raw. There were also soft buns containing grilled mincemeat, soft boiled sausages in bread with mustard, and other specialities of the American cuisine. Marcel tried some of everything, washed down with plenty of Bourbon.

Drifting along with the continuous swirl and eddy of the

crowd, he found himself by chance standing next to Bonavista again. The Minister for Transport and Maritime Affairs looked very elegant in his white silk dinner-jacket and with diamond studs down the front of his shirt. He put an arm round Marcel's shoulders, as if they were old friends, and greeted him most cordially. He introduced him to the group of local sycophants and hangers-on standing about him, and Marcel noted their names in his memory for possible future use. But it was more interesting to be introduced to Bonavista's wife Lucreza. In Marcel's private opinion, Madame Bonavista was exquisite.

He put her age at about thirty, two or three years younger than her husband. Her face was a perfect oval, framed by very dark straight hair, worn long, and parted in the middle to descend to her bare shoulders. Her complexion was the delicate coffee-cream tint of the best Santa Sabina families, her mouth a subtle curve that hinted at passion and cruelty, her eyes a lustrous black. Or so, as he bowed over her hand and touched his lips to it, did Marcel describe her to himself, in terms so excessively romantic that eve he was surprised. She was not very tall; the islanders never were, but her body was marvellously proportioned inside her amber-gold party frock.

Half an hour later, Marcel was standing alone under a tree by the swimming-pool, waiting for her. They had exchanged no more than six words when they were introduced, but their eyes had met and he was certain she would find him. Arrogant though his assumption might be considered, it was well-founded; he had waited no more than five minutes before she and another woman strolled towards him, ostensibly deep in conversation. They passed him with a casual glance, but thirty seconds later the companion had walked on alone, her cover role in the comedy complete. Lucreza Bonavista turned back and, under the black shadow of the tree, was in Marcel's arms. 'You are beautiful, beautiful,' she murmured softly to him, her velvet lips brushing against his cheek, while her hands stroked his chest inside his jacket.

'And you, you are adorable,' he whispered back. His

fingers caressed the bare warm skin of her back, above her straight-cut frock and his heart was pounding as her mouth closed on his in a long kiss. He sighed when she reached down to undo his trousers and he slid his tongue into her wet mouth as her fingers closed on his swelling *zimbriq*. She plunged both hands into his underwear and his head was spinning dizzily with pleasure at the touch. 'Lucreza, *je t'adore*,' he murmured as she took out his stiffness, squeezing its throbbing length with one hand while she slid the other under his pompoms and held them.

'But we shall be seen,' he said. 'People are everywhere.'

Over her shoulder he could see other guests strolling about together, only twenty metres away from where the tree's bulk hid them. She led him by the handle she was holding, staying under cover of the trees, right past the empty swimming pool, to an unlit area at the end of the gardens. They found a small, open-fronted shed of bamboo, in which gardeners kept the implements for planting flower-beds and cutting grass. No one else was likely to venture this far away from the bar and the area was dark enough to inspire a lover's confidence.

In the absence of anything better, Lucreza steered him to a wooden wheelbarrow and sat him in it. The position was utterly ridiculous, far too low for comfort and with no support for the back, so that Marcel found he could do no other than sprawl with his knees up. Lucreza did not hesitate for a moment; she pulled up her frock, flung a shapely leg over his middle and sat down across his thighs. She stroked his *zimbriq* with short and nervous little movements which delighted him, and leaned forward for him to find the zipper of her frock and run it down to expose her black lace brassiere. He unhooked that and cupped her soft breasts in his hands.

Though the light was dim, it was enough for him to gaze up with rapture at Lucreza's beautiful face.

'I have always wanted you,' she whispered, 'I have seen you before at diplomatic parties, but this is the first time I have been able to meet you.'

Words like that from a beautiful young woman were

incredibly flattering. And spoken to the accompaniment of little spasms of delight from the touch of her hands on his *zimbriq*, there was no reason to doubt that she was speaking the truth. But even if there had been cause to wonder whether her conduct was perhaps just a little too accommodating, the fact was that by this time Marcel's reason was submerged in a sea of pleasure. Murmuring that he adored her to distraction, he rolled the balls of his thumbs gently over the delicate buds of her breasts until he felt them stiffening. '*Cheri, cheri*!' she sighed. 'You are enchanting!'

Marcel's head was whirling with pleasure and he paid no attention to this reversal of roles. He strained upwards to suck the tips of Lucreza's breasts one after the other, proud to hear her little gasps of delight and feel the beat of her hand quicken on his *zimbriq*. His hands between her thighs, he touched the warm skin above her stocking-tops and her legs opened even wider. Through thin silk he felt the springy curls between her legs and pulled her frock higher to get a hand down her knickers and play with her *kuft*.

'Oh, I must have you!' she exclaimed. 'I must!'

She let go of his throbbing *zimbriq* and dismounted from her ungraceful seat to bend over and slide her underwear quickly down her legs. She straddled him again, her wide-splayed thighs displaying the thick black fleece between them, then sank onto him, her hand reaching down to grasp his *zimbriq* and hold it at the best angle to impale herself. Her knees bent far outwards as she pushed herself down to force him in deep. It did not enter his mind that so beautiful and cultured a woman had with this action reverted to the true Santa Sabina tradition, whereby it was the women who controlled the men and used them for their pleasure.

Even if it had occurred to him, he would have dismissed the thought as irrelevant, for by then he was too greatly aroused to want anything different. As was the way with the women of this country, Lucreza bounced up and down, panting and gasping, her eyes wide open and wild with excitement. It was for all the world as if she were not a sophisticated member of the Hundred Families but a bored

little housewife picked up in a cafe. Her unsupported breasts were flopping up and down before his eyes, their engorged buds showing black against her skin in the half-light. Faster and stronger grew the rhythm of her furious *zeqqing*, until she pushed him past the point of no return and drained him in jolting spurts.

After her wild climax was over she murmured breathlessly that it had been ravishing beyond words and that Marcel was even more charming a lover than she had imagined. But she did not linger; she was up and off him and fastening her brassiere and zipping up her amber-gold frock. She gazed down at him with a smile as he half-lay in the wheelbarrow, his trousers gaping wide to reveal his *zimbriq* wilting against his belly.

'When can we meet again?' she asked, not waiting for Marcel to pose the question. Delighted by the experience and anxious to repeat it at the earliest possible opportunity, he said he would telephone her the next day.

'There is much I have to say to you,' said Lucreza. The words were no sooner out of her mouth than she reached down to trail a finger the length of his soft *zimbriq* by way of farewell. Marcel scrambled awkwardly out of the wheelbarrow, sure it had never been put to that use before. Her touch had been light and casual, but more than enough to reawaken his excitement, so vivid was the memory of the ecstasy she had given him. She thought he wanted to kiss her *au revoir*, and giggled with surprise when he took her hand and guided it down into his open trousers, to feel how strong he was again. While their mouths met in a long hot kiss, her clasped hand slid up and down what it held.

'You are adorable,' she murmured, forestalling him again. In another moment she had turned herself round completely, to present her back to him, leaving his bone-hard *zimbriq* sticking out of his trousers. She gathered her frock up round her waist and held it there with one hand while she sank to her knees on the grass. '*Cheri*,' she murmured, turning her head to smile at him over her shoulder, before she went all the way down on her hands and knees. He saw then that she had not put on her knickers and the pale roundness of

her bare bottom was presented to him in an invitation it would be impossible for any man to decline.

His *zimbriq* jerked stiffly as he threw himself with instant enthusiasm to his knees behind her and put his hands on her bottom to feel the warm flesh of her cheeks. Down between her thighs, even in the semi-darkness of the garden, he caught a glimpse of lips of her dark-haired, plump and pouting *kuft*. He bent down to kiss her bottom, but he was too aroused to wait any longer. He gripped her tightly by the hips while he thrust his loins forward and slid straight into her wet warmth. The smooth clasp of her *kuft* was so exciting that he butted at her like a wild goat, and she braced herself on straight arms to withstand his assault, moaning and sighing all the while.

'Lucreza, Lucreza, *je t'adore*!' he was babbling, and she pushed her bottom at him to receive his thrusts.

She was completely open to him, drawing him in deeper and deeper, as if her hot *kuft* would swallow him. This degree of elevated sensation could not possibly endure for long; Marcel's belly convulsed against her bottom and both their bodies bucked in release as his rapture jetted into her. Almost before his last wet throb, she had escaped from his grasp, murmuring that she would be missed and that he was to phone her. Then she was on her feet, her frock dropped to conceal her sensual charms. She disappeared into the darkness while Marcel was still on his knees, a final twitch or two stirring his wet *zimbriq*.

With a shrug of resignation at being so cruelly deserted, he fastened his trousers and got to his feet. The next time he met her he would make certain that she did not get away from him before he had his fill of her. It was then he noticed Lucreza's knickers still lying on the grass, where she had thrown them in her eagerness to bestride him on the wheelbarrow. He picked up the scrap of black silk and lace, and was delighted by the delicate trace of Chanel No. 5 that clung to the silk. He pressed the fragile knickers to his lips in a kiss of exultation and put them in his pocket.

Later on, back at the party, he found himself talking to a

man he had not met before, a lanky American in his thirties, with crew-cut straw-coloured hair. He spoke hardly any French at all, giving Marcel an opportunity to demonstrate his command of English. But engrossed in this, and elated by his adventure with the beautiful Lucreza and several glasses of Bourbon whisky, he failed to notice that while they were chatting the American was with great skill edging them out of the crowd. But there came a moment when the American put his hand on Marcel's arm and pulled him round a hitherto unnoticed corner of the Embassy building and through an unobtrusive door.

Marcel glanced round in surprise. They were in a small and square room where a hard-faced man in US Marine Corps uniform sat before a metal panel that carried a pattern of little red lights, some on, some off, some flickering.

'OK soldier, take five,' said the man who had edged Marcel into the office, 'I'll mind the store for you.'

Without a word the Marine got up and went out, closing the door firmly behind him.

'But why are we here?' Marcel demanded. 'And who are you?'

'Windhover's the name. You can call me Hank. I know a lot about you, Marcel. You're the Frog who screwed the Ambassador's daughter in the movies. And you're the guy who made Colonel Hochheimer foul up on his mission here. We've got you pegged as an operator for some branch of French intelligence. No point in denying it – we're here to talk turkey.'

'I have nothing to do with espionage,' said Marcel hastily, 'and as for the charming daughter of the last US Ambassador – the one who was recalled to Washington – that is not your concern. What is this turkey you wish to speak about?'

'We know you took your Frog buddy to meet Bonavista in a whorehouse. We ran a check on him and he's a wanted man in practically every French territory round the world, including some I've never heard of. Your pal turns out to be a high-octane con artist. And you're backing his rip-off, right?'

‘This is intolerable,’ Marcel exclaimed. ‘Are you mad, to accuse me? Tomorrow I shall report this conversation and a formal complaint will be made to your Ambassador.

‘Hold your water,’ said the American, completely undaunted by the threat. ‘We’re not out to get *you* – all we want is a little co-operation. And we can make it worth your while.’

‘What do you mean?’ Marcel asked suspiciously.

‘Let’s just say there are reasons why we don’t want to see Bonavista’s ass in a sling. It suits us better for him to stay squeaky-clean and keep his job in the government.’

‘Why? If he’s replaced, it will be by someone like him.’

‘That’s true,’ Hank conceded, ‘but it’s more economical to deal with one guy than to keep starting fresh.’

‘I am well aware that all this plotting and scheming is part of United States long-range strategy to persuade the government of Santa Sabina to permit you to build a naval base here for your warships and submarines.’

‘Slow down there, Marcel, boy! That stuff’s way above my level,’ said the American. ‘My job’s baby-sitting Bonavista, not planning World War Three. Does your Ambassador know this guy Murville is a crook?’

‘Really!’ Marcel exclaimed indignantly. ‘How dare you speak of His Excellency with such insolence! Let me inform you of one very important difference between an Ambassador of the Republic of France and a representative of your own country. It is not our custom in France to send abroad as Ambassadors men of dubious origin who have made themselves millionaires by selling chewing-gum to school children or collaborating with the Mafia to build sub-standard tenements . . .’

‘OK, OK,’ Hank cut in quickly to stem the tirade of outrage, ‘I guess what you’re trying to tell me is that Ducour’s not in on the action. OK by me. No agent in his right mind would tell his Ambassador what’s going on. But you personally put a known crook like Murville up to Bonavista as the man with the money, so it has to be a French intelligence action. And by targeting Bonavista you’re getting your wires crossed with ours.’

‘What am I to conclude from this farrago?’ Marcel asked. ‘That permission is required from the Americans before anything is done? You seem to forget that France is not a colony of yours, like Britain. We do as we like. So how do you say it, Hank – take the running jump.’

‘Easy on, fella, while I lay it out for you. This is not me talking, you understand, this comes straight from the head man in person. If Bonavista gets caught by his boss with his hand in the cash-drawer and goes belly-up, a copy of Murville’s record will find its way on to the desk of President da Cunha to show him that the whole thing was a Frog set-up.

‘The name is *de* Murville,’ Marcel said weakly, his mind almost paralysed with dread.

‘Who cares – a fink is a fink whatever he calls himself. You can bet your whole stack that if the evidence comes to light, your Ambassador will be kicked out on his ass, and you with him. What do they do with French agents who mess up – do they send you to Devil’s Island? Or post you to a Bedouin hell-hole where they’re still running prohibition and there’s not a white woman within a thousand miles? I guess you’ve got the picture.’

Marcel by this time was feeling extremely depressed. Turn as he might, every road seemed to lead straight to disaster and ruin, thanks to Olivier de Murville. In the depths of his heart he cursed the man to damnation and back.

‘You must understand that I admit nothing,’ he said to Hank, playing for time to collect his thoughts. ‘I have nothing to do with intelligence matters and it was the merest chance that I was present at a meeting between de Murville and Bonavista. If anything dishonest was discussed, I have no knowledge of it.’

‘OK, that’s enough bullshit for now,’ said the American, ‘What are you going to *do*?’

‘The decision is at a higher level,’ said Marcel, trying to sound important and vague at the same time, ‘I shall report the position as you have explained it to me and recommend that we abandon any plan that may exist involving Monsieur Bonavista, though I strongly deny that there is any such official plan.’

'That sounds fair enough,' said Hank, who seemed to believe this nonsense. 'We all have to get clearance from the top-brass in our line of work. But I want a cast-iron guarantee from you in person by the end of the week that Bonavista is off the hook and the plan to destabilise him has been junked. OK?'

'OK,' said Marcel gloomily.

He had just remembered that he was under orders to report to Ducour in the morning to explain why he had been invited to the party and what approaches had been made to him. It would be necessary to invent some tissue of lies to keep the Ambassador quiet – it was out of the question to inform him that the CIA were aware that de Murville intended to defraud the Santa Sabina government and took it to be an official French action, which they were insisting must be stopped at once.

The evening was very hot, of course, but the trickling drops of perspiration on Marcel's forehead had more to do with the appalling prospect of shame and disgrace that faced him. He reached into the inside pocket of his jacket for a handkerchief to dab his brow.

'Holy shit!' Hank exclaimed, his eyes bulging, 'Everybody says you Frogs are degenerates, but that beats all!'

Dumbstruck with embarrassment, Marcel realised that he had just dabbed his forehead dry with Lucreza's perfumed and lace-edged black knickers.

'I've been keeping you under surveillance since you got here tonight,' said the American, 'waiting for a chance to talk to you. I was following you down past the pool to watch what you were up to, and when I saw who met you there, I figured she was slipping you a message from her old man.'

'You were spying on us?' Marcel gasped, finding his voice at this new evidence of American treachery.

In a sense, Hank was right. Lucreza had brought a message from her husband, for reflection had persuaded Marcel that it was not so much sexual desire that had brought her to him but Bonavista's instructions. Perhaps the message had not been in words, but he had little doubt that it would be made clear to him at their next encounter.

'Yeah, and here I was kicking myself because I couldn't risk getting close enough to hear what you were saying when you went behind the shack. I didn't guess you went back there to fool around with her.'

'But this is a monstrous invasion of diplomatic privilege!' was the best that Marcel could think of to say.

'You're a lulu, you really are,' said Hank, a trace of reluctant admiration in his voice. 'You set Bonavista up to take a fall, and all the time you're screwing the ass off his wife right under his nose! Right here on the Fourth of July, goddammit! And grabbing her panties for your souvenir chest! In twelve years service I thought I'd seen everything, but I've never come across an operator like you! You're a real sicko, you know that?'

Marcel drew himself to his full height and, with whatever remnants of dignity he could collect, informed the impertinent American that he should for the future restrict his spying to whichever cheap whorehouse would permit him to peep through the keyholes of its bedroom doors. And having delivered himself of this useful advice, he strode out of the room, past the Marine who was leaning on the wall outside the door, smoking a cigarette. In the circumstances the only practical course of action that presented itself to Marcel was to return to one of the bars in the garden and get drunk.

He was unused to large quantities of whisky and, towards the end of the evening he found himself wandering round inside the guest wing of the US Embassy, with no idea of how he got there and even less of where he wanted to go. He opened a door at random and found himself in a bedroom, dimly lit by a bedside lamp. On the beige satin bedcover a fully-dressed woman lay on her side, snoring slightly, evidently dead drunk and dumped there to sleep it off. Her face was turned away from Marcel, as he stood swaying on unsteady legs.

After immense concentration he recognised her as the friend who had accompanied Lucreza on her stroll down the garden to meet him. He knew it was her by the black and white taffeta frock she was wearing. Her shoes had been

taken off and dropped by the bed, displaying her long thin stockinged feet. Marcel's interest was caught by them, and by the delicacy of her ankles, and without being wholly aware of what he was doing, he sat on the end of the bed and gently massaged her feet. Her toenails were painted crimson and the colour showed through the flesh-coloured nylon of her stockings.

His touch on her feet roused her a little – but only enough to turn away from him and until she lay face down on the low bed, with one bare arm hanging down over the side to the floor. Marcel took her thin ankles in his hands and stroked them, enjoying the feel of smooth nylon against his palms. In his condition of intoxication he had now lost contact with reality and soon he was stroking her legs up to her calves. They were elegant legs, no mistake about that, very slender, well-shaped, delicately sensual. It was exciting to stroke them; so much so that before long he was on the bed, straddling one of these fine legs on his hands and knees.

He had not seen the woman's face and had no idea of who she could be. In so far as he was capable of coherent thought, he took her to be a Santa Sabina friend of Lucreza Bonavista. What was in his mind, who can say? Nothing, perhaps, but a Bourbon-induced fantasy of eroticism. His *zimbriq* was so hard in his underwear that it was uncomfortable, and he was compelled to rip open his trousers to set it free, quivering and throbbing in its eagerness. He reached forward with both hands to massage the sleeping woman's leg higher, up to her stocking-tops where the suspenders were attached, and then he turned up her frock to reach higher still, to touch the bare flesh of her thigh.

His knees seemed to have folded under him, though he had no recollection of that happening. With each massaging movement of his hands on her warm thigh, the engorged head of his *zimbriq* was rubbing along the calf of her leg. It felt very good and he kept on doing it, sliding up and down the glassy nylon, until she stirred and sighed. The leg he was not stroking twitched, but she did not wake up. Marcel's

hands were high up her left thigh, touching the frilled edge of her knickers.

Lucreza, *je t'adore*, he muttered, for everything was completely muddled in his mind by then. The sensations that jabbed through him from his *zimbriq* were becoming stronger and stronger with each movement along her stocking. The woman face-down under his hands moaned and trembled; perhaps she was dreaming that a handsome man was making love to her. '*Cherie, cherie*,' Marcel gurgled, almost overcome by a surge of tender feeling towards her. He slid his body up her legs to push his jerking *zimbriq* into her knickers and tried to get it into her.

He was too drunk to achieve so complicated a manoeuvre by himself on an unconscious companion. His *zimbriq* slid over her smooth flesh and, without warning, his belly pulsed in urgent climax and squirted his hot lust between the tiny cheeks of her bottom. She moaned, but slept on as if nothing of interest had happened. Marcel gasped and jerked like a gaffed fish, and then passed out on the bed beside her.

8

Fortunate the Man Who Knows the Countryside

Sitting at a battered metal table outside a small cafe in Vasco da Gama Square, where the buses started from, Marcel realised that Olivier de Murville's scheme was a stroke of the purest inspiration. Santa Sabina's so-called buses were decrepit trucks acquired ten years before, at an unofficial auction of American army surplus sales equipment in Rangoon. Passengers climbed in and out by wooden steps fixed at the back, and sat on hard benches along each side, sheltered from the elements only by slats at their back and a battered tarpaulin top.

Tight-fisted though President da Cunha was known to be, it seemed possible that his Minister of Transport might be able to persuade him, for the good of the people, to replace these worn-out relics with more modern vehicles. Presumably, Marcel speculated, this was the key to Olivier's successful career of crime; in whichever country he found himself, he looked round for what was most needed and approached the authorities with an offer to supply the need at a reasonable price and offered the personal inducement that made them want to deal with him.

On a stone plinth in the middle of the Square there was a statue of Vasco da Gama himself. It had always seemed to Marcel that the sculptor had inadvertently given the great voyager an expression of dismayed surprise. But on reflection, it would have been entirely appropriate if da Gama could have foreseen how unpleasant the Square would be. The cobbles were stained and darkened with oil that had leaked from engines, and there were rust-streaks where water

had dripped from rotting cooling systems. The palm trees that lined the Square had been poisoned for years by exhaust fumes and resembled vegetation in a mad Surrealist painting.

A driver in a shiny-peaked uniform cap and a short-sleeved shirt came out of a bar and climbed into one of the half dozen buses that had been standing idle for the past thirty minutes. He made a great performance of adjusting the rearview mirror and then started the engine, in preparation for moving off. Marcel finished his glass of mint tea and climbed aboard. It was early afternoon and there were only two other passengers – a boy and a girl, both about sixteen years of age. As the local etiquette required, Marcel greeted them both politely when he took his seat opposite them. There was a wickerwork basket under their bench and from it came an indignant squawking of hens when the bus lurched forward.

According to the faded timetable displayed outside the ticket-office in the Square they were just leaving, this was the one-forty bus to Selvas. Marcel glanced at his wristwatch and saw that it was five minutes past two and resigned himself to being late for his meeting. Selvas was a fishing port on the west coast of Santa Sabina, and with the blessing of Providence and a fair wind the bus ought to arrive there sometime after nine that evening. Marcel's destination was much closer.

The bus ground from stop to stop through the suburbs and on past the Reserved Beach. Marcel observed, between the palm trees that divided road from beach, twenty or thirty people lying on the sand and as many again splashing about in the sea. He thought it likely that Lisette was there and told himself that it was high time he carried matters to a conclusion with that young woman. But not today, there being another call on his time and energy.

The road moved away from the shore and ran parallel with it, through clumps of vivid bougainvillaea and frangipani flowers, and then through groves of coconut palms. On the seat opposite Marcel the boy and girl were locked without shame in a loving embrace, her arms round his neck and his hand between her open thighs under her

electric-blue frock. Naturally, girls like her wore no underwear, and Marcel's *zimbriq* was growing hard at the thought of what she was encouraging the boy to feel. Her little *kuft* would be wet by now, under his fingers.

Marcel turned away from the engrossed couple and stared out between the wooden slats, trying to keep his attention focused on the white-washed kilometre stones as they passed. The youth of Santa Sabina were completely without shame in their interest in love and it was obvious that, as soon as he got off the bus, the girl would sit herself astride her boyfriend's lap and let him pierce her. She had her hand down the front of his trousers already. Marcel sighed in relief when the fifth kilometre stone appeared by the roadside and stood up immediately to tug on the greasy cord dangling under the tarpaulin, conveying to the driver that he wished to descend.

The bus growled to a halt and Marcel waved goodbye to his travelling companions and they smiled back at him with a gleam in their eyes that told of their intentions. The girl made no effort to hide what she was doing as she jerked her friend's trousers open while Marcel was still climbing down the rickety steps to the road. With his jacket over his arm, he walked back slowly to the kilometre marker, his *zimbriq* so stiff that it rubbed uncomfortably against his underwear with each step that he took, and the friction roused him further. He was glad to sit on the grass verge by the stone and wait.

He was half an hour late, but nothing and no one were ever on time in this country, and another ten minutes passed before a bright red open car came racing along the road and screeched to a halt by him. Lucreza Bonavista was driving and, Marcel saw with distaste, the car was American made. To his mind, it was vulgarly ostentatious in size, colour and chromium-plating. But Lucreza herself! His heart leaped to see her again and although he remembered her as exquisite from their meeting at the US Embassy, the reality far surpassed memory and fantasy. She was wearing a brief and sleeveless summer frock of pale jade-green silk that enhanced the delicious coffee-cream tint of her face and arms.

Susceptible as ever to women's charms, Marcel fell in love with her on the spot.

'Have you been waiting long?' she asked, with a smile so enchanting that his head spun, 'I'm sorry to be so late.'

Marcel got into the car, assuring her that he would wait for all eternity for the delight of seeing her if he had to. Before he could take her in his arms, she kissed his cheek and drove on, accelerating as if she were competing at Rheims or Monaco. The few who owned cars in Santa Sabina were fortunate in that they generally had the roads to themselves. The ordinary people walked or used the infrequent buses; country people who could afford them had mule-carts, or rode tiny thin-legged donkeys. And bicycles were sometimes to be seen, imported through Goa from heaven knew where.

Lucreza's long black hair was flying out behind her as she sent the car hurtling along the road with a casual skill that made Marcel very uneasy. They roared through a village without slowing down, and Marcel looked out for a tiny cafe he knew. Three people sat at one of the small tables outside in the street and the faded wooden sign still said *Xavier's Bar*, though fat Xavier had sold it to his niece and retired.

They were out of the village and heading west far too fast for the narrow road, the rush of wind howling over the windscreen. Lucreza's frock had crept up her bare legs, almost into her lap, and Marcel stopped being aware of their speed. His *zimbriq* had collapsed under the stress before they reached the village, but the pale green frock crept higher and his stiffness reasserted itself. Before long her golden thighs were totally uncovered and he could see how the thin white silk of her close-fitting knickers was stretched over her mound.

She caught the direction of his gaze and grinned at him as she moved her left leg a little away to the side. Marcel could not contain his exclamation of pleasure to see the silk pulled taut enough to outline the split of her *kuft*. His *zimbriq* was twitching desperately, like a chained animal struggling to break free. Lucreza saw and her little laugh was swallowed by the slip-stream. She reached down into

his lap, feeling his hardness through his trousers, and Marcel's heart was pounding in his chest at her touch.

'Lucreza, stop the car!' he begged her, but she squeezed him hard between her fingers and laughed again.

'Not yet!' she said exultantly, 'I want to drive you insane with desire for me!'

'You have succeeded!' he assured her, but she drove faster, one hand on the steering-wheel and the other in her own lap.

With the tip of her middle finger she began to stroke the lips of her *kuft* through the silk of her knickers. Marcel could hardly breathe as he watched open-mouthed, his thighs wide apart on the car-seat in an effort to ease the maddening pressure of his trousers on his upright *zimbriq*.

'Lucreza . . .' he gasped as she raised her frock to her hips and slipped her hand inside the elastic of her knickers. Marcel saw her palm slide down her smooth belly until her fingers were between her thighs and a knuckle jutted outwards against the silk as she sank her finger into her *kuft* and caressed herself.

The sight of Lucreza playing with herself was too much to contemplate in inactivity. Marcel reached across to put his hand down her knickers and feel her, but she laughed at him and told him to watch and not touch. The car swerved crazily across the road and almost off it when she lifted her bottom from the seat and pushed her knickers halfway down her thighs. But she dragged one-handed at the steering-wheel and stamped hard on the accelerator, and the car slid sideways for fifteen metres before it was racing straight down the road once more.

Of their near-approach to high-speed disaster, Marcel knew nothing. At that moment nothing existed for him outside the car. He was staring with undivided attention at the bush of curly black hair between Lucreza's thighs and at the full lips of her pouting *kuft*. When he called to her over the roar of the engine and the howl of the wind that she had achieved her aim of driving him insane with desire for her, she shook her head and answered, 'Take my knickers off for me.' He could hardly believe what he heard

and looked at her questioningly until she nodded and repeated her words.

Then he was down on his knees on the bucking floor, wedged in tightly between dashboard and seat, his trembling hands on the satin skin of her thighs. He pulled her knickers over her knees and down her bare legs until he could get them over her feet and off. At once, as if revelling in her freedom, Lucreza spread her legs, so that from where he was crouched, Marcel saw the pink inner lips of her *kuft* exposed to him, and their moistness. He was desperate to feel her; he moaned softly to himself as he put his hand between her thighs, but she pushed him away and thrust two fingers into herself.

'Lucreza, I am dying . . .' Marcel gasped.

He was clutching at his *zimbriq*, vibrating in his underwear. Lucreza was feeling the effect of her own stimulation and the car was slowing down and wandering from side to side of the road. She ran it up a cart-track along a grassy slope, and when they were well away from the road, drove round behind a clump of mango trees and stopped. There was no one in sight at all, not for as far as the eye could reach. They were screened from the road and ahead of them the ground sloped gently upwards to the far distance. Small plantations of fruit trees were dotted about in a curiously haphazard manner and, a flock of fifteen or twenty goats grazed and bleated not far away from the car.

Almost before Lucreza had set the handbrake and turned off the ignition, Marcel was up on the seat beside her, an arm about her waist to hold her close to him and a hand thrust into the deep-cut neck of her green frock to feel her breasts and their hard little tips. She gasped loudly and her shining black eyes half-closed as her neck folded over the seatback until she was staring straight up into the sky. Marcel rolled a warm breast in the palm of his hand and her bare legs jerked upwards under the dashboard in a convulsive kick.

He put his hand up her frock and found her *kuft* so open and slippery wet that there could be no doubt her climax had already come. Her head turned on the seatback and she

stared at him with eyes full of desire. He kissed her open mouth and, as soon as he touched her bud, she went into the convulsions of urgent release again. In moments it was over, and she murmured his name again and again while she climbed up and straddled him on the car-seat. She ripped his trousers open with a savage tug and put her arms round his neck. Marcel took the fleshy cheeks of her bare bottom in his hands and kneaded them lovingly.

'Yes, I've made you insane with desire for me!' she said with a little grin of triumph, while she rubbed her belly against his throbbing *zimbriq*.

'And you are mad with desire for me,' Marcel gasped.

On fire for her though he undoubtedly was, he was not wholly convinced he was the subject of the raging desire that was consuming her. She had aroused herself deliberately with her fingers, and she could as easily pleasure herself with them if he were not present. But that was of little importance to a man in his condition, and of no importance whatsoever to a *zimbriq* as stiff as his. He reached down between their bodies, to steer its purple and swollen head to her wet *kuft* and she gasped and shivered as she pushed her belly at him to help him slide in.

'Don't move,' she whispered fiercely. 'Sit absolutely still and wait! For me!'

His hands were on the cheeks of her bottom again, fondling them and kneading them. Lucreza pressed her mouth to his in a never-ending kiss, her wet tongue in his mouth. Deep inside his belly a delicious pressure was mounting and he could feel her *kuft* gripping him like a hand and milking him gently. He sighed to her mouth and his back went rigid against the car seat as the most acute pang of pleasure he had ever felt tore through him. He wanted to tell Lucreza that he adored her, but his sensations were too intense and the words of love turned into a gurgle as her *kuft* sucked his desire from him in long spurts.

When the two of them were rational again, Lucreza climbed off him and flopped limply in the corner between white leather seat and car door, to cool down. Her frock

was up in her lap still, revealing the enticing length of her bare thighs.

'You make love so beautifully,' she said, turning her head on the seatback to look at him. 'I adore you for that.'

With all his heart Marcel wanted to believe that she meant what she said, for his feelings about her were tender and true. But he had himself said words like hers to many women in the after-glow of love-making, and knew how little they meant. And as if to confirm his misgivings about her truthfulness, she at once plunged into the real concern that had brought her to him.

'There is something we must talk about,' she said, her smile so adoring that it would have been a cold-hearted man who could resist it, 'something very important. Do you understand me?'

'I can guess what it is,' he answered, resigned to tasting the sour now that he had enjoyed the sweet, 'but tell me.'

'It concerns your friend Olivier de Murville.'

'I don't doubt it,' he said wryly. 'What of him, Lucreza?'

'My husband has received some very disturbing information about him. It seems that Monsieur de Murville has stolen money in more than one country. He is an international criminal. And now he is here in Santa Sabina asking my husband for a contract to supply new buses.'

'Do you know from whom Monsieur Bonavista received this distressing information?' Marcel asked. 'Was it from the Americans, by any chance?'

'He didn't tell me. But what does it matter where the report came from, if it is true?'

But it had to be the Americans, Marcel thought. Evidently Hank Windhover had divulged his information to Bonavista to get his shot in first. The offer he had made to wait until he heard that the supposed official plan had been cancelled – that was bogus, a deception.

'To be frank with you,' he said, not being frank at all, 'I have heard a similar report about de Murville, but I don't know for certain whether it is true or false.'

Lucreza gave him a look of total disbelief.

'He came to my husband with the recommendation of the

French Embassy,' she said. 'You introduced the two of them. And as all the world knows, you are the head of the French Secret Service in Santa Sabina. So what is going on?'

'I have nothing to do with spying,' said Marcel wearily.

He knew she wouldn't believe him; no one ever did now. The rumour had started a year before, when he was engaged in a passionate love-affair with the wife of a German diplomat. By chance she had involved him in a family squabble to replace President da Cunha by a cousin of his named D'Cruz. In self-protection Marcel reported what he knew to his Ambassador and, to the astonishment of them both, in the unmasking that followed, the Santa Sabinans had credited Marcel with foiling a *coup d'etat*. Since his actual role had been too ludicrous for rational minds to accept, the whole of the local political and diplomatic communities decided that he was a French master-spy.

'I know you have to deny it,' said Lucreza, resting her hand on his thigh. 'But what I have to tell you is this – my husband regards you as his guarantee that the business with Monsieur de Murville will be carried through properly. The money will be paid over and the buses will be delivered – do you understand? He holds you personally responsible.'

'But I cannot be responsible for de Murville's actions,' said Marcel in dismay. 'I know almost nothing about him and his business affairs!'

'If that's true, why did you introduce him to my husband?' Lucreza asked sceptically. 'Did he pay you?'

'Of course not! I was acting on the instructions of . . .'

He was going to say *of the Ambassador*, but he broke off when he realised that he was about to incriminate His Excellency, the Embassy and its policy, and his beloved France.

'Yes, on the instructions of your superiors in the Secret Service,' said Lucreza with a smile. 'I am not stupid, but I do not understand the purpose of this plan, nor does my husband. But that is of no significance, just as long as the business of the buses goes through as promised. Otherwise . . .' and she shrugged her shoulders delicately.

'Otherwise?' Marcel asked, his heart sinking.

'You can imagine for yourself some of the unpleasant things that might happen to foreigners involved in stealing money from the government. It would be too serious a matter for the police and the Bureau of Public Information would take over. Their agents seize suspects in the streets and carry them off to secret places for interrogation. Many are never seen again. Those that survive always sign full confessions for use at their trial.'

'You seem to forget that I have diplomatic immunity,' Marcel said, feeling very uneasy at her account of the activities of the thugs of the Secret Police.

'Naturally,' she agreed. 'But mistakes are sometimes made. A Swedish diplomat vanished about three years ago – you must have heard of the affair, because at the time it was notorious. This diplomat was thought to be implicated in bribing a member of the Chamber of Deputies to pass confidential documents to him – he was suspected of being a spy, in effect. When no one could find him, there were official complaints and protests and even an ultimatum from his Embassy. They were convinced that he had been taken by the Bureau but there was no proof. President da Cunha ordered a full investigation to be carried out, to please them, but no trace of the man was found and who can say whether he was interrogated or not?'

'No, this is too ridiculous,' said Marcel, 'I refuse to be intimidated by threats of violence!'

'Threats?' said Lucreza, her jet-black eyebrows rising up her forehead in surprise. 'But how can you think such a thing? All I am trying to explain to you is that my husband wants you to know he is your friend. He is confident that you will protect his interests, as a good friend, so that he can protect yours. And I too am confident that you will look after him.' Her hand was stroking his thigh slowly as she spoke.

'Come into the back seat,' Marcel suggested.

She smiled and nodded and they moved into the rear of the open car. He took her in his arms and she snuggled against him, her hand dipping into his open trousers to take hold of his upright *zimbriq*.

'How enchanting, the way you are strong again so soon,' she murmured. 'I suppose you want me to lie down for you, so you can make love in your strange and uncomfortable foreign way.'

'The women of my country do not find it uncomfortable,' he said defensively, feeling her breasts through her pale green frock. 'In my experience they find it very satisfactory.'

'How peculiar they must be, if they permit themselves to be dominated by their men in this way,' Lucreza retorted. 'Do you Europeans beat your women to make them lie down for you?'

Marcel knew there was no point in trying to explain to her that man-above, woman-below was the most natural way in the world of making love. He had failed many a time in the past to convey to Santa Sabina women the good sense and natural logic of the time-honoured position. Their own traditions and culture convinced them that man-below, women-above was the proper way. And who was to say which belief was correct, or whether there could be any such concept as 'correct' in a matter of pleasure?

'Our women lie down to be loved because they enjoy it, no other reason,' he said, his smile charming as Lucreza slid her diamond-ringed hand up and down his *zimbriq*.

'How can they possibly enjoy being crushed under the weight of a heavy man?' she sighed. 'What strange women you have in your country! But because I adore you to distraction, you shall have your way . . .'

She unzipped her frock and pulled it over her head, threw it over into the front seat and arranged herself naked on the white leather. Marcel knelt on the car-floor to kiss her soft breasts and lick their coffee-bean buds. Her thighs parted and he put his hand between them, to find that her dark curls were plastered wetly to her flesh. He played with her deftly until she began to shake under his touch and he knew her crisis had come. Her eyes were closed and she was gasping when he lay on her and split her with his *zimbriq*.

The car seat was not wide enough for his height and he was compelled to lie half on her and half across her. He had one leg hanging over the edge of the seat, with his foot

on the floor, while his other leg, bent at the knee, stuck up in the air like the periscope of a submarine. But as the old saying goes, true love finds its own way. The comic awkwardness of his position did not hinder Marcel from riding in and out of her slippery *kuft* with tremendous zest, until he flooded it with his gratification and heard Lucreza's ecstatic cry.

'That was fascinating!' she surprised him by saying, when she was speaking again. 'But I prefer the proper way. Tell me that you adore me and then I must be going – this evening we have a big dinner-party and I am due at the hairdresser at four-thirty.'

It was then that the truth of another old saying was forced upon their attention; love may find its own way, but love's way is never entirely free from obstacles. Lucreza's frock, thrown casually over into the front seat when she took it off, was not to be found. It was not on the seat, not on the car-floor, not on the grass outside the car; in a word, nowhere.

'But this is ridiculous!' she exclaimed sharply.

To the delectation of Marcel she threw herself down naked on the grass and searched underneath the car, the round cheeks of her bottom clenching and unclenching in the most delightful way when she slid and wriggled herself under it to the waist. The temptation was enormous to get down beside her and feel her bottom, but her temper was fast deteriorating. The mystery of the vanishing frock puzzled him as much as it puzzled her, and the unwelcome thought was in his mind that someone had crept up to the car and taken it while they were intimately involved with each other on the back seat.

The wordly-wise Duc de la Rochefoucauld was the first to point out that, in the misfortune of even our best friends, we always find something which is not displeasing to us. Marcel felt the truth of this when Lucreza ran naked right round the car, her beautiful breasts joggling rhythmically up and down. But it was very necessary to hide this feeling as he joined in the hunt for the missing frock. He stood on the car seat and turned slowly, to stare out in all directions

for any sign of a retreating intruder. And the awful truth dawned on him.

'Lucreza – we left the doors wide open when we got into the back of the car,' he said. 'Look over there!'

She stared in the direction of his pointing finger and shrieked, 'The goats have got it!'

The little flock had moved further away, but it was obvious that curiosity had brought one of the goats right up to the car while Marcel and Lucreza were at their amusements in the back and, finding the doors open, had put her head inside. The green frock had evidently attracted her interest and she had clamped her teeth on it and carried it away. And now another goat was disputing possession of it with her, as could be seen all too well from the car. The frock was being torn apart by the two of them, their heads down and their front legs splayed out as they fought their tug-of-war.

'No!' Lucreza cried in anger. 'That's a Balmain original!'

Naked as she was, she went dashing up the hill towards the goats. Marcel stood motionless on the car seat, spellbound by the deliciously reciprocal movement of the cheeks of her bottom as she ran. Incidents like these constituted the truly magical moments in life, he knew; unforgettable glimpses of enchantment that would never return. To see the bare bottom of so beautiful a woman in motion across a green countryside had, for him, all the emotional impact that a vision of the Holy Grail or the True Cross would hold for a Crusader.

His heart bursting with joy, he sprang from the leather seat, over the side of the car, and ran in pursuit of Lucreza. Unlike her, he was fully clothed, except for his jacket, and the heat soon slowed his pace. Even so, he was a faster runner than she, and soon began to reduce her lead, letting her soft and wobbling bottom be the magnetic pole towards which his compass needle was pointing. But neither she nor he got any closer to the goats; the disobliging creatures had taken fright and were running away up the slope as fast as their skinny legs would carry them.

The hill was not steep, but to the top of the slope was

the best part of a kilometre. Marcel gained on Lucreza and had almost overtaken her when she stopped abruptly and sat down on the grass, her breasts rising and falling delightfully to her breathless panting. Marcel drew level and halted to stretch out a hand to help her to her feet, but she shook her head.

'I can't run any more,' she gasped. 'Get it for me, Marcel.'

He nodded and smiled and ran on, his legs aching miserably. The goats had vanished over the brow of the hill and he could no longer hear their alarmed bleating. He pounded to the top an paused, bent over and hands on his knees, to relieve his breathing, while he stared down into a green valley. Not very far off he could see the gleam of light on water, where a brook wound its roundabout course, and beside it there stood a small house. The goats had taken refuge in an open yard at the side of the house.

Clearly, there was no point in exhausting himself by more running, and Marcel resumed his pursuit of the idiotic animals at a walking pace. Now that his mind was functioning again, he pondered what Lucreza had said to him. Obviously, in the affair of the buses there were no secrets at all! Everyone knew that Olivier de Murville was a professional swindler, even the man he proposed to swindle. And by some strange sleight of hand that was incomprehensible, the blame for Olivier's criminality had been shifted sideways on to Marcel's shoulders!

When he reached the stream he threw himself down on the grassy bank to drink from his cupped hands and bathe his sweating face. Slightly refreshed, he ambled on along the bank until he came to the house, a typical small farmer's home with white-washed walls, a roof thatched with palm leaves, and wooden shutters for windows. At present the shutters were all open, as was the door. He moved slowly, so as not to startle the goats and set them running again, though he could see no sign of the green frock. If they had not dropped it in their flight, they must have eaten it.

While he stood pondering this problem, a woman came round the side of thc house and stared at him. She had a

baby cradled in one arm and her sleeveless white blouse was open to bare her full breasts. She was about twenty, Marcel thought, a typical Santa Sabinan peasant woman, with a mop of coarse black hair and dark eyes in a broad face. From the way her brown-skinned breasts hung low and slack it was evident that she had several children. And while he was enjoying looking at her dark-budded breasts, she halted almost within arm's length and gave him a hard stare of accusation.

'Why are you chasing my goats?' she demanded in very strongly accented French. 'Are you a thief?'

Marcel wished her a polite *bon jour* and regretted to inform her that her goats had taken his friend's frock and he had been chasing them only to recover it. She cast a glance at her flock and naturally the miserable creatures had a look of innocence about them. She stared suspiciously at Marcel and he noticed the ripple of muscle in her arms and shoulders and the sturdiness of her legs under her short brown skirt. Women of her sort worked long days in the fields from childhood onwards, he remembered, and developed a formidable strength of body. She would be more than a match for him if she decided that he was harbouring criminal intentions towards her livestock.

'The frock will never be recovered now,' he said with a shrug, giving her his most charming smile, 'but no matter, other possibilities exist. My name is Marcel – and yours?'

His smile and friendly manner, to say nothing of his good looks, did much to reduce her antagonism. 'Zita,' she answered, her broad face relaxing into a faint smile. 'Where did your woman take her clothes off?'

'Over the hill, by a clump of mango trees near the road.'

She grinned at that and shook herself to make her breasts wobble, aware at last of the circumstances in which the garment was lost. The baby slept on undisturbed in the crook of her arm, his appetite evidently satisfied earlier. Marcel grinned back at her, but with a certain wariness. He knew well enough that when a Santa Sabina woman became aroused she turned into a carnivorous beast. He had no wish to satisfy this one, so soon after making love twice to the

woman he most adored in the world, and he must take care not to raise her expectations.

'My friend cannot go back to the city naked, you understand that, Zita,' he said. 'Is it possible that you can sell me something of yours for her to wear? You and she are about the same height, but she is somewhat thinner than you.'

'If I could help you, I would,' she replied, making her breasts shake again to hold his attention, 'but all I have is what I have on and what I wear for church on Sunday.'

Marcel had seen many a time the hand-embroidered, flounced-skirt and scarlet-waistcoated outfits that country women wore for church and for festivals. They represented months of work by several women working together and it was almost impossible to set a price on them.

'What you are wearing would serve very well,' he said, reaching into his back pocket for his bundle of paper money.

The bank-notes of Santa Sabina were large and colourful, perhaps to compensate for the uncertainty of their relationship to any other known currency. Marcel peeled fifty-tikkoo notes, one by one, off his folded stack, deliberately slowly to make sure Zita was impressed. To be honest, the notes were worth only a little over five francs each, though they were the size of a handkerchief and printed with a portrait of President da Cunha wearing the uniform of a Field-Marshal. Marcel held out four of them fan-wise to Zita.

'For your blouse,' he said. 'Will you sell it?'

He knew that he was offering five times the price when the blouse was new, and to judge by its appearance, it had been worn and washed many, many times. Zita did not hesitate for an instant; she laid her baby down on the grass, where he slept on peacefully with a thumb in his mouth, and stripped off her blouse. She stood grinning as she held it out towards Marcel, her big brown breasts rolling to her movement.

'Where is your husband, Zita?' he asked.

'He's working,' she answered, and waved an arm vaguely in a westerly direction.

Marcel felt that it was in order to indulge a little his lifelong interest in the female body, although he was completely determined not to permit it to go beyond looking. It would be amusing to get Zita to strip naked for him for the equivalent of a few francs. He handed her the money and took the blouse.

'You like my *gublas*?' she asked, instinctively aware of his interest. 'You want to feel them? Suck them maybe?'

Marcel dismissed her question with a smile and peeled off four more highly-coloured bank-notes.

'Will you sell me your skirt?' he asked.

Her response was to pull open a button at her hip and let the loose black skirt fall round her ankles. She stepped out of it nimbly and flicked it upwards with a bare foot, to catch and offer to him. When he reached for it, she stepped closer and, with her free hand, took hold of him between the legs. 'You're hard,' she said. 'You want to *zeqq* me.'

Before he had time to pull away with a grin and a shake of his head, Zita squatted on her haunches, dragging him down with her by her firm grasp on his pompoms. A moment later he found himself pushed flat on his back by her strong arm, while she was astride his thighs. She grinned down at him, tore open his trousers and took his *zimbriq* between her hard work-roughened fingers. At this point, there being no alternative, Marcel resigned himself to what was going to happen.

He watched as she raised herself on her knees in order to position the engorged head of his *zimbriq*, and he gasped when she sat down hard and drove it up into her. And at once she jerked herself up and down furiously, her mouth hanging wide open and her hands tugging at her long brown breasts. He gave himself up to sensation, knowing that in Santa Sabina *zeqqing* of this sort was quickly over, with only seconds of enjoyment for a vast outlay of energy. At least he had the satisfaction of knowing that his self-sacrifice was not in vain – he had acquired clothes for Lucreza to go home in.

9

Odd Figures Glimpsed Swimming, as Virgil Said

When Marcel learned that Bonavista knew Olivier was a swindler, he concluded that the information had been passed over by the American, Windhover. In consequence his opinion of Windhover suffered a severe decline, from rude and arrogant to untruthful and treacherous. It went without saying that there was no longer any point in making contact with the man to pretend that the non-existent intelligence operation directed against he Minister of Transport and Maritime Affairs had been cancelled.

But Marcel was to learn that agents like Windhover are not so easily shaken off and forgotten. He was sitting with Lisette and Olivier on the terrace of the Gran'Caffe Camille, enjoying an after-dinner cognac, when a boy of ten or eleven came to the table and asked which of the gentlemen was Monsieur Lamont. Somewhat surprised, Marcel identified himself and the boy said he had a message to deliver, but it was for him alone. Even more surprised by this, Marcel excused himself and rose from the table.

The boy was not content to withdraw a few paces beyond the cafe terrace; he led Marcel right across Martyrs' Square, and it was not until they stood under the shadow of the church front that he seemed to feel secure enough to halt and inform Marcel in a dramatic whisper, 'Somebody wants to speak to you.'

'Who?'

'He didn't tell me his name, but he's foreign, like you,' said the boy, deriving considerable enjoyment from his role as go-between in a matter of formidable importance.

'For the past half-hour I have been sitting at that table with my friends,' said Marcel, not at all pleased by what he heard. 'Whoever he is, he could have approached me.'

'No, he says this is a matter of secrecy,' said the boy. 'He gave me 25 tikkoos, so it must be very important. He is waiting for you over there,' and he indicated somewhere behind him.

'What does he look like?'

The boy threw his hands up, as if to say *what do foreigners look like*? When Marcel persisted, he said that the man was thin and had hair like a sweeping-brush. That established him as Windhover in Marcel's mind, and he reached into his pocket.

'Here are another 25 tikkoos for you,' he said. 'Go back to this idiot and tell him that I have no wish to speak to him now or at any other time and he can make the big running jump.'

'Shall I call him an idiot to his face, Monsieur?'

'I insist on it!' and Marcel marched back across the cobbled square to where Lisette and Olivier awaited his return.

They looked at him with a question in their eyes, and when he gave no explanation, Olivier chuckled and suggested that an assignation had been made with a lady. Marcel smiled vaguely and said nothing. He thought he had detected signs of tension between Olivier and Lisette and he was hoping that any lack of sympathy that might have developed could be turned to his own advantage. The truth was that Lisette was looking extremely desirable that evening in a little white silk frock that draped over her superb breasts in a manner that was breath-taking.

But less than ten minutes passed before the same boy was back beside the table. 'Go away,' said Marcel, even before he had time to deliver whatever message he brought this time.

'Monsieur, excuse the interruption,' said the lad, grinning mischievously, 'but the idiot-gentleman told me to say that if you refuse to come with me, I must repeat his message in front of your friends.'

'What message!' Marcel exclaimed, infuriated by all this.

'It is about what you did when you were dead drunk,' the boy answered, his grin stretching wider. 'Shall I say i?'

'Wait!' said Marcel, his thoughts racing.

He had been incapacitated-drunk only once in the past year, and that was on the night of the US Embassy reception, when he had too much Bourbon whisky. He had woken up the next morning in his bed at the Grand Hotel Orient with a disabling hang-over and uneasy half-memories of having made certain advances to an unconscious woman who was a complete stranger to him. It would not advance his cause with Lisette to have any of that divulged now, and as for Olivier, he was sure to make crude and insufferable jokes at Marcel's expense, if he ever got to know of that episode.

'Very well, I will accompany you, you little blackmailer,' he told the boy, and again presented his apologies to Lisette and Olivier, both of whom stared at him in open-mouthed amazement.

'Evidently the lady is impatient for your embrace,' Olivier said unnecessarily. 'I wish you good-night and good luck!'

'There is no question of an assignation,' Marcel retorted. 'This is official Embassy business.'

Lisette burst into laughter and Olivier shook his head in solemn disbelief. There was nothing Marcel could do to retrieve the situation and he hurried away from the table, following the boy across the cobbles for the second time.

'Where is this cretin?' he demanded. 'I have things to say to him that he will not enjoy hearing!'

'Turn right on the Avenue of the Constitution, Monsieur. He is waiting for you at the fifth tree down.'

His mission accomplished, the boy trotted away into the night and Marcel, teeth gritted in rage, strode out of Martyrs' Square into the Avenue and along it. It was planted with palm trees every twenty metres and they had been there so long that they had grown very large. Marcel approached the fifth one from the corner, but he could see no one there, even though for once the overcast had cleared and a three-quarters full moon made the streets almost as light as day.

It was not until he drew level with the tree and halted that

Windhover stepped out from his cover behind the trunk and put a finger to his lips to enjoin silence. The American had dressed to be inconspicuous, in dark grey trousers and jacket, but his peculiar hair-cut made him the easiest man in the entire city to identify. He kept his right hand inside his jacket, as if he were holding the butt of a revolver in a shoulder-holster, as perhaps he was.

'Windhover – what idiot game are you playing?' Marcel asked in angry English. 'What is this stupidity of secret meetings?'

'Throttle back, Frog,' said the American, his tone of voice registering dislike, distaste and even disgust. 'In my line of work I can't afford to be watched.'

'Who on earth would be watching us?' Marcel demanded.

'You know damn well who,' said Windhover, 'goons from the Bureau of Public Information. They've got every non-national under twenty-four hour surveillance. There's one on my tail every time I step outside the Embassy grounds, but I've shaken him. Have you shaken yours?'

'What do you want?' said Marcel, exasperated by the Secret Service nonsense. 'You've given de Murville's record to the Minister. We have no more to say to each other.'

'Don't give me that, you Frog degenerate,' Windhover said in derision. 'Maybe you've forgotten you raped an American citizen the night of the Fourth of July, but we haven't.

'What do you mean?' said Marcel, trying to bluff it out, but to no avail. Hank Windhover sneered at him under the pale yellow street-lights.

'After our talk that night I lost you for a while,' he said, 'and when I went searching round everywhere for you, where had you got to? Goddam it to hell, you were out cold alongside Dr Prout, with her clothes up round her belly and you with your dick hanging out! Course, I don't know the lady that well and I figured it was an invitation-match, so to cover up for her I bundled you into an Embassy car and dumped you at your hotel.'

'I have you to thank for that, have I' said Marcel. 'Why couldn't you mind your own business?'

'Anything tending to bring the Embassy of the United States and its personnel into disrepute *is* my business,' Hank replied, 'and Dr Prout screwed unconscious by a liquored-up foreigner is pretty damned disreputable in my book.'

'How dare you say that to me' Marcel squawked, appalled by the crudeness of Windhover's mind. The American glanced round nervously, to see if the outburst had drawn the attention of anyone walking nearby on the Avenue.

'Keep your voice down,' he hissed, 'and cut the bullshit. I gave you a ride home not knowing what you'd done. And holy hell, when I got back and looked in to see if Dr Prout was OK, she came to and started screaming blue murder, thinking I'd raped her. My god, she had me sweating! It took some doing to straighten her out and let her know who the perpetrator was. Why'd you abuse her, you mentally-deficient creep – can't you ever control yourself?'

'If this lady has a complaint to make against me, that is for her to say,' said Marcel, pretending an unconcern he was far from feeling. 'Tell me what you want, Windhover, or I walk away now.'

'You don't get off that easy, Frog. First, she wants to see what a sex-fiend capable of what you did looks like. Second, she wants a full explanation, if you're up to it. Third, she expects the most grovelling apology you're capable of. After that, she'll decide whether or not to press charges.'

'There's something not right about this,' said Marcel. 'Why is it *you* who is sent to threaten me with this travesty? You're a species of CIA espionage operator, not a detective and not a policeman – not even a security guard. So why are you here, Hank, dear old friend? Explain, if you please.'

'Do you see somebody right across the Avenue watching us?' the American said hastily. 'Under that tree, hiding behind the trunk – see where I mean? He's your tail and he's had us under surveillance all the time we've been here!'

'Rubbish!' Marcel said, not even bothering to look across the Avenue. 'You are evading my question, Hank, and that tells me the answer.'

'I'm only the courier,' Hank said huffily, 'I've passed the message over and it's no part of my job to explain policy.'

In Marcel's mind an idea was forming that he found extremely amusing. Hank said that he had gone back to the unknown woman's room to see if she was OK. But by his own admission, he thought that an ordinary act of love-making had taken place by consent. There was no reason to return to the room where she was asleep unless . . . unless Hank had gone there to do exactly what Marcel had attempted to do – to enjoy her sleeping body. Suppose that she had woken up while Hank was *in flagrante delicto*? Or half-woken? Then it made sense that she had accused him of rape.

'It is I who am receiving the bullshit now, and it is you who are delivering it,' Marcel observed with a smile in which triumph and malice were about equally mixed.

'Gotta go now,' said Hank, but Marcel held on to his sleeve to detain him.

'This Dr Prout,' he asked, 'who is she?'

'She's an Embassy guest,' said Hank. 'Let go my sleeve.'

'I know she's a guest because she has a room in the wing you use for important visitors from America. Why is she important? And of what is she a doctor? Is she political?'

'I guess you don't know much,' Hank said with a sneer in his voice. 'She's a doctor of philosophy three times over and just about the most famous art expert in the world. Don't you have any paintings in France? She teaches at the University of Southern California and she's the Director of the Feigenbaum Museum of Art in San Diego. She's big news.'

'Why has she come to Santa Sabina?'

'Hell, I don't know. To look at pictures, I guess.'

'I would like to make the acquaintance of this lady,' Marcel announced.

The beautiful blonde German woman with whom he had been in love a year ago had been very interested in paintings. Before she deserted him, and her husband, to disappear back to Europe on her own, leaving Marcel broken hearted for weeks, she had succeeded in stealing a painting which she said was worth a fortune. According to her it was a lost masterpiece by El Greco, that had been hanging in a side-

chapel of the Church of the Four Crowned Martyrs for hundreds of years, so blackened by dust and candle-smoke that it was hardly recognisable.

In view of Windhover's information, it must be presumed that the stolen picture had been sold, perhaps in the United States, for the arrival of another art expert in so unlikely a country as Santa Sabina could surely be no coincidence.

'You wanna make Dr Prout's acquaintance!' Hank snorted. 'That's rich – after what you did to her when she was out cold, you low-life freak!'

'Please, let us dispense with the compliments,' said Marcel. 'How do I get in touch with her, telephone the Residence?'

'I'm here to take you to her now. We'll grab a cab.'

But now that Hank had told him what he wanted to know, Marcel had no further need for him and no wish to prolong the dubious pleasure of his company.

'You were right, Hank,' he said in an urgent whisper, 'we're being watched from across the Avenue! But he's not behind the tree, he's in the shadow of the Convent doorway. Over there – can you see him?'

'Forget it,' said Hank in a voice heavy with scorn. 'I just tried that one on you.'

'I am not trying to deceive you,' Marcel assured him with great seriousness. 'Watch the doorway for a moment or two.'

While they had been conversing by the palm tree, he had seen behind Hank's back a young couple stroll along the Avenue, arm in arm. When they reached the baroque frontage of the Convent of the Precious Blood, they had darted under the ornate and deep-shadowed porch, though not for any religious reason. Hank peered sceptically across at the doorway, and then grunted.

'Goddammit – you're right! I can see movement there! You didn't shake your tail off and he followed you to this meet!'

'No, my goon for today is wearing a black leather hat,' said Marcel, using his powers of invention. 'The one over there must be yours – he's outwitted you, Hank.'

'Holy shit!' said the American in deep disgust at his own carelessness. 'We'll split. I'll lead him down the Avenue and then ditch him, while you make it back to Martyrs' Square. I'll pick you up there after I've dumped the goon.'

'You'll never see him tailing you,' said Marcel. 'He's too good for you.'

'Don't have to see him,' Hank retorted, 'I know he's there – and he'll only see me while I want him to. I'll take him as far as the Grand Boulevard movie-house and lose him in the crowd.'

Off he set on his foolish mission, leaving Marcel alone under the palm tree. When Hank was out of sight, he made his way down the Avenue in the opposite direction, to the cab-rank outside Madame da Silva's and was at the American Embassy in less than ten minutes. The Marine sergeant on the gate phoned through to the Residence for Dr Prout's authority to let him in, gave him a printed pass to wear on his jacket lapel and directions to the visitors' wing.

On his previous, unauthorised visit to Dr Prout's quarters, he had entered through the building. On the instructions of the Marine he went round the outside of the single-storey visitors' wing and found it had a long verandah overlooking the gardens, furnished with bamboo tables and chairs. Dr Prout, in a roll-neck white silk sweater and linen slacks, was sitting out with a long cool drink, enjoying the brilliant moonlight. Sitting with her, to Marcel's astonishment, was Lucreza Bonavista.

'You didn't expect to see me here, did you?' she asked, her smile dazzling. 'But when Darlene told who had *zeqqed* her while she was resting, I was so amused that I begged her to let me be here to see her accuse you face to face. This is the man, Darlene – let me introduce him – Monsieur Marcel Lamont.'

Dr Prout stared up at him from her bamboo chair.

'But you're not at all what I expected from Hank Windhover's description,' she said at last, in passable French.

And truth to tell, she was not what Marcel had expected.

The words director of the Museum of Art and university professor conjured up in his mind a picture of an unmarried woman of fifty, unattractive, boring, and plainly dressed. But this picture, he was compelled to admit to himself now, had been formed by male prejudice. At their previous encounter he had not got much of a look at her, her face being turned away from him. All that had lodged in his mind was that she had light brown hair and thin ankles. He seemed to recall it was the fineness of her ankles that triggered off a wish to touch them, and that had led on to a drunken exploration of her underwear.

Her hair was light brown, that memory was based on fact. She wore it straight, parted on the right and hanging to below her ears, in an attractively simple style. Since she was wearing slacks this evening, it was impossible to confirm that her ankles were as thin as he remembered, but it was reasonable to assume that they were, for her entire body was thin, almost to the point of ugliness. Through the silk of her sweater her tiny breasts showed as pointed buds, and the hand holding her glass seemed too fragile to support the weight. She was about forty, Marcel judged, and unlike any woman he had met before.

She did not offer him her hand to kiss or to shake, and she did not invite him to sit down. She stared at him as if he were a dangerous criminal and came straight to the point.

'So why did you do it?'

Marcel shrugged his shoulders a fraction, just enough to impress his Frenchness on her, and treated her to his most charming smile. 'Ah Madame,' he said, 'I could make a thousand excuses, but I refuse to do so. The simple truth of the matter is that when I saw you at the Embassy reception I was overcome by a passion so exquisite that all sense of reason and proportion deserted me. I sought you out, to make your acquaintance, but this I did not achieve. In an agony of desire I followed you here to your room and gazed on you as you slept . . . what can I say? Madness seized me and I could do no other than follow the prompting of my nature. There, now you know everything!'

'But you're Lucreza's boy-friend!' Darlene protested,

lapsing into English in her surprise. 'You'd just screwed her in the gardens. Twice, she told me. And you come straight into my room where I'm lying crocked on the bed and jump on me! What kind of stud are you, for God's sake?'

Marcel was not sure he understood her words completely, but that was of no importance. He could hear the underlying emotion in her voice and it was not indignation – it was admiration.

'I am a man who loves beautiful and intelligent women,' he answered, smiling at her again with such charm that no woman in the world could have withstood his appeal. 'Lucreza will tell you that is so. There is much we could discuss about love – may I sit down, Madame?'

'She's already told me a lot about you, that's why I wanted to see you for myself.'

Lucreza giggled and kissed her diamond-ringed hand towards Marcel, somewhat spoiling the gravity of the moment.

'Sit down and pour yourself a drink,' said Dr Prout, her face relaxing into a grin at last. 'You can call me Darlene.'

They were drinking gin with lemonade and lemon-slices. The bottle had evidently been bought from the Embassy commissariat, for the label was printed in English and the quality was good – not at all like the malignant version sold in the city bars. An English origin was claimed for that, but everyone knew it was an illegal distillation imported from Calcutta.

When cordiality had been established, Marcel enquired what had brought her to Santa Sabina. He pointed out with regret that the while the island had enjoyed the benefits of having been colonised by the Arabs, the Portuguese, the Genoese and the French, it had the misfortune of never having created any music, literature, drama, or painting, above the level of folk-art. Darlene explained that she had been able to acquire, at a knock-down price of a couple of million dollars, a totally unknown El Greco for the Feigenbaum Museum of Art in San Diego. Finding that it came in some unexplained way from Santa Sabina, she had come to see if there were any more lost treasures to be found.

At that, Marcel professed a total ignorance of paintings and changed the subject. He knew where at least three unrecognised master-pieces were to be seen in churches, but he had no desire to be involved.

The three of them chattered away in French and English while they emptied the gin bottle between them, though Darlene seemed to drink the most. Eventually, like all visitors, she began to complain of the oppressive heat and suggested they cool off with a dip in the pool.

'But we have no swimsuits,' said Marcel, grinning at her.

'Who needs a swimsuit on a night like this?' she exclaimed in a devil-may-care tone inspired as much perhaps by the gin as the tropical night. 'Will you just look at that moonlight! What do you say, Lucreza, you too shy to swim naked?'

To ask a Santa Sabina woman if she was too shy to take her clothes off for any reason was a question completely without meaning, but Darlene had not yet been there long enough to know that. Marcel translated her question into French for Lucreza's benefit, and was rewarded with a knowing grin.

'Let's go, then,' he said, 'let us cool ourselves.'

They started towards the pool, the three of them arm in arm with Marcel in the middle. On their way down through the silent Embassy gardens the embrace became even more friendly, so that they had their arms round each other's waists. He did not entirely believe that the American meant what she said about bathing nude in the moonlight. He thought it more probable that there would be a last-minute compromise and she would keep on her underwear, expecting him and Lucreza to do the same. But he was sure that the objections of insulted modesty would not be too loud or compelling if he stripped naked before he dived in.

They reached the pool and stood close to the side, gazing at the undisturbed water for a while. 'That looks good,' Darlene said at last and, while Marcel and Lucreza looked on, she took off her shoes, pulled her thin sweater over her head and dropped her slacks. And then, as if deliberately to confound Marcel's assessment of American women, she

removed her brassiere and slid her small white knickers down her legs.

She stood with her head up and her arms hanging at her sides, defying him wordlessly to look at her body. Whether she was lean by nature or slimmed excessively, she seemed to Marcel to be practically transparent – he could swear that in the strong moonlight her bones showed through her meagre flesh. Her spiky little *gublas* would not make a handful for a lover, and her bony hips poked prominently through her skin. The hair between her parted legs was no more than a wispy little powder-puff that exposed the split of her *kuft* completely.

She turned away from his stare, took three running steps to the edge of the pool and dived. As her long pale body slipped into the water with hardly a splash, Marcel looked at Lucreza, only to discover that she too had taken her clothes off. She was not a plump woman, but in contrast to her American friend her breasts appeared lusciously full and her belly a delight. She grinned at him and ran to throw herself bottom-first into the water, sending waves hurtling over the side of the pool. Without wasting another moment, Marcel undressed and dived into water that felt as warm as soup.

Darlene swam two lengths of the pool with an easy and expert front crawl while Lucreza, who had not the least idea of how to swim, struggled and paddled her way, laughing and whooping, towards the shallow end. And there the three of them stood in a closed group, with their arms about each other's shoulders, in warm water up to their waists. Who started it, Marcel could not say, but in another moment they were kissing each other's cheeks and mouths and, soon after that, each of the women put a hand below the surface where the moonlight danced and shone, one to tug at his soft *zimbriq* and the other to feel between his thighs and cradle his pompoms.

'It is time to pay your debts, Marcel,' Lucreza announced. 'You *zeqqed* Darlene at a time when she was in no condition to enjoy it. Now you must make amends.'

'Damn right,' Darlene agreed at once. 'You started

something and now you've got to finish it.' The hand holding his *zimbriq* massaged it to full stretch, while the hand between his legs slid further underneath and a fingers probed between the cheeks of his backside. He let go of Lucreza altogether to hold Darlene close with an arm round her shoulders, while he fondled her tiny *gublas* and put his hand between her legs.

'You goddam evil rapist!' she moaned when she felt him prise her *kuft* open, so that the tepid water flooded in . 'Rape-fiend!' she gasped when his fingers penetrated it.

'Her *kuft* looks just like a little girl's,' Lucreza observed unexpectedly. 'Does it feel like that?'

'It feels hot and nervous,' said Marcel, with a smile.

Lucreza waded around slowly in the water until she was behind Darlene and could put her arms about her. She pulled her against her plump wet breasts, and ran her palms down Darlene's narrow belly to her thighs.

'Her *kuft* is nervous?' she asked. 'Let me feel.'

Marcel took his hand away and heard Darlene moan lightly as Lucreza's fingers found their way inside her, to play with her bud. He put his hands on her bony hips below the water and bent forward to suck the hard wet tips of her spiky little breasts.

'You're perverts, the pair of you!' Darlene exclaimed in a shrill voice, her thin body shaking as if she had a high fever.

With Lucreza's expert hand agitating between her legs and Marcel stimulating her *gublas*, her climax did not take long to come. She squirmed in their grasp, her thin belly bulging as she thrust her loins at Marcel, and her hands beat the water into foam around them. For three seconds, five, eight seconds, twelve, her throes continued, not decreasing in their intensity at all. Then with a final little shriek she subsided against Lucreza and was still. Her eyes had been open, but sightless, throughout, and now she turned them towards Marcel and showed her teeth in what was either a snarl or a smile.

'Now you must *zeqq* her,' said Lucreza, slipping her hands up under Darlene's arm-pits.

Marcel took his throbbing *zimbriq* in his hand and spread Darlene's slender legs. She was not a tall woman, and to lodge himself between the lips of her *kuft*, he found it necessary to hold her by her narrow waist and assist Lucreza to lift her until her feet were off the bottom of the pool. When he had her correctly positioned, he went all the way in with a strong push. Darlene gave a long shuddering sigh and rested her head on Lucreza's shoulder, letting her legs float up in the water until she could clasp them round Marcel's waist.

He thrust in and out with commanding authority, and Darlene babbled English obscenities that he had never expected to hear from a woman, especially not an art historian with a doctorate in philosophy who taught at a major university, to say nothing of her connection with the Feigenbaum Museum of Art. Lucreza's face was staring at him over Darlene's shoulder, her tongue thrust out towards him and vibrating rapidly. He saw her hands slide from under Darlene's arms to clasp her tiny *gublas* and squeeze them like oranges. And very soon, sooner than he thought, Darlene gave a loud cry to proclaim the onset of her crisis and, two moments later, his hot excitement fountained into her.

'Oh my God, you wonderful, wonderful pair of sex-freaks!' Darlene murmured. 'I haven't been done like that since I was on vacation in Mexico City!' She made bicycling movements with her skinny legs to get her feet down on to the bottom of the pool and turn within the arms that enfolded her to kiss Lucreza. 'Your boyfriend is a class act,' she said in English, which Marcel took to be some species of American compliment.

She pushed and tugged at the other woman until they had exchanged places and she was behind Lucreza, with her thin arms round her body and her hands cupping her plump breasts. Lucreza reached out to put her arms round Marcel's neck and urge him closer to her. He kissed her and took the soft cheeks of her bottom in his hands and kneaded them lovingly. His *zimbriq* was already beginning to stiffen again, and Lucreza rubbed her bare wet belly against it, below the

surface of the pool, until it was throbbing with life and strength.

'Is he hard yet?' Darlene asked, her fingers plucking at the dark tips of Lucreza's breasts.

Lucreza understood what the English word hard meant and said 'Oh, yes, hard and strong! as she took hold of Marcel's *zimbriq* with both hands and rolled it between her palms.

'Come on, you pervert, stick it right up her,' the American said shrilly to Marcel, and Lucreza changed her grip so that she clasped him in one hand and jerked up and down until he was trembling wildly.

He moved in closer, to allow her to steer him up between her open thighs. Her mouth pressed over his in a hot kiss while she held her *kuft* open for him with her fingers. But he lifted her by his grip on her bottom, until she bent her knees and let her feet float upwards and outwards, until the black bush of curls between her thighs broke the surface of the water. He grinned at her and pushed up into her welcoming softness, sinking his finger-nails into the flesh of her bottom, making her writhe and moan and smack her belly against his.

'That's it!' Darlene exclaimed, and stared over Lucreza's shoulder to catch a glimpse of his long *zimbriq* penetrating her friend. 'You're being screwed, Lucreza – how about that!'

'*Zeqq* me hard . . .' Lucreza moaned, 'hard, Marcel!'

He rose up on his toes and began almost to dance, the most exquisite sensations fluttering in his belly. He pressed his legs tightly together, like a ram-rod of steel, and he danced a ballet on the smooth tiles at the bottom of the pool, bending and straightening his knees and ankles and hips in a powerful rhythm of desire that made Lucreza utter little staccato cries of pleasure.

'Screw her hard!' Darlene urged him breathlessly, the whites of her eyes brilliant in the moonlight as she stared at Lucreza's *gublas* bouncing up and down to Marcel's thrusts.

Marcel could feel his climax approaching, and he dug his

nails with passionate cruelty into Lucreza's fleshy bottom. She had his nipples between her finger-tips and was pinching them unmercifully, gasping loudly all the while, *'Je t'adore, cheri, je t'adore!'* Marcel's belly clenched in violent spasms and he shot his delight into her.

'Fill her belly full!' Darlene squealed, her eyes bulging.

Lucreza shrieked and beat her fists against Marcel's chest, while Darlene gasped and sobbed and almost twisted her friend's dark-tipped *gublas* right off in her sympathetic excitement. The pool sides magnified their passionate outcries and sent back the echoes:

'Je t'adore, Marcel . . .'

'Shoot her full!'

'Lucreza, je t'aime . . .'

'More, more . . .'

When it was all over, Lucreza's arms slacked their hold at last and slipped away from Marcel's neck. He released his grip on her bottom and she slid off his softening *zimbriq* and away from him, and disappeared beneath the water. At once Darlene dived to rescue her, the moon gleaming for a moment on the wet and tight little cheeks of her bottom as she up-ended herself and went under. Marcel staggered a step or two backwards to get out of the way, and waited for the women's heads to break the surface side by side, Darlene's arm round Lucreza to raise her.

Between them they helped her to the side and out of the pool, where she sat giggling with an arm round each of them.

'She must have swallowed a lot of water,' said Darlene, shaking her head anxiously. 'Do you know anything about giving lifesaver resuscitation?'

Without waiting for an answer, she pressed Lucreza down flat on her back and spread her arms and legs, instructing Marcel to kneel between her thighs, while she herself took up her place with her knees on either side of Lucreza's head. She leaned forward, her spiky little breasts jiggling beneath her, and put her palms flat together on Lucreza's chest, telling Marcel to put his on her diaphragm.

'We do this by the numbers,' she said, speaking slowly to permit him to understand the significance of the English

words, 'press down firmly but gently to the count of three, keeping your shoulders above your hands. Got that? Then you swing up and back for a count of five, OK? Then we go down again for three . . . understand? OK, let's go! Down . . . one . . . two . . . three . Up . . . one . . . two . . . three . . . four . . . five. Down . . .'

Lucreza, whether or not she had swallowed water in the pool, was completely conscious and in no discomfort. She closed her eyes and her lips were curved in a faint smile as she lay quiet under their rescue ministrations. Before long, of course, Darlene's hands had crept from their position on her chest to her plump wet *gublas*, and Marcel's hands had slithered down from her diaphragm to her soft belly and were well on their way towards her *kuft*. Lucreza sighed in pleasure and was content to let herself be resuscitated for as long as her friends desired.

10

A Feast of Nectared Sweets

To be invited to a private supper by a man of importance, with whose wife you are on terms of exquisite intimacy, is an event that contains a certain potential for social awkwardness. Even if, and especially if, you have reason to suspect that the man knows all about his wife's intimacy with you. Naturally, you accept the invitation, partly because you want to find out why he has asked you, but mainly because he is important anyway. It was obvious that Salvador Bonavista's little supper-party was really for Olivier, and Marcel was included in order to bring a touch of official French backing to the occasion, spurious as it necessarily was.

The invitation was for ten o'clock, at Madame da Silva's on the Avenue of the Constitution. Olivier asked Marcel to have dinner with him before they went there together, and at eight that evening, handsomely dressed in a new white suit, Marcel accompanied Olivier to Paladio's restaurant by the harbour. Marcel suggested a table at the back, away from the view of anyone outside who might be keeping an eye out for him, for he knew enough not to dismiss Hank Windhover's account of Secret Police goons as entirely fantasy.

Over the grilled sword-fish Olivier began to speak about the affair of the buses more confidentially than he ever had before – and the reason soon became clear. Bonavista had suddenly become suspicious of Olivier's good faith.

'Have you said anything that could account for this attitude of distrust?' Olivier demanded, his cold grey eyes boring into Marcel's as if to penetrate to his innermost secrets.

'I? What could I possibly say about you?' Marcel replied 'I know nothing of your business affairs?'

'It's damned strange,' said Olivier, shaking his over-large head in an accusing manner. 'Everything was going well until a few days ago – and for no reason I can pin down there was a sudden reversal of attitude at the Ministry. I went to talk to an official about technicalities yesterday and he kept me waiting for over an hour. That he should dare do so was a clear indication that all is not well.'

'Perhaps a competitor is also negotiating with Bonavista,' Marcel suggested. 'Have you considered that? It is well known that the Americans would like to do business here, and there must be others who manufacture and export buses.'

'It was my first thought,' said Olivier, refilling their glasses with wine. 'To be kept waiting an hour by a government functionary is a sign which a businessman recognises. There was nothing for it but to take immediate action, of course.'

'Of course,' Marcel agreed. 'What action?'

Olivier glanced round the half-full terrace to make sure he would not be overheard.

'You understand that the Minister has been promised certain personal financial benefits on the completion of this deal,' he said, lowering his voice and leaning forward to tap the table close to Marcel with the thick fingers of a hand backed with dark hair. 'Very considerable benefits, in effect, equivalent to a significant percentage of the total cost of the goods.'

'I guessed that much,' said Marcel, displeased to be taken for a fool. 'What did you offer him, ten per cent?'

'You are very frank,' said Olivier, who evidently did not like to have delicate matters stated so plainly. 'That was the inducement I proposed at first, but this Minister of Transport is not an innocent in business arrangements. It was remiss of you to give me no warning of that. He demanded a full third and eventually we compromised at fifteen per cent, though with much reluctance on my side, I can assure you.'

He made Bonavista sound like an extortionist, and it was

all Marcel could do to keep a straight face. It didn't matter in the least what percentage Olivier promised, since his intention was to disappear with all the money anyway. But the Americans had passed over the file on Olivier's past swindles, exactly as Windhover had threatened, and that put Salvador Bonavista in a position of strength.

'But what action have you taken?' Marcel asked again.

Olivier huffed and puffed for a time, ran his hand over his brush-cut dark hair, emptied his wine glass and ordered another bottle. But at last he overcame his resistance to passing on information that concerned himself. 'In order to retrieve my standing with Bonavista,' he said, 'and to reinstate the deal, I agreed to pay him in advance half the sum due to him on completion of the transaction.'

'My God, you're going to give him cash before anything is signed?' Marcel asked in amazement and alarm.

'I am a financier and an entrepreneur,' said Olivier, taking offence at Marcel's tone of voice. 'It is sometimes necessary to take great risks, in order to gain even greater rewards. I do not expect you to understand that, for you are protected from the imperatives of the real world by your profession. And therefore you will never be as rich as I am.'

'Alas, I do not expect to become rich,' Marcel agreed. 'But this money you are handing over – is it your own?'

'Not precisely. I have a bank borrowing facility in Paris.'

'Ah, I understand now,' said Marcel, his faith in Olivier's fundamental dishonesty fully restored. 'You will give the bank's money to Bonavista.'

'It is a routine matter of bank financing,' Olivier hastened to assure him. 'The loan will be repaid when the Santa Sabina authorities make payment for the buses.'

'Of course,' said Marcel, suppressing his laughter. 'It must be a very interesting amount, this seven and a half per cent advance payment. Have you handed it over yet?'

'It is to be this evening,' Olivier explained. 'Personally, I would have preferred a private meeting and a much less public place. But your friend Bonavista insists on giving a party to celebrate the transfer of funds, and you and I are his guests.'

Marcel sipped his fresh glass of wine while he entertained himself for some moments with the farcical situation Olivier had revealed. The confidence trickster was being tricked by his dupe, who knew that he was the other's dupe. The only cash that was flowing was from Olivier's pocket to Salvador Bonavista's pocket. Except that Olivier was also swindling a bank.

His voice was shaky and he was hardly able to stop himself laughing his head off as he enquired when the Minister had promised to sign a contract to buy the buses.

'In a day or two,' Olivier answered. 'The form of contract is being examined by the Ministry's legal advisers before Bonavista puts his signature on it on behalf of his government. And then half the purchase price will be paid into a European bank, as evidence of good faith and to cover preliminary costs, documentation, and shipping.'

Except that it will instantly vanish from the account and no one will be able to trace it, thought Marcel. Aloud he asked in what form Bonavista's commission would be handed over. Olivier became red of face and angry at the question and he spoke most impolitely of Third World politicians too backward to grasp the principle of payment into a numbered bank account elsewhere in the world, and who would take nothing but actual cash.

'Cash?' Marcel exclaimed. 'But that much money in tikkoos would require all of your hundred buses to transport it!'

'He's not stupid enough to want his own worthless currency,' said Olivier, angrier than ever, 'nor will he take francs. He wants his money in American dollars.'

'You have arranged this?' Marcel asked.

Under the table Olivier kicked the fat brown leather briefcase that he had refused to leave in the restaurant cloakroom.

'It has cost me a considerable amount in commissions and fees to get this much in dollars delivered here in so short a time,' he said. 'I doubt if anyone else could have done it. But in overseas business affairs, I have the experience of years.'

'My congratulations, Olivier. There is no doubt in my mind that as an entrepreneur you are in a class of your own.' While Olivier was preening himself on his abilities, Marcel pretended to recognise a man walking slowly past outside the restaurant. 'Ah, take care!' he whispered urgently across the table. 'Is your briefcase out of sight?'

'I think so. Why?' Olivier asked, craning his neck to see who Marcel was looking at. 'Who is that?'

'He's an agent of the Bureau of Public Information,' Marcel lied. 'I've noticed him lurking about before when I've been with you. He must be assigned to watch you permanently.'

'Me? But why – I am a businessman, not a spy.'

A wonderful scheme to sabotage Olivier's felonious operation had formed itself in Marcel's mind. It sprang from the comical recollection of Hank Windhover's paranoid fear of being under surveillance by the Secret Police.

'Yes, you are a businessman, Olivier,' he said, 'but in the course of your business arrangements you intend to commit what is a very serious criminal offence in Santa Sabina law.'

'Serious offence? In an underdeveloped country like this?' said Olivier scornfully. 'Don't be a fool – in places like this the officials are always interested in their own gain and there can be no kind of commercial activity without inducements. Do you suppose that this is the first contract I have negotiated in a country like this? Give me credit for understanding my own business.'

'What you say is perfectly true,' Marcel answered mildly 'Politicians here are as corrupt as those we elect back home. Civil servants are not even expected to live on their salaries – they are allowed to sell licences and permits for whatever they can get. All this you have seen before in your travels around the world. But there is one big difference here, which is why you must take care.'

'And that is?'

'President da Cunha is hostile to foreign influences. He is not merely hostile in the manner of old-time reactionaries – he is insanely hostile. Bonavista has been able to obtain

permission to import buses not because they are needed badly but because he is da Cunha's favourite nephew. If it were ever discovered that he had accepted money from a foreigner . . . that would be the end of him.'

'He would lose his job,' Olivier commented in an utterly unsympathetic voice, shrugging his shoulders. 'Politicians come and politicians go – it is the way of things.'

'I meant literally his end,' Marcel said. 'Only last year the Minister of Commerce was found to be in the pay of the Americans. I had the honour of attending his execution as the representative of the Ambassador, who had qualms about seeing a man garrotted. And he was the President's cousin.'

At that Olivier hastily drained his glass and called to the nearest waiter to bring a bottle of cognac.

'But this is terrible,' he said. 'And you were there?'

'With many thousands of others. Executions here are public, as a deterrent to others. On this occasion, the entire foreign Diplomatic Corps were invited, as a warning against emulating the American example of corrupting a government Minister.

'But from the severity of the punishment I assume there was more to the affair than a simple business transaction, even for a Minister of Commerce.'

'Much was never fully revealed,' said Marcel mysteriously. 'There was a case not long before I arrived here to take up my post, which was related to me as a warning to be careful in my dealings with local politicians. The matter concerned a member of the Swedish Embassy, who had complete diplomatic immunity, but nevertheless disappeared one day. It was rumoured that he had paid money to a senior official in a Ministry and had been snatched in the street by the agents of the Bureau of Public Information. Our American colleagues call them *goons*.

'What happened to him?' Olivier asked, downing a generous measure of cognac.

'No one knows. The President ordered a full investigation to pacify the Swedes, but the head of the Secret Police stated on oath that his goons had not arrested the man and no trace

of him was ever found. Unless a sock with a foot in it that was washed ashore on the Reserved Beach belonged to him.'

'Good god!' Olivier exclaimed. 'Just one foot?'

'You must understand,' said Marcel, satisfied that he was creating a useful uneasiness, 'after interrogation by the thugs of the Bureau of Public Information some suspects are too badly injured to be brought to trial or to be set free if they are innocent. They are never seen again. Folklore has it that they are dumped well out at sea for the sharks to dispose of.'

'You think this is what happened to the Swede?'

'Who can say? According to a report in the *Daily Chronicle* the toenails were still attached to the foot, which is unusual for anyone interrogated by the goons.'

'Are you trying to frighten me?'

'I am trying to impress on you that care is required in your business dealings with Bonavista. You said yourself that it is necessary in business to take great risks to gain great rewards – here in Santa Sabina the risk you are running is not merely financial. If any suspicion arose and you were taken in for questioning by the Bureau, there is nothing any of us could do to assist you, not even the Ambassador in person. I salute you as a man with the courage to stake your life in the cause of business and profit!' and Marcel raised his glass to Olivier.

For the next half hour Olivier was in a subdued mood, which was most uncharacteristic for him. But a few cognacs helped restore his normal attitude of superiority and he was himself again when they left Paladio's and took a rattle-trap of a taxi to the Avenue of the Constitution. Serafina da Silva greeted them and conducted them in person to one of the large private rooms kept for special functions. Salvador Bonavista was there already, much to Marcel's surprise, and he looked very prosperous in a suit of gunmetal-grey silk and a scarlet cummerbund.

He was a most cordial host, greeting them as old friends and handing them glasses of champagne. It was not a good vintage, but nothing in Santa Sabina was ever of the best. Olivier, well primed already with wine and cognac, was soon in a suitably elated frame of mind for a party of this nature

and grinned broadly when Salvador asked if he had anything to give him. He handed over his briefcase with a few meaningless words to the effect that he respected and admired the Minister for his modern attitudes and efficiency.

Salvador opened the lid of the briefcase only a centimetre or two, just enough for him to glance inside and assure himself that it truly contained wads of American hundred dollar notes. He closed it again and, with a grin of satisfaction, handed it to Serafina da Silva, with the request that she put it in her safe, until he was ready to leave. Marcel remembered the safe as a monstrous cube of brown-painted steel, made in, according to the inscription on the door, in Stuttgart in 1887. It stood in a corner of the office where he *zeqqed* Serafina and made the little gold bells chime on her breasts.

Ten men would be needed to lift and carry off that mighty safe and, without the key, nothing less than dynamite would open it. Salvador's American dollars would be secure while he was amusing himself with the girls of the house.

In three or four minutes Serafina came back and handed the safe key to the Minister. It was a large and heavy key, and it dragged down his elegant jacket when he put it in a pocket.

He tried it in a trouser pocket, only to withdraw it at once with a grimace and a joking remark about disabling himself even before the fun began. Serafina took it from him and dropped it down the front of her low-cut black frock, between her dangling breasts. The whole company watched in fascination the silk of her frock bulge out as the steel shape slid down her narrow belly. She clapped a hand to her *kuft* to stop the descent and push the key between her legs to grip it with her thighs.

'That's the most dangerous place in the house to hide it,' said Salvador, smiling at her. 'You'll have your legs apart a dozen times before morning and someone is sure to steal the key from you. Give it back to me.'

She let it fall down inside her frock, to appear with a thud on the floor between her feet. When she bent over to pick it up her long slack breasts slipped out of her frock, to the

general amusement of the company. She handed the key to Salvador, who bowed his thanks and pressed a kiss to the golden-ringed tip of each bare breast. To satisfy Olivier's curiosity and to please Marcel, she lifted her breasts on her hands for each to inspect in turn the pretty gold ornaments hanging from their coffee brown tips, before tucking them back inside her frock.

'Put the key on the sideboard, Monsieur Bonavista,' she suggested. 'It will be safe enough there. Only your friends and my trusted employees will be in the room.'

He put the key inside an empty drawer of the sideboard and, while Serafina poured more champagne into their glasses, he invited Olivier and Marcel to take their seats with him at a round table that occupied the centre of the room. It was covered with a fine damask tablecloth, but there were no place-settings or even a floral decoration.

'Well then, I see you are ready, gentlemen,' said Serafina, looking at Salvador. 'Shall I serve supper now, Monsieur?'

He asked her to proceed and she left the room again, to return accompanied by the waiter who kept clients well supplied with drinks in the *salon*, and a young man dressed in the white hat and apron of a *chef de cuisine*. Between them they carried the largest covered dish Marcel had ever seen in his life. Olivier stared at it unimpressed, for he and Marcel had dined well together, and asked if supper was a whole roast sheep.

'Not a sheep,' said Salvador happily, exchanging smiles with Serafina, who supervised the placing of the gargantuan silver dish on the table. 'A tender young lamb for your enjoyment. I wish you good appetite, gentlemen.'

He gestured to the servants, who bowed and removed the vast domed lid of the serving dish, to reveal a naked girl. She was a black-haired seventeen or eighteen year-old, with full breasts and a plump bottom, and she lay on her side, propped on an elbow, her knees drawn up to fit her inside the dish. Her body was skilfully decorated with sugar and marzipan flowers, foliage and tracery, in pink and white and green and blue. As the three men stared at her with round eyes and mouths open in admiration, she opened her own

black eyes and gave them a smile of such innocent mischievousness that Marcel could not contain the sigh of pleasure that rose to his lips.

'This is Adriana, served for your enjoyment,' Serafina said, her face displaying the satisfaction she felt at astounding the company with her offering. 'I shall leave you to your meal,' and she and her staff left the room, closing the door quietly behind them.

The provider of the feast, Salvador Bonavista, was the first to recover himself. With a deliberately casual movement he reached for the candied grape in Adriana's belly-button and slipped it into his mouth.

'But how exquisite, my dear Salvador,' Marcel exclaimed and he leaned forward over the table to taste a pink-petalled marzipan daisy that adorned the soft bud of the girl's left breast and then to lick it away with the tip of his tongue. Olivier's mouth was still gaping in astonishment, as when the cover had been lifted, but to see Marcel delicately licking Adriana's little decoration inflamed him furiously. With a groan of delight, he pressed her lower thigh flat to the silver dish and raised the other.

Marcel sat back from his delicious task and let the sweet marzipan dissolve on his tongue. His heart skipped a beat when he saw the *bonne bouche* that Olivier had revealed by spreading Adriana's rounded thighs. Her soft *kuft* had been shaved smooth for this special occasion and in it was set the prettiest little pink sugar rose imaginable. Olivier, his face crimson with emotion, put his head between her thighs and his mouth to the split between them, to nibble at her flower. Marcel sighed again, and he thought he heard a faint moan from Salvador, as the two of them watched Olivier's wet tongue lapping the petals into his mouth and then licked the protruding lips of her *kuft*.

One reason for Marcel's fervent interest was that the inner lips of Adriana's pretty *kuft* were long and plump and protruded between her permanently parted outer lips. Olivier too became entranced by this little genetic attraction and sat back to admire it while he stroked it with a wet fingertip.

'You like that?' Marcel asked him. 'For myself, I find it irresistible.'

'I find it very exciting – to look at and to touch,' Olivier confessed, his face still flushed and his voice ragged. 'I have seen girls shaped like this before, of course, but the complete removal of her curls throws her charms into greater prominence – she is delightful!'

'This interesting little physical characteristic is fairly common among the women of Santa Sabina,' said Marcel. 'It is a question of inherited traits, I suppose. I have noted it very often, but it retains its power to arouse me.'

Throughout this exchange of opinions Olivier continued to stroke Adriana, opening the inner lips of her bare *kuft* with an expert fingertip, until he was caressing her secret bud. Her dark eyes opened widely, the whites almost luminescent against her beautiful coffee-coloured skin, and her red-painted mouth gaped in delight. With her knee bent upwards to raise her thigh and permit Olivier full access to her *kuft*, she reached behind her and stroked her bottom, soft and round with satin skin of a delicious light coffee colour.

Salvador moved round the table, to take a chair behind her, and slowly her fingers parted the warm cheeks to display the little knot of muscle set deep between them. It was surrounded with tiny white petals of sugar stuck to her skin, a perfect embellishment that was the work of a master confectioner. Marcel's *zimbriq* had been shaking wildly in his trousers ever since the dishcover had been removed, and at this new delight it throbbed with such emphasis that he knew that decisive action to relieve its tension would be necessary very soon.

Olivier too had been affected by the sight of the tiny white flower in the cleft of Adriana's bottom. The shade of his complexion deepened from crimson to purple when he saw Salvador bend down to lick it away, and he put his head back between her legs and used his own tongue on her bud. Thus relentlessly assailed by Olivier in front and Salvador behind, while Marcel was devoting his best efforts to sucking the pink daisy from her other breast, the girl began to utter

gasping little cries, feeling her critical moment approach.

Marcel raised his face from her sticky breast just in time to observe her legs spread as wide as they would go. Olivier's tongue was flicking at her bare and wet little *kuft* with the speed of a striking snake and, compelling the little spasms of release to begin in her belly. She reached out to seize Marcel by his hair and drag his face close to hers. Their parted lips met and she pushed her tongue so far into his mouth that it was as if he could feel it vibrating in his throat. His hands were cupped over her plump breasts, opening and closing convulsively to enjoy the feel of her soft flesh.

His entire body was aflame with sensation, his mind was in a delirium of pleasure. His *zimbriq* was throbbing furiously out of control inside his trousers and when he felt Adriana's hand clutch at it and squeeze it hard through the thin cloth, his overloaded nervous system could sustain no more. He moaned into her mouth as his *zimbriq* leaped and fountained his desire into his underwear, a long hot gush against the skin of his belly. The frantic jerking between her fingers told Adriana what was happening to him, and she screamed loud and long, her back arching to push her *kuft* hard against Olivier's lips.

When she released her grip on him, Marcel sagged back in his chair, his eyes closed and his mind happily dazed by the intensity of his release. When he opened them again, he saw that Olivier and Salvador were so aroused by Adriana's noisy little climax that they were using their fingers and tongues on every part of her squirming body, cleaning away all traces of sugar and marzipan adornment, until her smooth skin shone with the moisture of their appreciation. They both wanted her now, and intended to have her. Marcel sat up straight in his chair and unzipped his trousers, his *zimbriq* stiffening again fast at the sight of the girl being so thoroughly licked and enjoyed.

Salvador's face appeared above her rounded hip, flushed red and split by a broad grin induced by the pleasure of devouring her decorations and tasting the girl herself. He gave Marcel a glance full of significance, and Marcel nodded his agreement. The guest of honour was Olivier, and he must

be allowed first option. Needless to say, Olivier was fully aware of his own importance and took immediate advantage of the situation. He lurched to his feet, breathing heavily, and in seconds he was undressed, his jacket, tie, shirt, trousers, underwear all cast to the floor behind him – all that is except his shoes and his black socks, which for some reason he kept on.

Marcel had seen Olivier undressed at the Reserved Beach and knew that his thick-set and muscular body was covered in a pelt of black hair, from his shoulders down to his belly and his thighs. To Salvador the sight came as a revelation, for the men of Santa Sabina rarely had much body hair. He stared amazed at Olivier, his features set in a fixed grin, especially when his gaze dropped below Olivier's waist, where a *zimbriq* as hard as a broom handle stood up at a sharp angle from a thick and curly bush of jet black hair.

Oblivious of the stare directed at him, Olivier scrambled on to the table and covered Adriana with his bulk, resting his weight on his elbows and settling his hairy belly down on hers. She spread her legs wide and drew them up, until her knees were pressing against her breasts, to open herself wide for him. From where he sat, Marcel had an unobstructed view of how she guided the purple head of his *zimbriq* to her naked slit. He held his breath while he watched it slipping into he and he observed how her *kuft* opened itself to take it in, as Olivier slid the entire length into her with a long hard push.

The moment that he was all the way in, Adriana wrapped her legs round his waist and gripped him tight with her thighs, as he began to *zeqq* her with strong and remorseless strokes. Marcel's *zimbriq* was quivering again like a trapped bird in a cage and, to bring a little relief to its sufferings, he freed it from its prison and allowed it to jut proudly upwards out of his open trousers. Olivier's heavy and hairy rump was thumping up and down in a rhythm as relentless as the pistons of a steam locomotive and he was contorting his body so that he could get his mouth to one of Adriana's breasts and suck it.

Your turn will come in a moment, my dear friend, Marcel

silently assured his stiff and throbbing *zimbriq*. It was impossible not to touch it, to comfort it just a little. And when he saw that Adriana's body was starting to tremble under Olivier, as if her climax was about to arrive, Marcel's own excitement was so very great that it compelled him to caress his *zimbriq* with gentle fingers. He gasped to see that Olivier was responding to the writhing of the girl underneath him with faster and more powerful thrusts into her *kuft*. A moment later they reached their crucial moments together in a flurry of cries and groans and spasms that seemed to go on and on.

Marcel's iron-hard *zimbriq* was jerking so frantically in his clasping hand that he was almost afraid to draw breath in case he precipitated another crisis prematurely. But Olivier at last slid off the girl and collapsed into his chair with a foolish grin on his face and at once, to forestall any possible claim of priority by Salvador, Marcel jumped to his feet and showed Adriana what he held. She grinned at him while she got up off her back and knelt on her huge silver serving dish, her hands on his shoulders while he kissed her belly fervently and felt her smooth-shaven and wet *kuft*.

'Come on, then!' she said, reaching down for his *zimbriq*. But Marcel knew for certain that in his condition of high arousal the touch of a girl's hand on his over-sensitive part would be enough by itself to set off a mighty explosion in his belly.

'Lie down, lie down, Adriana!' he was sighing, 'Lie down for me, *cherie*, I implore you!' she grinned and let him push her down on her back again, and his hands felt for her knees. He was standing so close to the table that his thighs pressed against it and, crouching forward a little, he threw her legs over his shoulders, steered his *zimbriq* to her *kuft* with a hand that trembled, and sank it into her hot and slippery depths.

For so young a girl she was well experienced in the arts of pleasuring men. Lying on her back, her legs in the air and her *kuft* engulfing him, her hands went to her plump brown breasts, to roll them and squeeze them and pluck at their coffee-bean tips, all this to enhance Marcel's

excitement. He was *zeqqing* her with tiny little strokes, riding in and out no more than a couple of centimetres each time, in an endeavour to retain some vestige of control for as long as was possible. But he was too far gone, and ten or twelve thrusts brought on the ultimate and Adriana shook to his gasping and jolting climax.

When he had his breath back, so to speak, he told her that she was delightful and thanked her for the pleasure she had given him. Then he sat down, his wet *zimbriq* starting to droop at last. Adriana sat up on the table and leaned over to kiss him in acknowledgment of his words and then pivoted round on her bare bottom to face Salvador.

'Monsieur . . . do you want me?' she asked politely.

Her hesitancy was not due merely from her awareness that Santa Sabina men over the age of thirty retained only a limited interest in *zeqqing*; there was also the consideration that he was a member of the government, which meant he was related to the President. In the closed society of Santa Sabina such persons enjoyed status and importance not accorded to European politicians and it was necessary to approach him with extreme respect. But Salvador was in an excellent mood, as well he might be with a briefcase full of American dollars locked in Serafina's safe for him.

He smiled at Adriana and held out his arms towards her in a gesture that indicated he was well-disposed. She climbed off the table to sit on his lap and removed his scarlet cummerbund so that she could open his trousers wide. Marcel watched with great interest, fascinated by the sexual customs of Santa Sabina, and sure that his soft *zimbriq* would soon stiffen again at the sight of Adriana being *zeqqed*. He glanced at Olivier, naked but for his shoes and socks slumped in his chair, his shrunken *zimbriq* almost concealed in the thicket of black hair between his thighs. His eyes were almost closed and, since it was unlikely that one act of love had felled him, Marcel guessed that the large amount of alcohol he had drunk must be responsible for his unusual quiescence.

Adriana was squeezing and tugging at Salvador's *zimbriq* to raise it to full hardness, while she breathed into his ears

and licked them. When she thought the time was right, she slid off his lap and pulled him from the chair and, while he was laughing at what she whispered to him, she turned him round and positioned him with the backs of his thighs against the edge of the table. He let her push him down until he was lying on his back over the silver serving dish, his feet still on the floor, and at once she bent over him to lick his upstanding *zimbriq*.

A pleasant tremor ran through Marcel's limp *zimbriq* when he saw Adriana get her knees on the table and perch herself astride Salvador's loins. There was an element of perversity, Marcel thought, in the spectacle of a fully dressed man in his elegant suit and tie, mounted by a completely naked girl of seventeen or eighteen, the bare lips between her spread thighs gleaming with the moisture of her excitement. She held Salvador's stiff *zimbriq* upright between her fingers while she lowered herself on to it, and Marcel saw how its pale coffee length disappeared into her wet pink folds. A pang of jealousy stabbed through him as he thought how often that *zimbriq* must have slid up into Lucreza just like that.

What followed was the traditional Santa Sabina mule-ride. As soon as Adriana was firmly in the saddle, she began to bounce up and down vigorously. Marcel stared in delight at her full breasts flopping up and down, his *zimbriq* lengthening and rearing its head. Salvador was responding to the *zeqqing* he was undergoing, his body heaving strongly under the girl, struggling to drive himself deeper into her. Suddenly he was groaning and his feet left the floor to thrash in the air as Adriana clenched the cheeks of her bottom and drained his essence from him.

Her eyes were wide open and her belly was convulsing in the spasms of her climax. At the sight of her pleasure, Marcel's iron-hard *zimbriq* was shaking so wildly that he held it in his hand to quieten it. He stared open-mouthed as the last slow shudders agitated Adriana's sweat-shiny body and she leaned forward, her hands on either side of Salvador to take her weight, as if she felt fatigued for the first time that evening. Between her legs Salvador was

sprawled limply, his eyes closed and his face peaceful, slipping gently into a doze after the excitement of his release. But young though she was, Adriana shared the heritage of all sexually insatiable Santa Sabina women and her relaxation was only momentary. Her dark-haired head swivelled round and she smiled invitingly over her bare brown shoulder at Marcel. Her smile became a chuckle of appreciation when she saw that he was fondling his upright *zimbriq*.

'Adriana, come to me,' he said softly, returning her smile, 'sit on my lap and *zeqq* me in the Santa Sabina way.'

11

Confession is Often Good for the Soul

Because Marcel had decided that he was in love with beautiful black-haired Lucreza, it did not follow that his interest had diminished in beautiful blonde Lisette. But opportunities to get her alone and advance his cause were difficult to arrange. He had thought after the episode on the Reserved Beach that he was wearing her down. She had, after all, allowed him to remove the top part of her red bikini and she took his *zimbriq* in her hand when he had aroused her. And although in the throes of her climax she had rolled away, to remove her nylon-covered modesty from the reach of his stiffness, she had not retreated far enough to prevent his desire from splashing on her bare bottom.

It was Marcel's experience that a woman who held his *zimbriq* in her hand would eventually hold it in her *kuft*. Perhaps not immediately, but he was prepared to be patient with Lisette and play with her as often as necessary to demolish the barriers in her mind. And this might have come about, but for her mother. More precisely, if it were not for the misunderstanding on the day of the *Suruq*, there was an excellent chance Lisette would have entrusted herself completely to him by now.

He shook his head over the comic memory of how he had crept silently across the room to kneel behind Denise and raise her slip, believing that it was Lisette leaning out of the window. Forever imprinted on his mind was an image of the peach silk of her knickers stuck in the cleft of her bottom. With what delight his lips had touched the bare flesh above the tops of her silk stockings, while under her slip his hands stroked her soft belly. And then the murderous

blow she struck him, and the terrible realisation that it was the wrong woman!

It had taken several hours in her bed and his most diligent endeavours to finally remove Denise's indignation and grievance against him. But he had been over-diligent in pleasuring her, he now saw. Denise was not a fool; she had guessed that it was her daughter he was pursuing, not herself, and having benefited once from his exuberance, she had every intention of enjoying his services again. She stayed close to Lisette at all times, so that whenever he tried his luck, there was always Denise smiling and making little gestures behind her daughter's back to indicate that she would like him to take her up to his room.

This complicated and vexing train of events ran through his mind at breakfast on the terrace of the Grand Hotel Orient when Lisette appeared and made straight for his table. She was alone for once, he saw with delight, and she looked very desirable. Her silver-blonde hair shone with brushing and her sumptuous breasts were well displayed in a blouse of cornflower-blue that matched the colour of her eyes. Beneath the silk they bobbed up and down to each step she took, in so charming a manner that every man on the terrace smiled in pleasure. But even as Marcel rose to his feet to greet her, he saw that all was not well. Lisette's expression was one of deep concern.

'It's Olivier,' she said, a note of worry in her voice 'He is very ill. He has a fever!'

'Then we must get a doctor for him,' said Marcel, pouring a cup of coffee for her. 'Drink this, it will help a little.'

'I am sure that the most terrible tropical diseases are rife here,' Lisette exclaimed 'Bubonic plague, cholera, blackwater fever, ringworm, sleeping sickness, leprosy . . .'

'No, no, no,' Marcel interrupted her with a smile, 'Santa Sabina is a very healthy country, considering its climate. I am sure that Olivier has nothing too serious.'

'Mama is with him,' said Lisette, not in the least reassured by his words. 'She is bathing his forehead and chest to reduce his temperature while I find a doctor. I came to you

instead of asking the hotel staff because I am sure you can 'recommend a first-class doctor.'

'But of course,' said Marcel in his most soothing tone. Truth to tell, his faith in the local practitioners was less than enthusiastic. For the most part they were graduates of little-known medical schools in Madagascar or Indo-China, who had scraped through their examinations. On the other hand, not much was required of them beyond simple midwifery and treatment for alcohol poisoning. 'Stay here,' he said. 'Order more coffee while I telephone Dr La Paz. He is a friend of mine and highly esteemed. He is the personal physician of the President's family.'

He made his call from the hotel reception-desk, where Concepcion was on duty in a white-flowered frock that she had left unbuttoned to halfway down between her brown-skinned breasts. After explaining the situation to Dr La Paz, he stayed to chat with Concepcion and, inspired by the soft bounce of her half-covered breasts, he almost promised to be in his room that afternoon if she had any free time – which at once she said she had. When he returned to his table on the terrace Denise Coty had joined her daughter there. She was wearing pale green and she too looked worried.

'Well, when will the doctor be here?' she demanded before he had time to wish her *bon jour, chere Madame* and sit down.

'Very shortly, I promise you,' he answered.

'Good – Olivier is far from well. He is asking for you.'

'For me? But why?'

'I suggest that you go and find out,' said Denise, none too friendly towards him, for he had disappointed her expectations of pleasure a number of times since the day he kissed her bare bottom in error. 'I've left the door unlocked for you.'

Marcel shrugged and left the table, to climb the stairs to Olivier's room. He tapped on the door and went straight in, to find Olivier flat on his back on the bed, wearing purple silk pyjama trousers. His unshaven face showed chalk-white through thick stubble and his eyes were dark-ringed and

sunken. Even his barrel of a chest seemed to have collapsed into flabbiness under its pelt of black hair.

'How do you feel, my dear fellow?' Marcel asked cautiously.

'Terrible,' Olivier croaked. 'Bring a chair and sit down. I must talk to you.'

'But you should conserve your strength,' said Marcel. 'I have sent for an excellent doctor and he will be here soon.'

'Damn the woman!' said Olivier, 'I told her I don't want a doctor fussing round me. I suppose she persuaded you to send for one – why must women meddle all the time!'

'Madame Coty is concerned for your state of health. And I must agree with her that you look to be in a bad way.'

'There's nothing the matter with me that a day or two's rest won't put right. Lisette must not find out the truth – and that means her interfering mother mustn't get even a hint of it, you understand? Promise you'll help me.'

Olivier tried to raise himself on a elbow, but his arm shook with weakness and he slid down flat again. Thinking to be of service, Marcel with some difficulty lifted his sweating bulk and propped him up with the pillows.

'Do not agitate yourself,' he advised Olivier, 'you have my word that I will do whatever I can to help you. Now what is it that must be kept secret from your fiancée?'

'The truth is,' said Olivier, his voice feeble, 'last night I made an experiment with your celebrated *datra*. Entirely as a matter of curiosity, of course, for a man of my strength needs no aphrodisiacs to boost his love-making. But it seemed to me, as a businessman, that there would be a profitable market for it in Paris, if it really worked.'

'Yes, yes,' said Marcel, smiling at Olivier's self-deluding hypocrisy. 'I understand that you tried it from intellectual curiosity in the interests of business. What happened?'

'There was no point in half-doing things. I went to one of the little cafe-bars in Vasco da Gama Square and soon got into conversation with two women. They were waiting for the sister of one of them, who was supposed to arrive on a bus from Vilanova. I bought them a drink or two and we agreed to go to the home of one of them as soon as the

sister arrived. I'd bought a packet of datra pills at a pharmacy in the afternoon and while we were waiting I swallowed a few of them with a glass or two of cognac.'

'A few?' said Marcel, raising his eyebrows in surprise. 'As I understand it, the usual dose is one.'

'So the pharmacist said, but when I opened the packet they were such insignificant little pills that I decided a larger dose was appropriate for a man of my size and height. The women laughed and made jokes about my *zimbriq*, as they called it, and how hard it would soon be. One of them felt me under the table, and told her friend nothing much was happening yet, but both of them seemed so impressed by the amount of datra I'd taken that I washed a few more pills down.'

'Good God!' Marcel said softly. 'You are lucky to be alive this morning!'

'Nothing much seemed to happen at first,' Olivier continued in a mournful tone. 'I was getting very bored sitting in this shabby little cafe waiting for an overdue bus to arrive. Then all of a sudden it was as if my whole body was on fire! I was so stiff inside my trousers that it was painful.'

'How inconvenient for you,' said Marcel. 'What did you do?'

'The women guessed from my expression what was going on and the one who felt me before put her hand under the table again and burst out laughing. She told me to follow her and we went through the back of the cafe into a very dark yard. Josefa, her name was, a short woman of about thirty, her head only just up to my shoulder.'

'You had a belly-to-belly at the back of a cafe in Vasco da Gama Square,' Marcel said grinning. 'It seems appropriate.'

'It was like ravishing her,' Olivier said weakly, his head rolling ponderously against the inlaid mahogany bed-head to stare at Marcel with half-closed eyes. 'I couldn't help myself – I got hold of her shoulders and crushed her to me to feel my *zimbriq* throbbing against her belly. She pulled her skirt up and I got my hands under her bottom and lifted

her feet off the ground. She gripped my waist with her legs and hung on with her arms round my neck while I skewered her – no underwear, of course! And you may find it difficult to believe, but I was hardly inside her before I was squirting like a hose-pipe!'

'Disappointing, that,' Marcel commented, 'but later on, when you had recovered . . .?'

'There was no question of waiting for later on.' Olivier said faintly. 'I was still painfully hard. Later on was right then. Josefa clung to me like a monkey on a coconut tree, with her legs locked round me, and I bored away at her without stopping for a moment. It took only a minute or two before I squirted up her again and in that time I rammed her so hard that I gave her half a dozen climaxes. Doing it that second time so soon after the first calmed me down and I felt it going limp. Josefa was so grateful that she kissed me forty or fifty times before I could get her off me, and when we went back inside the cafe she babbled away to her friend how marvellous I was. So Nina wanted her share and slipped her hand between my legs – and as soon as she touched me, I was hard as an iron bar again! I knew there was a fortune to be made out of datra.'

'You took the second woman, Nina, out into the yard?'

'On the spot! She was bigger than her friend, too heavy to lift for long, so I had her with her back against the nearest wall and her legs well apart, and rammed away until I squirted again. It was too quick for her, can you believe that? And it hadn't winded me, so I did it again, trying to slow down a bit, and she enjoyed herself that time. I was burning to do it again, but she wanted to see if the bus had arrived yet, so we could go to her home together and take our clothes off.'

'And had it? Or was there time to take her into the back-yard for another bout?'

'It was just pulling into the Square, so we waited outside for the sister – Rosalita her name was, and she was a couple of years younger than Nina. She had a heavy suitcase with her, so I piled all three women into a cab and off we went to Nina's apartment. We were packed close together in the

cab and I was on fire again, and while Nina was explaining the state of affairs to her sister, my hands were up Josefa's skirt for a feel. She was so wet and hot! She had hold of my ramrod and we were wriggling about trying to get it up her, but I squirted in her hand. She told the others and they all had a good laugh.'

'But this is astonishing!' said Marcel. 'To do it so many times in such a short a period of time! How many datra pills did you swallow?'

'I don't really know. About half a dozen the first time. And when I saw the impression that made on the two women, perhaps another six. As you can imagine, Rosalita wanted to find out what my tireless *zimbriq* could do for her, and her hand was in my trouser-pocket while we were climbing the stairs to her sister's apartment We were hardly through the door before she had me on my back on the floor and was astride me with her clothes round her neck.'

'But it was nothing less than an orgy!' Marcel exclaimed, admiration and envy in his voice. 'It is not surprising that you are fatigued this morning! How long did you hold out?'

'All night! We stripped naked and rolled around the living-room floor together, me and the three women! I was speechless with desire for them and my body felt as if it was wrapped in fire! As for my ramrod, it was twenty centimetres long and as thick as my wrist! It was like being the Caliph of Baghdad in his harem, lying on my back while my women climbed on me, one after the other, and *zeqqed* me. How many rides each of them had, it is impossible to say. I was in a condition of such continuous ecstasy that I fainted several times – and came to my senses again to find Nina or Rosalita or Josefa sliding up and down my shaft.'

'Incredible!' said Marcel, his imagination ablaze with the images of eroticism Olivier had conjured up. 'Who lasted the longest, you or the women?'

'By dawn two of them lay beside me on the floor in the sleep of total exhaustion. But Nina crouched over me and tried to mount again. She looked terrible – her body was drenched in perspiration and her hair straggled all over her face. At last my *zimbriq* had collapsed, and she flicked it

with her fingers to try to raise it one more time. But it was finished and she gave a long sigh of victory and fell down unconscious across my belly. I too passed out, as you can imagine.'

'You were still there at dawn. How did you get back here?'

'The shutters were wide open and the noise of people talking in the street woke me. All three women were fast asleep on the floor and though I could hardly stand, I got my clothes on somehow. I think I fell down the stairs. I remember sitting on the doorstep until a cab came by and I managed to attract the driver's attention.'

'In effect, you have had no sleep at all?' said Marcel.

'It required an unimaginable effort to undress when I got here,' said Olivier, his voice hardly audible. 'I fell on to the bed and was unconscious before my head struck the pillow . . . and a quarter of an hour later Lisette was trying to rouse me to go down to breakfast with her. The rest you know.'

'An extraordinary and enthralling story, my dear fellow,' said Marcel thoughtfully. 'Sleep a little and I will go down to wait for the doctor in the lobby, so that I can explain to him the confidential nature of your indisposition.'

Manoel La Paz arrived before long, the most fashionable doctor in the city, a man of forty in a well-cut suit of white linen. He was completely bald when he removed his Panama hat, and as if to compensate for that, he wore thick black moustache that drooped over the corners of his mouth. Marcel greeted him as an old acquaintance and outlined the situation to him while they made their way up to Olivier's room. Olivier was so deeply asleep that he hardly stirred when the doctor took his wrist and felt for his pulse.

'How much datra did he take – do you know?' La Paz asked Marcel, staring at his watch to time Olivier's heartbeats.

'He doesn't know himself with any degree of certainty. But from his account, I would guess no less than nine pills and perhaps as many as twelve.'

'It is fortunate that he has a large and strong body,' said La Paz. 'A Santa Sabinan taking that much would have died of a seizure or of a heart-failure while he was *zeqqing*. Your

rash friend will recover, but he will be in bed for at least a week. Did he tell you how many times he did it before he collapsed?'

'I'm sure he doesn't know that either,' Marcel answered with a grin. 'There were three women with him, all Santa Sabinans, and you and I know their capacity for *zeqqing*. If I had to make estimate, based on what he told me, own experience of the charming women of this country, I would say that they took advantage of the frenzy brought on by his overdose of datra to have him twenty times or so.'

The doctor had opened the front of Olivier's purple pyjama trousers and was staring pensively at the wrinkled *zimbriq* that sagged between his legs.

'Twenty times, you think?' he said. 'Then he will have some pleasant memories, which is just as well, since it is memory alone that must sustain him for a long time to come.'

'What do you mean' Marcel asked.

He edged closer to the bed, to catch a glimpse of Olivier's over-used *zimbriq*. Gone was the long thick ramrod he had seen rearing upward at full stretch in Serafina's private dining-room, when they had shared pretty little Adriana with Salvador Bonavista. The adventures of the night had withered it to a pitiful and shrivelled appendage the size of a little finger.

'Good God!' Marcel exclaimed. 'Will it ever recover?'

'That I cannot say,' La Paz replied, shaking his bald head doubtfully. 'With a lot of rest and a high protein diet, there is the possibility that after some months it may eventually stand up again. But there is also the possibility that he has ruined himself forever. Datra is a dangerous stimulant, though I have never seen the results of an overdose in one of my own countrymen. It is only foreigners, like your friend here, who misuse it. There is no treatment for this condition.'

'His fiancée and his future mother-in-law are waiting in great anxiety downstairs,' said Marcel. 'What will you say to them, Manoel? I know I can rely on your discretion.'

'Your friend is suffering from a mild attack of fruit-bat fever,' La Paz said. 'It is a rare malady and only ever affects foreigners, who have no natural immunity to it.'

'Does it exist at all?' Marcel asked doubtfully.

'Who can say? Perhaps it has not yet been recognised.'

'But how would he have come into contact with a fruit-bat?' Marcel asked, trying not to laugh in case he woke up Olivier.

'There are many of them flying about after dark – perhaps he had a drink on a cafe terrace contaminated by their droppings. I shall reassure the ladies that with plenty of rest and food, he will make a good recovery. To whom shall I send my bill?'

About midday, Lisette asked Marcel to walk with her while her mother watched over the sleeping Olivier. The heat by then was intolerable, but they strolled as far as the Gran'Caffe Camille and sat talking over a cool drink. Lisette appeared to be uneasy of mind, and Marcel asked himself if she had perhaps guessed that the fruit-bats were not responsible for Olivier's condition and had awkward questions to ask.

'What I have to say is confidential and cannot possible be discussed here in public,' she said, confirming his fears.

'The hotel? We could talk in my room.'

She shook her head at that.

'I have it,' said Marcel, 'This cafe still keeps one or two private dining rooms for lovers – we will have lunch here.'

'A private room for lovers?' said Lisette with a charming smile. 'But how delightfully *belle epoque*. I've never seen one of these legendary private rooms. What are they like?'

As she soon saw for herself, the private rooms upstairs in the Gran'Caffe were small and intimate, furnished in red plush, crystal mirrors and well-polished mahogany inlaid with marquetry. Full-length draped curtains framed the large window overlooking the Square, and fine muslin hanging close to the glass guaranteed privacy. Beneath the window was a long and broad bench padded and cushioned, serving to seat two. Marcel ordered a bottle of champagne while they consulted the menu and decided what to eat.

The rich and elaborate meals of Paris were inappropriate in the climate of Santa Sabina, no matter how *belle epoque* the mood, nor was there any local tradition of fine cooking.

Smoked cuttle-fish, sliced and served in its own ink, with a salad of chicory leaves and chopped radish, proved to be the speciality of the day. The waiter assigned to them flitted silently in and out of the room, serving the food and keeping the glasses filled. But it was not until the meal was ended, and the waiter had finally withdrawn, leaving them with coffee and cognac on the table, that Lisette was ready to open her mind. By then, under Marcel's imperceptible guidance, she had drunk just the right amount to make her eyes sparkle and her cheeks to glow in the prettiest manner possible.

'You know that Olivier and I were invited to dine the other evening with the Bonavistas,' she began. 'Well, after dinner, while the men were talking business together, Lucreza and I sat in the garden and she told me – in the greatest of confidence, of course – that you and she are lovers.'

Marcel said nothing, though his eyebrows arched in surprise.

'Anyway,' Lisette continued, 'we got on well with each other and she asked me to visit her again, so we could enjoy a good gossip. I was there at her home yesterday, in the afternoon.'

There had crept into Lisette's voice a note of uncertainty that caused Marcel to listen carefully while he poured a little more cognac into her glass. 'No doubt you had a pleasant visit,' he said casually, 'and Lucreza was able to inform you about my qualities as a lover.'

'I don't know how to tell you this,' Lisette blurted out and blushed bright red, 'but I must tell someone or go mad! The truth is that Lucreza started to make passionate love to me!'

'Really?' said Marcel, his attention fully engaged at this unexpected admission. 'You must feel free to tell me everything – you will feel better afterwards.'

Still blushing, her eyes averted and her prominent breasts heaving with emotion inside her blue blouse, Lisette told how she and Lucreza were in the garden of the Bonavista mansion, chatting together on a lounging swing under a striped awning.

'She was so charming towards me that I took it for casual friendship when she put an arm round my waist and squeezed and kissed me,' said Lisette, 'and thinking nothing of it, I kissed on the cheek, and we giggled and hugged each other like schoolgirls. But after a while she turned her head so that our lips touched, and she kissed me full on the mouth, as a man would. It surprised me and shocked me, but at the same time it was delicious, for she is such a beautiful woman.'

Marcel could hardly believe what he was hearing. He sat up straight on the bench cushions and looked at Lisette's blushing cheeks with curiosity and secret amusement.

'When I felt her tongue press itself between my lips and into my mouth, I thought I would die,' Lisette continued. 'Then she started to tell me that no one as blonde and pretty as me had visited Santa Sabina for longer than she could remember, and she was very complimentary about my complexion and my figure and the colour of my hair. But all the time she was talking, she was trying to undress me! I was wearing my pretty rose-pink blouse and she pulled it right out of my skirt and undid all the buttons . . .'

'Well, well!' Marcel murmured, his head on one side.

'I'm sure my face must have been crimson with embarrassment when she unclipped my brassiere,' said Lisette, as if to excuse herself. 'I tried to catch hold of her hands but she was much too quick and agile for me. Before I could stop her, she had uncovered my bosom completely.'

'But why not?' Marcel asked softly and leaned back on the bench to spread his thighs apart and allow his stiff *zimbriq* to accommodate itself more comfortably inside his underwear. 'You have the most enchanting *gublas*, and it comes as no surprise to me to hear that others find them appealing – women included.'

Lisette glanced down at his lap and saw the evidence of his arousal bulging in his trousers. 'Like you, Lucreza was excited by them,' she observed dryly. 'She said she'd never seen breasts as beautiful as mine. She begged me to let her touch them.'

'Naturally,' Marcel murmured, 'and did you let her?'

'In some strange way, you see, I didn't really believe that any of this was happening to me. It was not difficult to half-convince myself that I was asleep and dreaming. I expected at every moment to wake up and find myself alone in bed.'

Marcel found it impossible not to lay the palm of his hand lightly over his *zimbriq* in an attempt to stop its leaping inside his clothes. Lisette looked down for a moment to see what he was doing and then her gaze came back to his face, her expression one of high seriousness.

'But when Lucreza kept on feeling me and telling me that I was beautiful, the moment came when I had to stop pretending to myself that it was only a dream and I would wake up in another minute. You cannot imagine how confused I was, Marcel!'

'Much as when you were a young girl and a boy felt you for the first time, I suppose,' he said, to be helpful.

'In a way . . . but I knew I must insist that Lucreza stopped what she was doing to me, because it was perverted and immoral. But, you understand, by then my nipples had grown sensitive and plump under her caressing fingers. My conscience informed me that what we were doing was wrong, but another part of me didn't want her to stop.'

'You do not have to explain the psychology of temptation to me,' said Marcel with a grin. 'All of my life I have been an expert in recognising what is wrong and then succumbing to it whole-heartedly.'

'You may make jokes if you wish,' Lisette said primly, 'but to me this is a matter of extreme seriousness. If only Olivier had been more attentive to me, none of this would ever have happened! But since we arrived here, he has neglected me. I have a nature that needs to be loved, like a flower that needs the warmth of the sun, or it will wither and fade. I am used to constant attention – after we became engaged he loved me every day when we were in Paris. And on the voyage here, when he had no business affairs to distract his attention and occupy his time, it was twice a day, and sometimes more. But all that came to an end when we landed! When I ask him why he no longer makes love to me, he says that the climate exhausts him.'

If only you knew! Marcel thought, keeping his expression solemn with an effort. *Your faithless fiancé has been* zeqqing *two or three different girls a day since I showed him how easy it is to pick them up. And if you had any suspicion of the orgy he enjoyed last night, with three women at the same time!*

'My poor Lisette,' he murmured sympathetically, 'you have suffered atrociously! And needlessly – when all the time you knew that I adored you and was desperate for a kind word and a little sign that you felt something for me. Why did you never accept my love and put an end to the inhuman frustration that led you to this encounter with Lucreza Bonavista?'

'It is a question of loyalty,' Lisette answered, her pale blue eyes fixed on him in an expression that pleaded with him to understand her difficulties of conscience. 'I said to myself that however attractive I find you, my duty is to my fiancé.'

'That is most commendable,' said Marcel, although privately he thought it was nothing of the kind, 'I have always respected you, Lisette, since the first moment we met. Now my respect has increased beyond measure. But please continue – you were strong enough to turn aside my heart-felt desires, but were your scruples powerful enough to enable you to resist being seduced by a beautiful woman?'

'She took my breasts in her hands and kissed them and sucked them until she drained away my strength of purpose! I was too weak to say a word to stop her. I knew I was lost when she undid my skirt and put a hand down the front, to caress me. All I was capable of was to moan and squirm while the swing rocked about under me as if we were in a small boat on a rough sea.'

Inside Marcel's trousers his hard *zimbriq* was twitching steadily, even under the restraining pressure of his hand. He sighed and slid his arm around Lisette's waist. There was a good chance, he thought, that she would ultimately try to atone for her little deviation by inviting him to make love to her. Though to whom she thought she was atoning was a complicated question and not worth enquiring into.

'In brief, you were a helpless victim,' he said, offering

an opportunity to salve her conscience. 'What was done to you was entirely without your consent?'

'To be truthful,' said Lisette, her cheeks a charming pink, 'after the first shock of being touched by a woman had passed, I wanted to find out what it would be like to go all the way. Would it be as nice as with a man? Could it be even nicer? One hears all sorts of strange whispers and rumours. In short, I was as willing to learn as she was to teach me, and my tongue was in her mouth while she stroked me between the legs.

'Ah, my God!' Marcel whispered in delight.

'What followed was what you would expect,' Lisette went on. 'Lucreza stripped me naked and knelt between my legs, her frock off to show me her own breasts. The colour of her skin is so perfect, like dark honey! She kissed my thighs until I became frantic, but she never once touched my . . . *kuft* . . . is that the right word, Marcel?'

'Most assuredly that is the right word,' he agree. His mind was dazzled by exciting images of the two beautiful women playing together.

'I can hardly speak of it now without dying of shame,' said Lisette, her eyes turned away from him again. 'I was writhing about on the swing, begging Lucreza to put her fingers into me, but she ignored me until my frenzy almost reached the point of madness. And then she forced my legs so wide apart I thought the sinews would break! My mind disintegrated into madness when she put her head down between my legs and I felt her tongue enter me! The sensation was tremendous and my climax came instantly – I could hear myself screaming in ecstasy and there was nothing I could do to stop myself, though I was terrified that the servants would hear me . . .'

'Well now,' Marcel murmured, putting a comforting arm about her when her story trailed off into confusion, 'it is good to know that Lucreza gave you as much pleasure as she gives me.'

Lisette was expecting her account to be taken more seriously than that and she gave a gasp of shock at his words. Before she recovered, Marcel was cupping a superb breast

in his hand while he told her she was beautiful and adorable and that it was only natural that Lucreza desired her as much as he did.

'But it was wrong, what I let her do to me,' she insisted.

She felt mildly guilty and made no effort to remove his hand from her breast, wanting him to confirm that she ought not have let herself be seduced. When he remained silent, she kissed him on the cheek and asked what he thought. Instead of words, he returned the kiss, on her lips. She struggled a little at first and then her mouth clung to his and their kisses became hot and passionate. He laid her down gently at full length on the cushions of the long bench, his *zimbriq* twitching vehemently in his trousers, demanding to be set free. When he started to undo the buttons of her blue silk blouse, she was overcome by doubt and asked him not to do that, because the waiter was sure to come in and see them.

'There is no need for alarm,' he assured her, his nimble fingers busy with the button, 'waiters do not enter private rooms until the are rung for,' and in anther moment he had her blouse open from throat to waist. It was evident that her senses were stirred by the story she had told him of her seduction by Lucreza Bonavista, for instead of repeating her protest, it was she herself who unhooked her transparent nylon brassiere for him.

'There!' she said, her voice quavering a little. 'You want to feel my *gublas*, just like Lucreza, and it was you who taught me that word. Very well, then, feel them all you wish!'

Marcel fondled her fleshy bounties with a swelling heart and put his face into their softness to suck their red-brown points until they stood up, long and swollen. He stretched out beside her on the cushions, squeezed her *gublas* together and licked the deep cleft between them. He was rewarded by the touch of her hand deftly inserting itself under his belt, slipping down into his trousers, gliding down inside his underwear, close to his hot belly, arousing him to an impossibly intense pitch of desire. Her hand stopped when it reached his curls, played with them and slid around his trembling *zimbriq* without touching it.

He was certain he would die of pleasure when she touched his *zimbriq*. His mouth gaped open with almost intolerable sensation when her finger-tips slid delicately up the shaft and, for the space of a heart-beat, glided over the smooth and sensitive skin of its engorged head. And when her fingers closed around his throbbing *zimbriq* at last, he experienced a shock of such intense pleasure that his back arched and he thought the crucial moment had arrived. He fumbled blindly under her linen skirt, wanting to touch her *kuft* and open her to him. His hand groped its way inside her knickers and his fingers touched her curls. At once she pressed her thighs together, not permitting his hand to advance further.

'Be still,' she whispered in his ear, her finger tips sliding up and down his *zimbriq*. He lay quietly, enjoying her caresses, and behind his closed eyelids he played out a fantasy in which he ripped away her blouse to bare her to the waist and suck her left breast until she spread her legs wide apart for him and he took down her white silk knickers to kiss the *kuft* he had never yet seen.

In his feverish imagination Lisette was adorned between the legs by a powder-puff of soft curls as silvery blonde as the hair of her head. He took her hand and helped her off the bench and round the table, until they stood naked, side by side, before one of the crystal mirrors on the wall, to stare in delight at their reflection. They turned towards each other, still looking into the mirror, while he handled her magnificent *gublas* and she played with his leaping *zimbriq*. She sank to her knees in front of him, to take it in her hot mouth and he felt the critical moment rushing towards him.

He put his hands on her bare shoulders and pushed her down on her back and flung himself on her belly. He was *zeqqing* her so frantically that she was sliding underneath him across the carpet and shrieking as multiple climaxes ravaged her . . . and while this erotic scenario was being played out in Marcel's head as he lay face to face with Lisette on the bench under the window, her hand was moving delicately up and down his *zimbriq* and he was kissing her face and licking her closed eyes in a delirium of sensation.

When she felt him throb in her hand with the first spasm

of his discharge, she exclaimed in a voice that shook with emotion, 'Now I've made you happy!'

'Aaah!'he moaned while her fingers flicked him rapidly and his hot sap flooded up inside his shirt, 'Lisette, *cheri*! The last throb of ecstasy was hardly over before she let go of him and sat up. She lifted her breasts into the cradle of her brassiere and he saw that their buds were still swollen and shiny-wet from his licking. He watched her button her blouse to hide her delights and, his shirt sticking to his belly, he gave silent thanks to heaven that Concepcion would be waiting for him at the Grand Hotel Orient, ready to be *zeqqed* properly.

12

A Double Pleasure to Cheat the Cheat

Marcel saw nothing wrong in making use of Gabrielle Delacoste's unusual sexual inclinations for the promotion of his scheme to thwart Olivier. She would, after all, derive very considerable pleasure from what he intended, even though it was pleasure of a type neither understood nor appreciated by most people. When a suitable moment arrived in the course of the morning's work at the Embassy, and they were alone together briefly, he told her that he wanted to examine Lafargue's dossier on Olivier. Gabrielle stared at him as if he had taken leave of his senses and reminded him that the document was confidential.

When 'naturally' was all Marcel said in reply, she informed him angrily that nothing in the world, nothing at all, would persuade her to betray her trust. Marcel was sitting casually on a corner of his desk while they talked. He smiled at her vehement refusal, and reached out to touch her bare arm while he told her that he would call at her apartment at nine that evening, to inspect the documents. At that she gasped and her plain face blushed bright red.

Before she could recover her self-possession, Marcel slid off the desk, to stand close to her and stretch out a hand to her plump bottom. He grasped a thick fold of flesh between his fingers and squeezed it cruelly while he repeated that he would call at nine. She tried to pull away, but he held on so tightly that she winced in pain and said it was her duty to report his unauthorised request to Lafargue. He gave her an insolent grin and, as soon as he let go, she stumbled out of his office, her face crimson with shock and shame, and her mouth opening and closing soundlessly.

For the rest of the working day she kept out of sight, but he was confident she would say nothing to Lafargue and almost confident that she would make a copy of the dossier for him to see. To unsettle her further and heighten her susceptibility to his suggestions, he arrived at her apartment twenty minutes late. She let him in without a word and stood facing him in her living-room, her expression one of seething anger. So much so that she would not let him kiss her cheek, nor even her hand, by way of greeting.

Something of her agitation of mind could be deduced from the fact that she had not changed the sleeveless white blouse and dark grey skirt she had worn all day at work. Nor did it seem that she had combed her hair since arriving home – it hung down untidily over her small ears from its central parting. As she stared at Marcel, her heavy breasts heaved under her blouse to the rhythm of her troubled breathing.

'Well, have you brought it?' Marcel asked casually.

'I can't give it to you,' she answered, speaking in a low and disturbed voice.

'Let me see it,' he said, holding his hand out.

Gabrielle wrestled with her conscience in silence for some moments, a succession of complex emotions showing on her face, before she went to a small writing-desk by the window and took from a locked drawer a thin sheaf of typewritten sheets. Marcel thought it courteous to spare her any further struggles with her conscience by crossing the room to her side and taking the papers gently from her shaking hand.

'This is so wrong!' she said, as if talking to herself.

Marcel ran his eye down the pages quickly. The information appeared to be comprehensive on Olivier's maraudings through French Guiana, Martinique, Upper Volta, Gabon and the Belgian Congo, with exact dates, names of politicians and government officials he had talked into bogus contracts, amounts of money he had made off with, names of banks and account numbers . . . enough material to send him to prison for many years, if he ever stood trial. There was also the unexpected information that Olivier had married a certain Marie Vigeron at Toulon six years before and had two children by her.

'My dear Gabrielle, your self-recrimination is needless,' said Marcel carefully, understanding now why Lisette was still Olivier's fiancée and not his wife. 'You have served the course of justice by permitting me to see these documents.'

'I've betrayed the trust placed in me,' she said miserably. 'What I have done is unpardonable and I shall resign my post first thing tomorrow morning.'

'Out of the question,' Marcel said at once. 'You have broken a rule by removing confidential documents from the Embassy, that is beyond dispute. And even though it was at my request, as a member of the Embassy staff I cannot condone what you have done. You must be punished for this breach of trust, punished severely. Do you understand that?'

She nodded dumbly, her eyes downcast, and took Marcel by the jacket-sleeve to tug him across the room, the papers still in his hand. She began to mumble to herself as she led him into the bedroom and before he could fold the documents and slip them into his pocket, she wrenched them away from him and threw them on to the dressing-table. A moment later she pushed him down to sit on the edge of the bed.

'I have done a terrible thing,' she said, lifting her skirt to roll her plain white knickers down her thighs.

She was standing half-facing him and he caught a glimpse of the broad expanse of thick curls between her legs. She threw herself heavily across his lap, her big round bottom bared for punishment. There was a purple bruise where he had gripped her so fiercely that morning, and at the sight of it Marcel forgot the unspoken rules of their game long enough to fondle her cheeks, running a finger down the crack between them, until Gabrielle shrieked at him that he was not there to indulge his degraded and vicious lusts but to chastise her for her wrong-doing.

At this rebuke he began spanking her, and understanding something of the perversity of her nature, he laid into her wobbling bottom with all the vigour of his right arm. Before long she was sobbing and squirming on his lap and, when his stroke slackened she gasped out for more. The spanking

lasted a long time, and so extensive were the motions of guilt racking Gabrielle that, long before she had purged them from her soul, Marcel's arm was aching painfully, while her cheeks were getting redder and redder, and hotter and hotter to the touch.

The truth was that the only emotion Marcel was experiencing just then was boredom. His *zimbriq* hung limply in his trousers and all that kept him at his task was an awareness of keeping his side of their tacit bargain. To disappoint her now would be to risk losing her usefulness in future. And so he kept on spanking until his arm ached so much he thought it was about to drop off and he stopped and put his hand down between her spread thighs to touch her hairy *kuft* and see how aroused she had become. She protested furiously at this molestation of her person and beat against his legs with her clenched fists.

'My arm is tired – I can't go on,' he excused himself.

'Beat me, beat me!' she exclaimed shrilly.

But for Marcel, enough was enough. With one hand flat on the base of her spine to hold her still, he used the other to pry open the plump lips of her *kuft* and rubbed her wet button with a finger-tip. She screamed loudly in outrage, her feet left the floor and her legs made swimming movements in the air. Her pudgy fists pounded at his shins, but he went on unrelenting with his manipulation until at last she was gripped and shaken by a long and noisy climax. When it was over she uttered a long and heart-felt sigh and then slumped over his lap, like washing thrown over a clothes-line to dry.

In the space of a few moments she had recovered herself and got up ponderously from his lap and stood with her back turned towards him while she pulled up her knickers and smoothed down her skirt. Marcel guessed that her bottom must be sore from the heavy smacking he had inflicted on it, but she gave no sign of discomfort. As soon as all was securely concealed, she told him that he too had betrayed his sacred trust and must be punished. Naturally, he had expected this and went along with it. She asked him to strip and while he was doing so she moved a bamboo armchair

from its place in a corner and placed it in the middle of the bedroom floor.

'Sit down,' she said, pushing him towards it.

There was no cushion on the chair and the woven strands of the seat were uncomfortable under his bare backside. Gabrielle was turned away from him, bending over to get something from inside the wardrobe and he wondered whether she would become angry when she observed that, for the first time, the privilege of spanking her had failed to stiffen his *zimbriq*. And indeed, she glared at it furiously, her face blushing again, but she made no comment. In her hand she held a dozen lengths of strong cord she had taken from the wardrobe.

This implied premeditation, he thought, for she had not only bought the cord, she had cut it into suitable lengths for her purpose. To speculate on what form of perversity this strange woman had in mind was intriguing in the extreme; more than that, it was exciting. While Gabrielle was standing behind him, tying a length of cord round his waist to hold him fast against the back of the chair, his *zimbriq* twitched between his thighs. And by the time she slid another cord under his armpits and round his chest, and tied that to the chair-back, he was stiffening rapidly.

'Put your arms flat on the arms of the chair,' she said and, when he obeyed her, she bound his elbows and wrists to the chair. 'Spread your legs,' she said angrily, and knelt at his feet to attach his legs to the chair-legs, tying him below the knee and at the ankle with more lengths of cord. During the operation she deliberately kept her gaze averted from what now stood stiffly upright his thighs. She got to her feet and moved right round him to test his bonds, and when she was satisfied that he was unable to move, she spoke to him severely, telling him to examine his conscience and contemplate his wrong-doing.

With that recommendation, she walked out of the room. Marcel sat astonished by this turn of events. In truth, to sit there was the only course open to him, for he was tied very securely to the chair. She had left the bedroom door open and soon he heard the shower running. He was hot

and uncomfortable from the exertion of dealing out as much punishment as she demanded and the thought of standing under the cool water was tantalising. He struggled a little against the bonds that held him, making the chair creak, but the cords cut unpleasantly into his flesh and he desisted.

It seemed to him a long time before Gabrielle returned. She had put on a thin and totally transparent night-dress, cut like a smock, with pale blue forget-me-nots on the shoulders. It was short, the hem well above her knees, offering a view of her sturdy thighs. And where those thighs joined, there was visible through the thin material a dark shadow where lay the broad expanse of her thick curls. Higher still, as Marcel raised his eyes, her breasts bulged out of the night-dress, their plump buds plainly visible.

She planted herself solidly in front of him, feet apart and her hands on her hips. There was a freshness and a fragrance about her after the shower, a coolness and a tempting trace of 'Muguet de Bois' perfume. She made no pretence of not looking at his stiff *zimbriq* now; she eyed its quivering with disdain and said, 'Wicked thing – such monstrous pride must be humbled!' Tied as he was, Marcel's legs wee held apart and there was nothing he could do to protect himself when Gabrielle sank to her knees and jerked his *zimbriq* up and down with such brutality that he feared she would rip it from his body.

'Gently, for the love of God!' he gasped.

'Be silent!' she responded, her dark eyes transfixing his with a malevolent glare. 'I betrayed my trust and have suffered for it – but I betrayed it on your orders, and your offence is greater than mine! You must be punished severely!'

Marcel's vision began to blur a little as he stared at her, her fat breasts swinging inside her night-dress to the rhythmic movement of her arm. A bead of perspiration appeared between them and trickled very slowly down towards her broad belly. She reached in between his open thighs with her free hand to hold his pompoms and roll them . . . and he was terrified that in her unthinking anger she might decide to crush them in her hand!

Fortunately, the barbarity of the suffering she inflicted on him did not extend that far. She jerked his *zimbriq* up and down cruelly, gasping out, 'You must be punished,' and he felt the hand gripping his pompoms release them and slide underneath him. A fingertip probed hard between the cheeks of his bottom and he gasped as he rose involuntarily above the chair-seat for the centimetre or two that his cruel bonds permitted. Gabrielle's fingertip forced open his tight little knot and slid into him and his moment had come – the violence with which she was handling him brought a torrent spurting from him.

Through the shuddering ecstasy that racked him, he saw the splatter of his passion between Gabrielle's breasts, on the pale skin exposed by the scooped neckline of her night-dress. The touch affected her instantly; her head went back and she moaned in a crisis of sensation, her breasts joggling and her hand wielding his gushing *zimbriq* with an insane energy. The intensity of her guilt overwhelmed her and she slumped forward with her head on the hard chair-seat between his parted thighs, her plump shoulders shaking to her dry sobs. Marcel heaved a deep sigh of relief that she had let go of his abused *zimbriq*.

'You are over-wrought, my dear,' he said, after her noisy fit of shame had continued for some time, 'untie me, now.'

'No!' she exclaimed, raising her head to stare up at him, white-faced with strong emotion. 'You are the Tempter!'

With that, she astonished and amused him by shuffling away from him on her knees, across the room. She kept her back to him while she climbed up on to the bed, switched off the light and collapsed on her side, facing away from him.

'But this is absurd! Come and untie me!' Marcel called to her, but there was no response and, after he had tried two or three times, he realised that he was not going to gain her attention. The violence of the emotions she had experienced had exhausted her so completely that she had fallen asleep and left him lashed naked to a chair!

Fortunately for him there was a little slack in the cord holding his left wrist to the chair-arm. It had not been like

that when she tied it, he was certain, but the force of his convulsive release had slipped the knot just enough for him to be able to worry at it, twisting and pulling his arm. It took an hour before he was able to slip his wrist out of the bonds and another hour to work the lashing below his elbow down to a point where he could free his arm completely. After that it was straight-forward, though the knots round his ankles had been pulled so tight that it took a long time to pick them apart.

Although his ordeal seemed to have lasted for an eternity, his wristwatch said it was not yet midnight. In the darkened room he stood at Gabrielle's bedside, looking down at her as she slept heavily with her knees drawn up towards her breasts. He was hot and sweaty from the long struggle to free himself, but he was too fatigued to take a shower right away. First he must rest a little, then he would have the energy to shower and return to his hotel. He lay down on the bed behind Gabrielle, closed his eyes and fell asleep in a moment.

When he awoke he could see through the open window that it was light outside. His *zimbriq* was hard and demanding; he knew he had been dreaming of something sexually arousing but couldn't remember what. Gabrielle was still curled up with her back towards him and her short nightdress had ridden up high enough to uncover her bottom. Without a moment's delay he slid forward on the bed until the swollen head of his *zimbriq* touched her between the fleshy cheeks.

Whether she was awake or asleep, she lay conveniently still while, with a little manoeuvring, he assumed the right angle of approach and pushed slowly into her *kuft*, until his belly was pressed firmly against her bottom. It was only when he reached over her to get a hand up inside her loose night-dress and clasp a big soft breast that Gabrielle stirred at last, her head rolling on the pillow while she moaned, 'Not that! Merciful God spare me this degradation!'

Marcel hushed and soothed her with meaningless murmurings while he eased his stiffness slowly and carefully in and out. 'It is the most natural thing in the world for a

man and a woman to do this together, Gabrielle,' he assured her. But she refused to be soothed or comforted and moaned how terribly wrong it was, her head rolling feverishly all the time on the pillow and her fingers clawing at the sheet. Wrong or not, she did nothing to hinder or disturb the steady rhythm of his *zeqqing*. In fact, after a while she began to sigh loudly, no doubt in her anguish of mind. This continued for some time, right up to the moment when she shuddered violently, in horror perhaps, and cried out in uncontrollable shame at the infamy that was being done to her body – unless by chance her shudder was caused by climactic pleasure.

In the case of so unnaturally complicated a person, who can say which convulsive emotion it was that Marcel's busy *zimbriq* stirred in her? Even she herself could not perhaps be certain. But whichever it was, it tore away Marcel's last little shred of self-control and, with a long gasp of relief, he discharged his excitement into her.

'Why, why, do you do this to me?' she moaned, her feeling of guilt blacker than ever at allowing herself to be *zeqqed*. Marcel chuckled and squeezed her fleshy *gublas* affectionately until she fell asleep again.

By six o'clock in the morning he was back in the Grand Hotel Orient and in his own bed. He dozed off without the least difficulty and was woken by an insistent hammering on his door. With a grin he pulled on his dressing-gown, for he slept naked because of the heat, and went to let in his early caller. As he had expected, it was Olivier, looking ghastly, and the time was not yet eight o'clock.

'What is it?' Marcel asked with a yawn. 'Do you feel worse? Shall I phone for the doctor to call again?'

Olivier pushed past him into the room on shaky legs and sat down heavily on the bed. He held a sheaf of papers in his hand and waved them wearily at Marcel. 'They're going to torture me,' he said in a voice laden with doom, 'just like the Swede you told me about! And then they'll murder me and feed me to the sharks! I'm done for!'

'Calm yourself,' said Marcel, pretending not to understand, 'What is the matter?'

Olivier detached the top sheet of paper and handed it over. It was a brief note in the old-fashioned florid style of handwriting used by the educated of Santa Sabina, addressed to Monsieur Olivier de Murville and inviting him to call at the writer's office at ten that morning. There was no heading or address or date on the paper, nor the least indication of the title or position of the sender, but the elaborate signature at the foot of the page was Emilio Sanches'.

'Good God!' Marcel exclaimed, sounding horrified. It was not easy to sound shocked convincingly by a note he had himself counterfeited only an hour or two before, copying the style from invitations to him from Santa Sabina friends. 'What on earth have you done, Olivier?'

'Nothing, I swear!'

'The chief of the Bureau of Public Information does not send personally for people who have done nothing, particularly not foreigners. He sends a couple of thugs to pick them up in the street and beat them unconscious if they resist. You must have committed some truly awful offence, to receive so sinister an invitation. What are those other papers you are holding?'

'Nothing,' Olivier said hastily, folding the papers Marcel had taken from Gabrielle which set out his fraudulent past and pushing them down into a pocket of his dressing-gown.

'Who delivered the note to you – one of Sanches' goons?'

'I suppose so. It was pushed under my door in the night. I found it when I woke up. What shall I do, tell me, Marcel!'

'You are not being entirely candid with me,' Marcel replied, 'It looks to me as if those papers you are hiding from me came with this note and refer to whatever you are to be interrogated about. Unless you are frank, I cannot advise you.'

Olivier's face was an unpleasant shade of yellow and there were beads of sweat on his forehead.

'To be absolutely truthful,' he said in a quavering voice, 'there is something in what you suggest. The papers were with the note and they refer to a certain indiscretion on my part. But that was last year, and it was in another country.

I cannot imagine how anyone here could know about any of this.'

'Policemen all round the world exchange information,' said Marcel solemnly, 'and though Sanches is a mad torturer who has nothing to do with the uniformed police force, he is still a policeman under the skin. This earlier episode – may I enquire if it was concerned with government contracts and bribes?'

Secretly he was amused by Olivier's description of a lengthy catalogue of financial swindling as an indiscretion. Even for a businessman, his bare-faced effrontery was astonishing.

'There were certain dealings with officials,' Olivier said with suitable vagueness, 'and commissions were involved.'

'Then be sure of it, Sanches has found out about the money you gave to Salvador Bonavista. I am afraid you are in serious difficulties. If you once enter the headquarters of the Bureau, you will never be seen alive again, and I dare not think what will be done to you to make you answer their questions. At what time does he want you there?'

'At ten,'said Olivier, sounding so miserable that Marcel almost burst out laughing, 'what do you think I should do?'

'Save yourself,' Marcel replied without any hesitation. 'Run away, now, this very instant. Stop for nothing, not even to bid your fiancée goodbye. Leave everything and disappear.'

'Out of the question!' said Olivier, obviously upset by the urgent directness of the advice. 'I have an important business investment here – I cannot abandon that!'

'Your *investment*, as you call it, in Bonavista's compliance – is lost anyway,' Marcel pointed out. 'He will be disgraced when Sanches passes the evidence of bribery to the President, but by then you will be maimed and perhaps dead. Besides, you told me it was bank money you gave Bonavista, not your own.'

'Even so . . .' Olivier muttered.

'Then you must do as you think best,' said Marcel, shrugging in a way that indicated he accepted no responsibility. 'If you refuse to save yourself by escaping,

I recommend you go at once to the Ambassador. He cannot protect you from the criminal law of the country, but he might be able to get you arrested by the police instead of the Bureau. That would spare you the torture, but their processes are notoriously slow and I fear you will be in prison for a long time, at least a year before they bring you to trial. After that, who can say?'

'Sit down,' said Olivier. 'Let me think.'

'Think for as long as you please,' Marcel answered. 'What I find impressive is that you have been invited to visit Bureau headquarters and incriminate yourself. This unnatural courtesy is not really intended for you, that is not their way. It is an act of formal politeness to the Ambassador, because of your engagement to a member of his family. Sanches does not want to embarrass His Excellency in public.'

'You're right!' Olivier exclaimed. 'I see it now. I'm being offered a chance to avoid scandal by making myself scarce!'

'I hope that's it,' said Marcel, shaking his head solemnly, 'but we must not pretend that Sanches is a civilised man – he is a sadistic murderer and he can change his mind at any moment and send a squad to arrest you. There is no doubt in my mind that he has a man waiting outside the hotel now.'

He knew this to be true, for the Bureau posted a man outside every hotel where foreigners stayed, as a matter of routine, to keep track of their comings and goings.

'How can I get out of Santa Sabina in a hurry, without being picked up?' Olivier asked, his mind made up at last.

'There is only one way – by sea. We must sneak you on board a cargo ship after dark, with a captain who asks no questions.'

'Is this possible?'

'Not impossible,' said Marcel, glancing at his wristwatch, 'But first we must get you out of this hotel, and quickly. You can be sure that the goons will kick your door down if you do not leave for Bureau headquarters in less than an hour's time.'

'But where can I go – where can I hide?' Olivier exclaimed, beginning to panic under this new pressure. 'You must help me – it is your duty to help a French citizen in distress!'

'I shall help you,' Marcel reassured him, 'but you must do what I say. When you are safely out of the hotel, I shall go to the harbour and make discreet enquiries until I find a captain about to sail who will take you as a passenger. His destination is of no consequence, only that he is sailing very soon.'

Because of his enfeebled condition, Olivier was susceptible to suggestion. On Marcel's instructions he returned to his own room to write a note to Lisette, explaining that he was leaving Santa Sabina for the sake of his health, being convinced that he would never shake off the fruit-bat fever in this climate. While he was composing this farewell, Marcel went downstairs to find the hotel porter and, for a few tikkoos, bought from him the disreputable cotton trousers and jacket he wore off-duty. Olivier stared at the garments in distaste but, believing that his only chance of escape was in disguise, he put them on.

Marcel explained how to get out of the hotel by the kitchen entrance, sending him alone, to increase his fear, and arranged to meet him in Vasco da Gama Square. When he found him there, poor Olivier looked hunted and shabby. He had been given no time to shower or shave before being bundled out of the hotel, and in the porter's ill-fitting clothes he resembled a fugitive from Devil's Island.

'Why here?' he asked as he tried to fortify himself with a cup black coffee and several glasses of *araq*.

Hardly able to contain the laughter that threatened to explode inside him, Marcel played his master-stroke. 'There is no safe place I can think of to hide you in,' he said, 'therefore you must keep moving. Take the next bus to Vilanova – that's it over there. The journey usually lasts for about three hours, sometimes four. But don't show yourself in the town. When you arrive, get on the next bus back here, you understand? You should arrive here by late afternoon. Be very careful not to be seen – get on the next bus out, whatever its destination. Meet me in this same cafe at eleven this evening and by then I hope to have arranged a ship for you. Good luck.'

Olivier nodded, his face ashen, shook Marcel's hand in

gratitude and lurched to the waiting bus. Marcel's belly was hurting from suppressed laughter; he had persuaded Olivier to spend a whole sweating day in unwashed rags, riding the noisy and unreliable buses on which he had based his confidence trick. As an example of poetic justice, it seemed perfect.

There were four tramp steamers tied up on the quayside and an official at the Customs House gave the useful information that two of them would be sailing on the early morning tide. Marcel chose the oldest and dirtiest, the *Wing Wang* bound for South Korea. The captain proved to be a short and thickset man, as wide as he was tall, with an aggressive stare and a minimal grasp of any language but his own. But money is independent of language, and Captain Hong Dow was happy enough to accommodate a passenger and pocket a fare that his owners would never know about. He and Marcel shook hands and drank to each other in Japanese whisky.

When he arrived at the Embassy, Marcel thought it wise to seek out Gabrielle to assure himself that she had got over her attack of conscience and renounced her intention of resigning. But she had telephoned to say she was not well and would not be in that day, and he sat at his desk, flicking idly through a document or two that had come in, his mind busy with thoughts of her. Was she nursing a bruised conscience or a well-spanked bottom? He called to mind how she had draped herself across his lap, with her big pale bottom bared for his attentions, and he began to be aroused.

He found it amusing that he was more excited by the memory of smacking Gabrielle's bottom than by the performance itself. One thought followed another until there were all too familiar sensations of congestion and pressure in his trousers. After that, he reached the not very surprising conclusion that it would be more pleasurable to return to her apartment than to remain in the Embassy pretending to read boring papers.

She opened the door and stared open-mouthed in surprise to see him. Although it was past ten in the morning, she had not combed her hair or dressed and was still in her night-

dress, a short blue dressing-gown over it, tied loosely round her waist. He ignored her immediate 'go away and leave me alone' and eased himself sideways past her and into her apartment. She followed him slowly into the sitting-room and sat down, her brown eyes never leaving his face.

'What do *you* want?' she asked.

Her face was far from friendly and she was sitting hunched over, as if to protect herself from a sudden blow. From where he stood Marcel was able to look down her dressing-gown and see her plump and loose *gublas* in her night-dress, all the way down to their dark buds. The sight renewed his excitement.

'They told me at the Embassy that you were unwell,' he said, his voice smooth as velvet with sincerity and sympathy. 'I came at once to see if there is anything I can do.'

'There's nothing I want from you,' she said.

But when Marcel chose to exert his very considerable charm, it was virtually impossible for any woman to remain hostile to him for long. He began to tell her how greatly he respected and admired her for her strength of character, how among their many colleagues at the Embassy she alone stood out as a person of high moral principles. She seemed indifferent to his praise, but she listened to it, and within five minutes he had talked himself on to the sofa alongside her.

She hunched over more, her arms about her knees to protect herself from his gaze. With a smile of pure friendly concern for her well-being, Marcel told her that she must calm herself. He put his hands gently on her shoulders and pressed her back against the sofa, murmuring to her as to a disturbed child.

'Be calm, Gabrielle, be calm, my dear, and let your tension go. Loosen these arms and lean back easily.' When she rested her head on the sofa-back and let her eyes close, he stroked her dark brown hair to soothe her, trying to comb it a little with his fingers . 'Breathe slowly and deeply,' he murmured, 'let your arms hang loose and unclench your fists. Good, good.'

By leaning back she pulled up her short dressing-gown

and night-dress showing legs above the knees. She shuddered when he rested his palm lightly on her bare thigh. 'Calm, calm,' he said. 'Your legs are as rigid as steel bars – relax them. Stretch them out and unwind the sinews.'

She breathed out heavily as she did as he said, letting her knees move apart a little. Marcel slid his hand between them and stroked the inside of her thigh with a light touch. But to dispel any illusions he might have about her attitude to him, she accused him of stealing official and confidential documents from her and demanded their instant return.

'But all I took were copies,' he said, 'and they have been destroyed. There is no cause for alarm.'

'That's easy for you to say,' she answered, letting her knees part a little wider as his hand moved very gently upwards another few centimetres, 'because you are without scruples or morals. But as for me, I can't stop thinking of the wrong I did and I couldn't go to work today and look Monsieur Lafargue in the face, knowing what I'd done.'

'But you were punished for that,' said Marcel, glad that her eyes were closed so that she did not see how her words made him grin. 'The question is closed.'

But for Gabrielle it was by no means finished. In halting words interspersed with many a sorrowful sigh, she made Marcel understand that one spanking was too trivial a punishment to wipe away her intense feelings of guilt. By this time his hand under her dressing-gown was so close to the join of her thighs that he could feel the touch of her curls against the side of his thumb. If he could keep her soothed and submissive for long enough to maintain this steady advance up the warm inside of her leg, he would be feeling her *kuft* in a few more moments.

His eager *zimbriq* was jumping in his underwear, but he knew very well that Gabrielle would not sit still for him while he played with her. At least, not until he had assuaged her guilt, as he had the previous evening, by smacking her bare bottom red and hot until his arm was numb with fatigue. It was only then, wriggling and complaining to appease her morbid conscience, that she had permitted him to touch her bud. Today he intended to purge her guilt more thoroughly

and suggested that she fetch the cords from her wardrobe.

When she returned with them he instructed her to lie face-down over the dining-table. He would have preferred her to strip naked, but he judged that was too much to ask so early in the encounter. When, with red blushes and downcast eyes, she spread her sturdy body on the table, her bare feet on the floor and her arms stretched above her head to grasp the far edge Marcel attached her wrists with lengths of cord to the table-legs, so that she was helpless. He knelt behind and pulled her feet wide apart so that he could tie her ankles to the other table-legs, immobilising her completely.

'Now you shall be punished as never before,' he announced in his most menacing tone. 'You will scream for mercy before I've finished with you. But scream as loudly as you like – it will make no difference, that I swear!'

He removed his jacket and tie before flipping Gabrielle's clothes up to expose her bottom. For some moments he stood in admiration of its generosity, of the magnificence of fully developed cheeks, not sagging or baggy, but firm-fleshed and smooth. He fondled those round cheeks heartily, ignoring her yelps of protest and accusations of depravity. There was no trace of reddening left over from yesterday's smacking and the bruise where he pinched her was already fading and yellowish.

He bent down to examine her *kuft* thoroughly while he had her at his mercy. In front, the curls were dark and thick on her belly, he knew, but they were sparse where the lips joined below her fundament. She groaned and her tethered body jerked on the table when she felt him slip a hand between her thighs to pinch her fleshy lips and then open them with probing fingers to find and touch her hidden bud.

'Prepare yourself now, Gabrielle,' he said solemnly. 'Your guilt cannot be expiated by smacking. What is about to happen to you is what you have truly deserved. Whether you scream for mercy or not, it will make no difference.'

She gave a little shriek when he used both hands to open her cheeks and reveal the pink-brown little node hidden between them. He began to finger it lightly and she twisted

her body from side to side in her bonds, and cried out, 'No, no, no!' in a vain attempt to escape his attention.

But Marcel was determined to pay her back in her own coin. When he had been totally at her mercy the evening before, bound to a chair, she had deliberately violated him with her finger; now she would learn what it felt like herself.

With his left hand he grasped her plump and hairy mound and kneaded it, enjoying her wailing protests. He prised the lips open and forced three fingers into her, as far up inside as he could reach, while the middle finger of his right hand probed into her other and smaller entrance. She was gasping, half fainting with shame and humiliation. But against her will she was becoming aroused; her *kuft* was slippery to his plunging fingers and the muscles of her tight little node were loosening to let his finger sink deeper.

Marcel's *zimbriq* jerked with passion inside his underwear and he opened his trousers and moved in close to Gabrielle to present its swollen head to her puckered knot. At this she began to whimper, but he closed his ears to the sound and, with his hands flat on the table-top to support him, he pushed slowly and relentlessly inside. She cried out in horror while this was being done to her, imploring him tearfully not to inflict this degradation on her. But by then, tight as this virgin passage was, he had penetrated it to a depth of about five centimetres and was *zeqqing* her with short, fast strokes.

'No more! You're splitting me open!' she shrieked in an agonised voice, but Marcel pushed in a little further.

His hands were underneath her body, inside her night-dress, massaging her plump breasts, plucking at their engorged tips, gripping the flesh of her belly, stroking inside her groins, prising her *kuft* open to let his fingers flicker over her bud. Soon the nervous contractions of the canal that gripped him so tightly forced on him an overwhelming awareness of the hot shamefulness of what he was doing to her. His *zimbriq* jerked frantically and poured his perverse desire into her.

'Oh, yes, yes . . . punish me!' she moaned.

13

Several Good Tunes Played on Old Fiddles

After Olivier's undignified departure Lisette did not appear in public for two days. Her mother could be seen at breakfast on the hotel terrace and in the dining-room in the evening, tight-lipped and with an angry scowl on her face. She responded only curtly to greetings and expressions of sympathy. By Saturday Marcel thought that the sulking had lasted long enough and presented himself at the door of the Coty suite. Denise let him in and waved him to a chair, sitting down opposite him with her hands clasped in her lap.

In a tone that made clear her abysmally low opinion of men, she told him that Lisette was in bed, prostrate with shock and headache. Undeterred, he talked on, exerting charm discreetly, until the strained expression left her face. She asked him what he thought of Olivier's disappearance and he shook his head and said gravely that he thought there was more to it than met the eye. Fruit-bat fever was a mild disease, he said, that ran its course in a week or so. Perhaps Olivier had involved himself in something he was ashamed to have known.

Not for the first time since reading the confidential report Gabrielle had shown him, he wondered if Denise knew or had any suspicion that Olivier had a wife and family in Toulon. If she did, she gave no hint of it, but confided, in the strictest secrecy, that she suspected that Olivier was involved with a Santa Sabina woman. Marcel asked if she had any thought who it might be and she lowered her voice to tell him she was fairly certain that Olivier had allowed himself to be ensnared by the wife of the Minister of Transport.

'Madame Bonavista?' Marcel exclaimed, stupefied.

If that was true, the situation was farcical beyond belief, after Lisette's confession of being *zeqqed* by Lucreza! But how much confidence could be placed in Denise's assertion?

'From the day he began making his business arrangements with the Minister, he neglected my poor Lisette shamefully,' Denise said, dabbing at her eyes with a tiny handkerchief. 'He was out of the hotel all day, every day, and out again in the evenings after dinner until very late. He had no time for her at all and when she asked him why, and when I asked him, all he would say was his business took time to arrange. Business arrangements indeed! He was with a woman, I am sure of that!'

'There may be something in what you say,' Marcel admitted, knowing full well that Olivier had passed days and nights with a variety of obliging women. 'But I do not see how that could be a reason for his departure.'

'Mark my words,' said Denise, pursing her lips, 'Monsieur Bonavista found out that his wife was unfaithful to him and he cancelled the business deal and planned some sort of reprisal. Olivier was warned in time by his mistress and took the first ship away from this country.'

'A remarkable theory,' said Marcel, hardly able to prevent himself chuckling, 'but is there any evidence?'

'There is. No one saw Olivier go – it must have been in the night and he left in such a hurry that he took nothing with him but his passport and money. Everything else was abandoned. I went though his belongings looking for some clue to his actions and I found more than enough to convince me that he had been having an affair with another woman.'

'Really?' said Marcel, his interest caught. 'What sort of evidence, if it is not too presumptuous of me to ask.'

'I trust you,' said Denise, 'but I will say no more – it is too humiliating for my daughter.'

'Mama,' a voice called faintly from behind a closed door, 'who are you talking to there?'

Denise got up and went to one of the bedroom doors. She opened it a little and looked in. 'It is Monsieur Lamont,'

she said, 'he came to see if he can do anything to assist us in our time of crisis.'

'He is very kind – I must thank him myself.'

Denise waved Marcel through into the bedroom and stood in the open doorway while he went to the bedside and smiled down at her daughter. The shutters were closed to keep out the sun and the room was dim, but he could see that Lisette's face was pale and there were dark rings round her eyes, either from sleeplessness or from weeping. She raised herself a little and smiled bravely back at him while she thanked him for calling to enquire about her. In turn he murmured a few words to try to relieve her disconsolate state of mind.

The telephone rang noisily in the suite's sitting-room and Denise went to answer it. Marcel heard her say, presumably to whichever Costa daughter was at the hotel switch-board that day 'Ask her to wait for a moment – I'll come down.' Then she was at the bedroom door again to say that she would be back in five minutes. She added that she knew Marcel had no wish to waste his day in a sick-room, but there was something she wished to tell him and she would be grateful if he would wait until she got back. She departed, leaving the bedroom door open, and at once Lisette said that her mother was going to tell him that Olivier was having an affair with Lucreza Bonavista.

'And was he?' Marcel asked, smiling as he sat on the bed.

Distraught and without make-up though she then was, Lisette could hardly fail to be a heart-warming sight, lying in her bed with her silvery-blonde hair spread out on the pillow, her big pointed breasts lifting the thin cotton sheet that was her only covering and their peaks showing boldly through it.

'No,' she said, he cheeks crimson. 'It's me Lucreza wants – I told you that after she had me the first time.'

'The *first* time!' said Marcel with an ironic chuckle, 'It seems that you and I have both been having her regularly.'

Lisette's eyes turned away from his in embarrassment and she said that she was terribly hot with the shutters closed and the heat had given her a vile head-ache. To cool herself, perhaps, she threw aside the sheet so that it lay slanting

across her body at waist level. Marcel saw that her short night-dress was of black silk, cut straight across, with shoulder-straps as narrow as strings, and more of her bosom on show than covered.

'I know why Olivier deserted me,' she said in a voice full of anguish, 'he found out about me and Lucreza. It was too much for him to bear – to be betrayed with another woman!'

There were tears in her pale blue eyes she stretched out a hand towards Marcel and clung to his arm. Pulling against him, she half-rose on an elbow and the sheet slid down her body to her knees, revealing that the hem of her night-dress reached only halfway down her slender thighs.

'It is my own fault,' she said feverishly. 'I can't blame him for abandoning me after finding out what I've done – any man would do the same.'

Distracted by her thoughts, she rolled from side to side and then turned on her side to face him, still clutching his arm. Her restlessness disturbed her night-dress and caused it to ride up, and there in front of Marcel was revealed a bare and rounded hip, the skin the colour of honey – and between her uncovered thighs, there at last was the treasure he had never yet seen. She had the prettiest *kuft* he could imagine – a neat little triangle of blonde curls that framed smooth pink lips that pouted excitingly. He was unable to control himself and he clasped it in his palm, sighing 'Oh, Lisette . . .'

So enchanted was he by the soft feel of it that he was not aware that she had released his arm until he felt her slide his zip down to let his formidably hard *zimbriq* emerge and jut out proudly. He gasped when she clasped it firmly, for her hand was dry and hot and trembling nervously. With delicate care he smoothed down the silky blonde curls between her legs and parted the lips of her *kuft* to find her bud and caress it, but her thighs closed on his hand and held it still, while she pumped his *zimbriq* up and down rapidly.

One of the narrow straps was displaced from her shoulder by the vigorous movement of her arm, and a superbly shaped breast was bared to Marcel's eager gaze, its bud a delicious

pink. He sighed and trembled and the moment was not far distant when his belly would convulse and his foam would fountain over her hand. Then with a speed that left him shocked and gasping in dismay, she thrust his vibrating *zimbriq* back into his trousers and flicked up his zipper. There was a step outside and he flushed with horror to realise that Denise had returned to the suite at the worst possible moment.

With a sweep of her slender arm Lisette covered herself with the sheet a heart-beat before the door opened and Denise came into the bedroom. She stared at her daughter, and then with suspicion at Marcel sitting on the bed.

'It is very hot in here,' he said, knowing that his face was flushed. 'I think you should open the shutters and let the air in.' But Denise insisted they must remain closed to ease Lisette's headache. She came closer to scrutinise the spots of bright colour on her daughter's pale cheeks and announced that her temperature was still high and that she must be left in peace to sleep.

Trying to control his breathing, Marcel said *au revoir* and stood up, hoping that his distended *zimbriq* did no show too obviously through his thin trousers. Denise followed him into the sitting-room, closing the bedroom door behind her and stared at him with an expression that meant she had guessed what had been going on between him and Lisette during her brief absence. He tried his charming smile, she advanced towards him wagging a finger ominously.

'You asked me to wait,' said Marcel hastily. 'You said you have something to tell me about Olivier and Madame Bonavista.'

'Never mind that now!' said Denise in a low and angry voice and, although she was as small a woman as her daughter, Marcel retreated step by step before her advance until is back was against the door to the corridor.

'You are a monster!' she said in disgust. 'My daughter lies suffering on her sick-bed and you try to take advantage of her – and I wasn't out of the room for more than a few minutes!'

'But you are mistaken,' he said, hoping to appease her

wrath and escape an unpleasant scene, 'I assure you that nothing at all happened while you were away.'

His untruthful words and the apologetic smile on his face had the reverse of the effect he intended. Denise took a step forward and pinned him to the door, her belly pushing against his. Marcel thought she was about to bring her knee up sharply between his legs to disable his offending parts and he tried to twist sideways away from her, but she surprised him by grasping his *zimbriq* through his trousers.

'What are you doing?' he said foolishly, unable or perhaps unwilling to believe that she would be so forward within ear-shot of her own daughter.

'As I thought!' she exclaimed. 'You are hard as iron! What were you doing to Lisette? I want to know!'

'Nothing,' he insisted, 'nothing at all.'

'Liar!' she said, unzipping him with a deft flick of her wrist and delving into his underwear with both hands.

'Denise – this is ridiculous!' he gasped as his stiff shaft of flesh twitched in her warm hands. 'Let go of me at once.'

Her only response was to handle him vigorously.

'What if Lisette comes in?' he whispered.

'Then she will see what you have between your legs,' Denise retorted, 'and not for the first time!'

She raised a hand to the neck of her ivory-white blouse and ripped open the buttons, revealing a white satin brassiere which she jerked sharply upwards to bare her flabby breasts.

'Feel them!' she commanded.

'No, not here,' he said. 'Come to my room later.'

'You may depend on it,' she said with a mirthless smile.

He thought she would release him then, but her hand still slid up and down the length of his *zimbriq* and with each pass his resolve weakened a little further. He had no idea of how they got there, but his hands were on her slack breasts and he was feeling them, while warm sensations throbbed in his belly.

'I think you should stop now, Denise,' he murmured.

'Don't be silly,' she answered, 'I'm not going to stop until I've had what I want from you.'

'And what is that?' he asked, surrendering languidly.

He leaned back against the door, with his eyes half-closed in pleasure, while he played with her breasts. They were not as large as Lisette's, but perhaps in her youth they had been just as excitingly pointed, he thought. He sighed again when, without ceasing for a moment her firm manipulate of him, Denise pulled up her skirt and fumbled under it to get her knickers halfway down her thighs. 'Feel me,' she whispered fiercely, and this time there was no reluctance on his part to comply. Without the least pretence at gentleness, he forced three joined fingers between the brown-haired lips of her *kuft* and found her wet bud. But before he could attend to it as he believed she craved, she was dragging at his *zimbriq* to guide it up between her legs. By this time neither he nor she cared whether Lisette got up and came into the room.

Marcel let himself slump heavily against the door, his feet wide apart and his knees bent outwards, in order to reduce his height and make it possible for Denise to spike herself on him. She could not separate her legs widely because of the confining knickers round her thighs and so Marcel held her wide open with his fingers while she inserted his distended *zimbriq*. Without a pause she rammed her belly and loins against him, forcing him straight up into her. 'Now I've got you', she hissed at him.

For the millionth time Marcel marvelled at the effect that the climate of this country had, especially on Europeans. This elegant, decent and well-to-do woman had fallen into a frenzy of lust so consuming that she was raping a man near where her daughter lay, taking the risk that she would be discovered in the act. Totally unconcerned, Denise swung herself forwards and backwards, *zeqqing* him as if she were a Santa Sabina woman enjoying a quick belly-to-belly up an alley. Marcel sighed to feel each forceful swing of her hips send her wet *kuft* slithering along his leaping *zimbriq*.

Denise was panting and moaning softly to the very energetic rhythm of her *zeqqing*, her hands deep inside Marcel's trousers and her fingernails clawing at the cheeks of his bottom. Her eyes were wide open and she was staring at his face to observe his strengthening emotion with the

fixity of obsession. 'I've got you now,' she repeated, 'and I won't let you get away from me before I've had everything you've got to give!'

This was the woman, Marcel told himself in feverish delight, who had lain on her back with her arms folded nonchalantly under her head the first time he had *zeqqed* her, experiencing a climax hardly more interesting than a mild sneeze. Now *she* was *zeqqing* him at a furious pace! Her nails bit hard into the flesh of his bottom and a long spasm shook her, as if she were a rabbit worried in the jaws of a hound. Marcel was instantly overwhelmed by her violent climax and flooded her with the thick jets of his release.

Her hot *kuft* was like a greedy mouth sucking out his essence and even after he had no more to give she continued to ram her belly against him. He became aware that the brute force of her thrusting was making the door behind him creak to her desperate rhythm and he became anxious in case the noise reached Lisette and brought her from her bed to investigate. But all was well and they remained undisturbed, while Denise's strong spasms of ecstasy slackened to tremors of waning delight and then to an occasional shudder of pleasure.

Finally she became tranquil, resting her weight against him, held up on her feet by his stiffness inside her and his arms about her waist. Her head was against his chest and he could not see her face, but he heard her long sighs of satisfaction. When at last his *zimbriq* softened and slithered out of her, he too sighed contentedly, to indicate that the pleasant episode had reached its natural conclusion and he was grateful to her. But to his consternation Denise fell to her knees and sucked his *zimbriq* into her mouth as if she were swallowing a strand of well-done spaghetti.

He stared in astonishment down at the back of her head. The aphrodisiac air of Santa Sabina had dissolved all restraint; her frustrations, resentments and her anger at Olivier's flight had been transformed into sexual desire. The after-glow of his own climax had not entirely faded yet and what Denise was doing to him soon aroused him again. A dozen passes of her tongue and he could feel himself

stiffening in her mouth. She put her head back to stare up in triumph at his face, her mouth gaping wide open to let him see the tip of her pink tongue licking under the uncovered purple head of his *zimbriq*.

'I haven't drained you yet,' she said softly, 'not by a long way! We'll go to your room and I'll have all I want from you.'

But this is absurd, Marcel thought, this is the second time I have been forced into *zeqqing* Denise instead of her daughter. Aloud he murmured that nothing would give him greater pleasure than to escort Denise to his room and make love to her until she sank into a deep and satisfied sleep, but alas, duty required him to be at the Embassy in a quarter of an hour and the pleasure must be deferred until later. Denise looked up at him with a disbelieving expression on her face and gripped him tighter between fingers and thumb to prevent him escaping from her, and her tongue flickered faster.

'Not again . . . not so soon,' Marcel sighed.

'Yes, again,' she answered, ceasing her stimulation to speak to him. But only for a moment, before she drew at least half of his *zimbriq* into her mouth, her hot and ragged breathing surging along its shaft, while her wet tongue lapped at it insistently. There was no point at all in resisting her, and so Marcel slid his back into a slightly more comfortable position against the door and abandoned himself to the thrills rippling through him. He stared down his body to where his wet shaft stood sharply upwards from the tuft of dark hair revealed by his open trousers, Denise's light-brunette head bobbing up and down its length.

Into his mind came the memory of mop-haired Concepcion Costa down on her knees performing the same pleasant office for him. If he gave himself the pleasure of comparing techniques, the Santa Sabina girl was the more expert, but Denise at this moment was driven by a determination to impose her will on him that he had to admit was extraordinarily exciting. And even if her skill in what she was doing was less than Concepcion's, it was effective enough to bring on the result she desired. Marcel's legs

shook under him and his belly clenched tight as she sucked his essence from him in quick throbs.

When he made his escape from Denise at last on the pretext that he was required at the Embassy, he thought it sensible to go there, even though it was Saturday afternoon and there was even less to do than usual. He would have liked to have taken a shower before leaving the hotel, but Denise was looking at him with such hunger in her eyes that he dare not go to his room in case she followed him there and got under the shower with him. At the Embassy door the security guard told him that only the duty officer and one secretary were in the building.

Even so, his arrival had been observed, he discovered when he reached his desk and the telephone rang. To his surprise it was Jacqueline Ducour, the Ambassador's wife, who had seen him from her balcony. She said there was a most important matter to be discussed and asked him to come to her sitting-room. The extensive Ambassadorial apartment took up the entire top floor of the building and was approached by a private staircase which led to a landing adorned by a large porcelain bowl of flowers on a small table. A smiling Santa Sabinan maid opened the door and conducted Marcel to Jacqueline's sitting-room.

It was not the apartment's main *salon*, which was furnished in the grand manner to impress the Ambassador's private guests, but a small and comfortable room which Jacqueline had made her own. The long windows to the balconies stood open, but not even the faintest of breezes stirred across King Alfonso Square. And if Marcel had been pleasantly surprised to be invited up to the Ambassadorial apartment, he was intrigued when he entered the sitting-room and saw how Madame Ducour was dressed.

It was well known that her elegant clothes were designed and made in Paris by a high-fashion *couturier* and, in the two years Marcel had known her, he had never seen her dressed less than exquisitely. Yet on this drowsy Saturday afternoon, alone at home, she was very casual indeed in a pink silk shirt and white linen shorts. She sat in a relaxed attitude on a sofa of green and gold brocade, her legs

stretched out and her sandalled feet up on a matching stool. She extended a hand to Marcel to kiss and he bent over it with a flattering murmured greeting.

He had to admit that for a woman of fifty Jacqueline had remarkably good legs, long, slender and well-shaped, displayed to advantage by her shorts. Unlike those who subject themselves to the sun's rays until they become indistinguishable from the darker Santa Sabinans, Jacqueline controlled her skin tone with great care, to maintain a light golden shade.

'You are alone?' Marcel asked, releasing her hand slowly.

'My husband is out sailing with his Danish friends,' she said. 'Perhaps you have seen Monsieur Jensen's yacht along the coast? I went on it once, but the effect of salt sea-wind on the hair is dreadful and the motion made me queasy. How anyone can imagine it is a pleasure to sail on small boats is beyond me. But enough of that – I asked you up here to discuss a very serious matter with you.'

She gestured towards an armchair facing her, but Marcel chose to ignore it and sat down on the sofa with her, though with a discreet metre of space between them. Jacqueline turned her head to stare at him in disapproval, 'I want the truth from you now,' she said. 'Why has Olivier de Murville run away in this ridiculous secrecy? Please don't try to deceive me – I know it's because of you.'

'Me? But what do you mean?' Marcel asked anxiously.

His heart had missed a beat at her question and his mind was whirling with unpleasant speculation that Olivier might have telephoned the Embassy to confess all before the ship sailed. But if he had, he would have talked to Jean-Jacques Ducour, not his wife – not unless they had been lovers and he had a need to burden someone with his criminal confidences! But that could not be possible; Olivier was bulky and muscular and aggressive – the very reverse of the type of slender and easygoing young man that Jacqueline enjoyed having. Marcel tried to picture in his mind Olivier's hairy body between Jacqueline's slim legs, thumping away at her, and he knew the scene to be unreal.

'How could I do anything to drive Olivier away?' he

asked, sure that Jacqueline knew nothing. Her next words proved that she was guessing.

'I know you too well,' she said, 'you have persuaded little Lisette to sleep with you – there is no point in denying it.'

'Is that what you think?' he asked, his smile charming.

'I'm sure of it. You have no honour and no respect at all for others. You see a pretty girl and your only thought is to get her into bed, without a care for the emotional upheaval and the atrocious suffering you inflict. Olivier found out that he had been betrayed by his fiancée and was heartbroken and in despair. All he could do in his agony of mind was run away from the scene of this wicked treachery.'

Jacqueline's apparent belief in Olivier's sensitivity amused Marcel greatly. It was Olivier, after all, who had *zeqqed* himself to a total standstill with the obliging women of Santa Sabina, and it was Lisette who had refused Marcel's advances, though she had not been as fastidiously virtuous as perhaps her fiancé would prefer. For a moment or two of deep delight he had touched her blonde-haired *kuft*, but as for achieving his ambition of making love to her, the nearest he had got was to *zeqq* her mother! Even that was an exaggeration; it was he who had been *zeqqed* by Denise, only an hour ago. 'Lisette has told you herself that she and I are lovers?' he asked, raising his eyebrows.

'She has no need to,' Jacqueline retorted. 'I see it in her eyes when she looks at you. She is a young girl and too easily led, perhaps, but there is no excuse for you. Your uncontrolled lust has destroyed an important and distinguished man.'

'What nonsense!' said Marcel. 'Olivier's importance lies in making himself rich at the expense of corrupt governments. I doubt if anything could damage his self-esteem.'

'I notice that you do not deny that you seduced Lisette!' Jacqueline observed coldly.

'I regret to inform you I have not had that pleasure,' said Marcel smiling, 'though I am sure it would be most enjoyable. But not every beautiful woman finds me irresistible, alas.'

'How can you tell such obvious lies?' Jacqueline exclaimed in high indignation. 'You've made love to her this afternoon.'

'You are mistaken,' he answered, grinning wryly at the irony of her words, 'more's the pity!'

'You must think I'm a fool!' said Jacqueline. 'The evidence is still upon you. You reek of her perfume – I could smell it the moment you came into the room. And if it came to a close examination, other traces of her would be detected on you.'

This was Jacqueline Ducour in a frame of mind Marcel did not normally associate with her sophisticated and predatory nature – this was Jacqueline experiencing jealousy! *But why*? he asked himself. Their love affair had been brief and was long past. It had been initiated by her and discontinued by her when he began to assert himself by taking her vigorously, rather than let her go on using him for her own languorous pleasures. But even so, she had continued to behave as if she owned him.

Could it, Marcel asked himself, unsure whether he should feel flattered or not, that the presence of Lisette, young, beautiful and desirable, had set off spasms of panic in Jacqueline's heart? A certain inadmissible fear that she was becoming almost too old to be able to have her way with many more handsome young men? That she was suffering the pangs of sexual jealousy at this moment was beyond doubt – her angry mention of other traces was a reference to his *zimbriq* and the moistness of Lisette's arousal clinging to it – except that it was Denise's arousal, as it was Denise's perfume.

Jacqueline was angry, no question of that. She was glaring at Marcel and her small breasts were rising and falling under her pink shirt in time with her irregular breathing. Her face was red and her dark brown eyes blazed. In a moment of insight, Marcel said nothing to her accusations, but put out his hand and looked at her eyes and she looked at his eyes, and then she slid across the sofa towards him and put an arm round his neck. 'Oh Jacqueline, there is nothing to be angry about,' he sighed, his cheek against her hot cheek.

She sobbed once, a dry and racking sound that suggested a vulnerability Marcel had never dreamed was within the range of her experience. She turned towards him as they sat and he hugged her so hard that she could only just breathe and certainly could not sob again. It felt to him as if he was hugging her with the whole of his body, a comforting and secure feeling. 'Oh my Marcel, what am I to do with you,' she sighed and her hand was in his lap. He did nothing to discourage her and in a moment she had his trousers open and a hand inside to hold his soft *zimbriq*. 'I knew it!' she said mournfully. 'Soft and small – worn out and useless from debauching pretty little Lisette! If only you had been content to go on loving me . . .'

It was in Marcel's mind to deny yet again that he had made love to Lisette, that afternoon or any other time, but before he could do so Jacqueline kissed him with a hard desperation that silenced him. And while she kissed him, her fingers were massaging his limpness very skilfully, so that it began to grow longer and stiffer in her hand. Little thrills rippled through his belly and Marcel knew from old experience how this 'discussion' she had wanted was going to end. He put is hand between her thighs, where the skin was like satin, and felt up inside the leg of her shorts, wondering if she was wearing knickers under them.

His unasked question was answered satisfactorily when his fingers encountered crisp curls and soft warm flesh. He touched her *kuft* very gently, using only the tip of his middle finger, and making no attempt to part the long lips or feel inside yet. Throughout the long kiss her eyes remained open, large and brown and so close to his, their expression sensuous and at the same time melancholy. The fragrance of her costly perfume made his head spin with excitement and all the time her sensitive and wheedling fingers traced enchanting little patterns along his throbbing *zimbriq*, making him shiver with sensation.

How very well he knew this routine of Jacqueline's from the days when they were lovers – and how he admired her adroitness, the graceful skill with which she could take a man on fire to push her on her back and *zeqq* her hard and

in moments reduce him to a passive plaything. Marcel was sighing continuously now, and she watched his face closely, a little smile on her lips. When she could see that he was totally bewitched, she was ready to exercise her powers further.

'Open my shirt, Marcel,' she murmured.

His hands were trembling as he fumbled at the buttons until he had it open to reveal her bare little breasts, slack but still desirable. Deliriously excited though he was, he had not forgotten that Jacqueline was too careful of her figure to ever go without a brassiere, and the conclusion forced itself on him that she had removed it, and her knickers, after she asked him up to her apartment. And that meant she had decided to have him before he even got there. Not that it mattered in the least that she was using him – what more delightful way of passing an idle afternoon?

'*Cheri, cheri*,' she whispered while he kissed the small and pink buds of her soft breasts, 'tell me that you love me or my heart will break.'

'Jacqueline, *ma cherie, je t'adore*,' he sighed, meaning it with complete sincerity at that moment.

She pressed her mouth delicately to his in a grateful kiss and made him lie on his back along the green and gold brocade of the sofa. She unbuckled his belt and slid his trousers and underwear down his legs to his knees, and ran her crimson-painted finger-nails along his swollen and shaking *zimbriq*.

'You are so beautiful,' she murmured, 'why are you so beautiful? You will break my heart! Tell me that you love me.' All this was a part of the intensely controlled game she played, Marcel knew well enough, but her skilfullness won his heart and he was content to surrender to being devoured.

'*Ma chere Jacqueline*,' he whispered lovingly, '*I adore you to distraction*!'

An exquisite contrast was floating in his mind between the dazzling refinement of Jacqueline's rapacity and the thrilling crudeness with which Denise had demanded and then looted what she wanted from him! The images excited him so highly that Jacqueline read the signs of impending

crisis in his staring eyes and twitching limbs and her thin and cajoling fingers released him. She knelt on the sofa beside him and put his hands on her hips, to let him grapple with the intricacies of the buttons that held up her white shorts. In a moment he had them down her thighs and was kissing her bare warm belly.

She wriggled out of her shorts and lay on her back beside him, her hand clasping his leaping *zimbriq* to prevent any initiative by him until the moment arrived that was the goal and culmination of her elaborate game. She pressed her mouth to his cheek and murmured that he might touch her. He contorted himself on the sofa to slide his trembling hands along her slim legs and touch the brown-haired delight between them, and then kiss the thin pink lips beneath the curls. She lay quivering slightly, her legs well parted, waiting for the exact moment. Marcel's wet tongue pressed between the lips of her *kuft* and she drew in a long gasping breath.

'Come to me, Marcel,' she said softly, raising her knees and parting them widely in invitation to him to lie on her belly, 'I am yours to do as you please with.' She held his leaping *zimbriq* and guided it to her *kuft* until he felt its hot and swollen head enveloped by soft lips. 'Slowly, slowly,' she sighed. 'Love me slowly and gently, as you used to . . .'

This was the most important part of her game and even though he was trembling on the brink of a climax, Marcel knew it well. Her words were part of the game too; Jacqueline was not his to do what he pleased with – she had played with him and excited him to the point where he was hers to do as she pleased with. The mere act of sliding into her would be enough to bring on an instant and tremendous climax, which was how she enjoyed love.

A lifetime of preying on handsome young men had taught her how to judge the moment to perfection. His entire body shaking with passion, Marcel pushed slowly up into the warm wetness of her *kuft* and the sensations were so prodigious that his crisis came at once and he spouted his frantic desire into her.

'Love me, love me!' she sighed.

Her long slender legs opened wider, her feet waving in the air, and she moaned softly in ecstasy as his hard and gushing *zimbriq* slithered right in to reach her depths. Marcel writhed on her belly and poured his youthful strength and virility into her with fast involuntary jerks, while she lay naked and shuddering beneath him, giving little mewling cries of triumph. 'Yes, you love me, Marcel,' she exclaimed, 'I can feel it!'

It was over very quickly for both of them and Marcel kissed her mouth gently and eased himself off her belly. From his past experience with her, he expected her to sit up and put on her shorts and button her blouse, as a prelude to dismissing him now that she had enjoyed what she wanted. But he was wrong this time; she turned on her side to face him, put her arms round his neck and kissed him warmly.

'It is always marvellous when you and I make love,' she said softly, 'you are so strong and you thrill me beyond words – I dissolve in your arms. The joy you give me is so overwhelming that I feel I am dying and entering paradise.'

She had never before spoken to Marcel about her satisfaction in love-making and he was fascinated to hear her version of her manipulation of her lovers. These sensations that she praised so extravagantly were in her head, not in her body, for he had been lodged in her *kuft* for a very short time – perhaps only a minute altogether, from penetration to the end of her spasms. Jacqueline's pleasure came from psychological triumph, not from physical gratification. But what of that?

'I am very glad that we have found each other again,' she said, taking much for granted that Marcel could not concede. 'A little fling with a pretty young girl is all very well in its way, but you are an intelligent man and by now you have found that Lisette has nothing except a pair of breasts too big for her height. Fortunately for you, she and her mother are leaving and so you do not have the embarrassment of ending an affair that has become boring.'

'They are going?' said Marcel, hiding his disappointment.

'But naturally! Now that Olivier has abandoned them and his business venture, there is nothing for them to stay here for. They leave for Djibouti on Monday, to get a ship to Marseilles. I persuaded Denise to stay and see the first day of the Festival tomorrow, since she will never have another chance.'

'Their visit to Santa Sabina has not been an entirely happy one,' said Marcel.

'I hold you to blame for that,' Jacqueline said, with a shrug of her bare shoulders. 'But what can one say – these things happen in life – and their visit has brought us together again. I forgive you your irresponsible seduction of Lisette and the collapse of her engagement to a distinguished man.'

Marcel saw that her belief was as unshakeable as the rumour that he worked for the French Secret Service – there was no point in denying it if no one would believe him. He sighed and let it go and then sighed again, though not in resignation this time, but because Jacqueline's cunning fingers were tracing patterns on his belly. This was out of character; always in the past she lost interest after one climax and his insistence on making love to her several times had caused her to discontinue the affair. At least, that was one of the reasons.

But she was tempting him to do it again, and that meant she was very anxious to keep him with her. Evidently his imaginary liaison with Lisette had affected her deeply – perhaps it had compelled her to confront the melancholy fact that she was approaching an age when she would no longer be able to attract and seduce young men, no matter how clever her techniques. She needed to be comforted, and Marcel knew exactly how to do that. He put his hand between her thighs and murmured, '*Je t'adore, Jacqueline*,' while with a finger-tip he gently stroked the warm and wet lips of her *kuft*.

14

Appetite Grows by Feeding, Said Rabelais

The celebrations to mark the Festival of Saint Sabina were said to begin at noon, with the firing of an official salute. Hardly more than ten minutes after the hour, the two ancient cannon at the entrance to the harbour were fired, one after the other, putting the lives of the gunners seriously at risk if the rusty barrels burst under the pressure of over-enthusiastic charges of gunpowder. But disaster was spared for another year and a double boom roared out over the city, to signal that the proceedings were now starting. In effect, most people had begun their celebrations hours before, as could be seen from the laughter and good natured drunkenness of the crowds rambling through the squares and streets.

The Festival procession assembled in Cathedral Square, where the statue of the Saint, dressed in a new blue robe and with her halo newly gilded, had been brought out on the church steps. A wooden throne stood there for the Cardinal-Archbishop and at an appropriate moment, two servitors hoisted the frail old fellow to his feet and held him up while he blessed the procession. A dozen priests in scarlet flicked holy water over the crowd and as many altar-boys swung brass thuribles on chains and sent incense smoke billowing out over the assembly.

Eventually, when the rites of the Church were complete, the procession moved off along the Avenue of the Constitution. Both sides of the wide Avenue were packed with people, cheering and waving their arms in the air, under the colourful bunting that had been strung between the palm trees along the pavement edge. Opposite the Convent of the

Sacred Blood, road viewing platform had been built for President da Cunha and his important guests, among whom were to be found His Excellency the French Ambassador and Madame Ducour.

At pavement level on either side of the raised platform was an enclosure with wooden rails to separate guests of lesser importance from the mob. Entrance to it was by ticket only and every kind of influence and outright bribery came into play to gain access. It was to this privileged place that Marcel, on the instructions of Jacqueline Ducour, escorted Lisette and her mother. From where they stood at the front railing Marcel was able to see, further along the Avenue, Madame da Silva and her girls, in their best frocks, on the balconies of her house.

The sky was completely overcast that day and the heat was oppressive in the extreme. It seemed hours before they heard at last the sound of approaching music, as the procession turned out of Cathedral Square into the Avenue. At the head of the procession was the man elected Grand Marshal of the Festival that year, riding a white horse. By tradition he wore 16th century Portuguese costume, an embroidered doublet, with velvet knee-breeches and black riding boots that came halfway up his thighs. His hat was a flat velvet creation with a very long feather and he brandished it in salutation to the crowd.

Behind the Grand-Marshal came the City Fire Bridge,band uniformed in tawdry splendour. Their bulging cheeks seemed almost to be bursting with the effort of the huge noise they produced from their polished trumpets and trombones and euphoniums. It was impossible to recognise the tune they were playing; it could have been *Alouette, The Skaters' Waltz*, or the National Anthem of Santa Sabina, but it had the merit of being cheerful. In the last row of bandsmen staggered a man with such an enormous drum strapped to his chest that he leaned over backwards to balance it while he thumped out a rhythm

Immediately after the band the first of the troupes of dancers came shimmying along the Avenue, wearing tall feathered head-dresses, almost like showgirls at the *Folies*

Bergeres, and little else – only a small loin-cloth of gold lamé for men and women alike. The Europeans in the crowd sighed, their eyes shining at the sight of a dozen pairs of *cafe-au-lait* breasts bouncing up and down to the music.

It amused Marcel that the so-called buses were used every year for the procession. They were transformed into floats by the removal of their tarpaulin tops and slatted sides, and it was a great pity, he thought, that Olivier could not be here to see them. Lisette had brought her camera and with gentle malice Marcel suggested she should take photographs of the floats to show her fiancé when next she saw him. It would have been most unkind to say *if she saw him again* but the possibility was in his mind that Olivier might think it prudent to remain out of sight for a long time.

The leading float was not a bus but an ancient wagon used only this one time in the year; a wooden-wheeled affair drawn by six mules that had little bells on their harness and nodding scarlet plumes on their heads. Naturally, it carried the traditional tableau of the triumph of Saint Sabina, and to represent the country's patron saint was the greatest possible honour that could be bestowed on a girl. So much so that every girl of the right age would cheerfully throttle her rivals.

'Oh. la la!, Denise exclaimed. 'That's a saint?'

Up on the float a delicious sixteen year old flaunted her pretty body naked before a group of four men in long robes, who represented the philosophers sent to convert her. Her mop of black hair was adorned with white gardenia and the thick fleece between her slender copper-hued thighs was sprinkled with gold dust that glittered. The crowd cheered themselves almost hoarse as she passed and threw flowers at her. She was savouring her day of triumph to the full, not standing like a statue but exhibiting her charms in a slow and circular little dance, and waving and smiling and blowing little kisses to the enthusiastic crowd.

'Sabina died a virgin martyr for her faith,' said Marcel in mild reproof of Denise's outburst.

'That is no reason for a schoolgirl to be paraded naked in public,' Denise replied. 'It is an offence against religion!'

'By no means,' said Marcel, amused by this show of modesty from a woman who had conducted herself most immodestly with him in private. 'Your attitude is excessively European. This float received the benediction of the Cardinal-Archbishop himself before the procession left the Square.'

'Disgraceful!' said Denise. 'He should be reported to the Holy Father for dereliction of duty.'

'Mama, you are being very old-fashioned,' said Lisette, and she smiled for the first time that day.

'As you may observe,' Marcel said dryly, 'across the road from us the nuns are standing outside the Convent to watch the procession pass. They have a dispensation for the Festival.'

'They should be made to whip themselves in penitence,' said Denise, her cheeks pink, putting into Marcel's mind the memory of Gabrielle's plump bottom bared in submission and he laughed.

Behind the Saint came more dancers and more floats, and then a second group of musicians, the band of the First Regiment of Santa Sabina Infantry. That the entire army consisted of only one regiment did not diminish the proud title or the loudness of the playing. Long before the parade was over Denise began to complain that she felt dizzy from the heat and was fainting with thirst. There was nothing that could be done in so large a crowd, Marcel pointed out, and slipped his arm under hers to support her a little.

It was not long before he could feel her hand down between their sides, her fingertips gently stroking along his thigh. They were completely hemmed in by people whose attention was on the procession, but even if anyone near them had looked down, it was improbable that they could have seen what she was doing. And for the same reason, Marcel thought gratefully, it was not possible for dear Denise to do more than touch him through his trousers. And if he stared straight ahead and pretended that it was Lisette's hand sliding along his thigh, the sensations were pleasant enough.

It occurred to him that two could play at that game. He

dropped his arm from under Denise's and slid a hand round her haunches to feel her bottom through her thin yellow frock. *Why not give her a little thrill*, he was thinking, *it can lead to nothing here, and so I can be generous and please her*. Denise's hand gripped his thigh hard, showing that his generosity was appreciated. That sent his thoughts further along the same road – and with his other hand he began to feel Lisette's bottom. Out of the corner of his eye he thought he detected a faint pink blush on her cheek, but she continued to stare at the passing parade and did nothing to dislodge his hand.

Perhaps it was the heat, perhaps the anonymity of the many strangers pushing and crowding round them, or perhaps it was the sight of so many bare-breasted girls dancing past, but soon Denise and Lisette were pressing themselves against Marcel, one on either side, and his fingers were deep in the clefts between the cheeks of two soft bottoms. The cheering and shouting of the crowd was as loud as ever, but Marcel thought he could just catch the whisper of faint sighs to his left and his right. Lisette's hands were fully occupied with her camera, but Denise had a firm grasp of his upright *zimbriq* through the trousers of his white linen suit.

On and on went the Festival procession, more brass bands huffing and puffing in the heat, float after float of waving and singing revellers, brandishing bunches of coloured balloons and bamboo sticks with tufts of feathers tied to the end, girls and young men naked except for a fragment of gilded or embroidered cloth at the fork of their thighs – and on more than one float even that had been dispensed with in favour of small sprays of flowers – white camellias and mauve wild orchids and pink bougainvillaea blossom – held fairly casually by a string about their hips. It would be a miracle if all those blossoms were still in place by the time the parade reached its dispersal point, Marcel thought with a smile.

Meanwhile, Denise was quietly disproving the validity of his generous thought that he could afford to give her a little thrill because nothing could possibly come of it in this public

place. He now discovered that his caressing fingers in the soft cleft of her bottom had aroused her beyond reasonable discretion. While the cheering crowd pressed tightly about them from all sides, she reached down to raise the hem of her white frock and guide Marcel's hand under it. His fingers touched her knickers and the warm flesh of plump cheeks through silk.

From the corner of his eye he cast a guarded glance and saw that Lisette was fully occupied with taking photographs. There was the prettiest pink flush on her cheeks, which he attributed to his surreptitious stroking of her bottom, but that would not go further, he decided with regret. But her mother – that was a very different story! Denise was wriggling her bottom against his hand, silently urging him to do more. He felt upwards under her frock until he found the elastic top of her knickers and plunged his hand down inside. She moved her feet apart to let him feel her soft-haired *kuft* from the rear.

It was not the most convenient of manoeuvres, but there was no doubt that Denise was enjoying his stealthy manipulations. In time her excitement made her become so slippy that he could push the tip of his longest finger inside her and touch her sensitive little button. She pressed her side against his, half leaning on him, as Lisette was on the other side, and into her eyes came the faraway expression Marcel knew so well. But she was not selfish about her pleasure; her hand was sliding up and down slowly, caressing the whole length of his upright *zimbriq* through the thin linen of his trousers.

A quarter of an hour passed, a time of secret caresses and of exquisite sensation, concealed by the jubilation of the crowd that surrounded them. And why not, Marcel thought dreamily, the most interesting thing in the entire world is a wet kuft. He saw that Denise's face was scarlet and she was breathing heavily through her open mouth, and at that he began to wonder whether, in these improbable circumstances, it was possible to make her go all the way. He rubbed her wet bud a little faster and only a minute later he had his answer – Denise's eyes bulged and her body shook in climactic throes.

Her legs were buckling under her and only by clinging to him fiercely did she remain upright. Marcel was immensely excited by his success in bringing her to a secret crisis in public and thrust his fingers as far into her hot wetness as the awkward position permitted. In his triumph he paid no attention to the fact that, even in her spasms of ecstasy, Denise still rubbed her palm over the stiff bulge in his trousers. A stab of purest delight through his belly made him gasp and he was shocked to realise that his *zimbriq* was leaping to the first spurt racing up its length.

He grabbed for Denise's hand, but it was already too late to stop what was happening to him. He clutched the bottoms of the women on either side of him to steady himself, his hot essence squirting up his belly inside his clothes, his teeth clenched to stop himself gasping. Lisette realised that something odd was going on, lowered her camera and stared at him and her mother clinging to each other in their shaking release. 'It is the heat,' Marcel managed to say, 'it is making your mother feel faint . . . we must get her to a café where she can sit down and recover.'

The Grand Parade wound its way through the city from noon till early evening and the next event of the Festival was the Masked Ball, though this was for the élite only, not for the people in general. It was held in the Theatre des Beaux Arts, a large baroque edifice intended as a Jesuit seminary centuries ago before folie de grandeur had overtaken the holy fathers and their chapel turned out to be as large and high-ceilinged as the Sistine Chapel in Rome. Suppressed by an alarmed and envious Archbishop, the Jesuits had deserted Santa Sabina for Macao, and their building was commandeered for secular uses, such as dramatic performances, musical recitals furniture auctions and cock-fighting tournaments.

It went without saying that Ambassador Jean-Jacques Ducour and his wife took one of the best boxes at the Masked Ball, it being considered one of the most important occasions in the social calendar of the capital. This year their guests included Denise Coty and her daughter, and so Marcel was invited to join the Ambassador's party to partner

Lisette. Before being driven to the Ball, the party of twelve met at the Embassy to dine in splendour and, seated beside Lisette, Marcel remembered how interesting he had found her when they had met at this same table, especially her sumptuous and pointed breasts.

Strange events had taken place in the three weeks since that first meeting. He had become an accomplice in the bribing of a Minister of State, he had been threatened by a CIA spy, he had fallen in love with one of the Hundred Families' most beautiful women, he had tried his hand at forgery, and he had *zeqqed* a mad American woman in a swimming pool. At least, these events would have been considered extraordinary in Europe, but here in Santa Sabina the standards of what was unusual and what was not were incomprehensible to an outsider.

With regret he was compelled to admit that he had failed in those three weeks to achieve what he had truly wanted – to make love to Lisette. Not for lack of trying, of course; he had more than once succeeded in seeing her marvellous breasts bare, and he had even been permitted to handle them. For a few enchanted moments he had been privileged to touch her blonde-haired *kuft* – an unforgettable delight! But that was the total of his achievements and tomorrow she and her mother were leaving Santa Sabina for ever. This one night was all that was left to him to accomplish his purpose, and the odds were against him.

For one thing, her mother had made it clear that she was eager to resume what they had started together at the Festival parade. In the cab that took them from the Grand Hotel Orient to the Embassy she stroked his thigh in the dark – with her own daughter sitting on the other side of him – and whispered hot invitations in his ear. And besides her, there was Jacqueline keeping a close watch on him all evening and looking for an opportunity to get him alone for her own cat-and-mouse style of love-making. There seemed little chance that he would insinuate himself between Lisette's legs before she departed.

It was well after ten o'clock when they reached the theatre and the festivities were in full progress. The tall pillars of

the ballroom were festooned with coloured lights and flowers, and the floor was crowded with couples circulating slowly in each other's arms to the music of a large dance band. But who was in whose arms, that was the fascinating question! With the usual local talent for getting things wrong, some dancers were costumed as historical personages, some wore brightly coloured domino robes, some wore ordinary evening clothes. But without exception, everyone was masked.

Simple masks of black velvet with eye-holes were considered unfashionable in good society here. The style was for birds and animals, half-masks shaped from papier mâché and painted in gaudy colours. The room was a zoological garden of lions, owls, hawks, goats, tigers, a menagerie of whiskers and beaks. While Lisette had chosen a demure tabby domestic cat for herself, her mother was more boldly masked as black panther, and Jacqueline appeared as a striped tiger. As a joke, Marcel was masquerading as a fruit-bat in a greyish-brown creation with sharp-standing ears and eyes painted red, but no one else found it amusing.

The champagne flowed generously in the Ambassador's box and Marcel did his duty by dancing first with Jacqueline and then with Denise. Each lady suggested that it would be pleasant if he escorted her outside for a breath of air, but he replied as charmingly as he knew how that it was early in the evening and that what she was proposing could perhaps be postponed for another hour. His private intentions was to lead Lisette on to the dancefloor, straight across it and out of the Theatre to the nearest conveniently dark corner where he might pursue his thwarted ambition.

While he was taking Denise back to the box she persisted in her demand for a 'quick breath of fresh air,' as she called it, and Marcel was relived when a small woman swathed in a red cloak darted out of nowhere and laid a hand on his arm.

'Marcel,' she exclaimed in English, 'dance with me!' She was masked as a green and blue parrot, but from her accent he knew it could be none other than Darlene Prout. With a quick word of excuse he left Denise to find her own way

back, took Darlene in his arms and whirled her into the throng of dancers.

It was a case of jumping out of the omelette-pan into the fire, of course. While they danced and Darlene was explaining how she had recognised him even in his bat-mask, she rubbed her belly against him, making his *zimbriq* stand up furiously. No more than five minutes after their meeting, they were out of the Theatre and squeezed close together, masks pushed up, in a dark niche between the plinth of a statue of King Henry the Navigator and the wall of the building.

'I must have you,' Darlene exclaimed, and drew his face down to hers to thrust her tongue into his mouth.

She smelt strongly of gin and Marcel realised as he unwound her red cloak that she was well on the way to being drunk. Under the cloak she was wearing a short frock of the same colour, cut low enough for him to be able to put a hand down the front and feel her spiky little breasts. 'Put your hand up my skirt,' she murmured, her breath hot on his face, and is fingers wandered above her knees and her stocking-tops, to stroke the smooth bare skin of her thighs.

A little higher and he expected to encounter her underwear, but instead he touched soft flesh and the wispy little fleece he remembered from their adventure by the American swimming pool. The split of her *kuft* was open and very wet, and she gave a sigh when his fingers slid in, almost by themselves.

'You have learned Santa Sabina ways very quickly,' he said.

'I started the evening wearing panties,' she told him with a giggle, 'but after I'd been laid a couple of times it seemed a waste of time to keep putting them on. This Festival is the greatest – I've been screwed five times since the Ball began – and I mean to be screwed another five times before it's over!'

She stood with her thin legs wide apart to be felt, her back against the stone plinth, enjoying it so much that in a very short time she moaned and twitched in a sudden climax.

'Ah, what an impatient woman you are to do it so quickly!'

Marcel exclaimed. 'But I know how to deal with you!'

'Let's see what you've got for me, you rape-fiend,' she sighed, dragging down his zipper to get at his hard *zimbriq*.

She played with him strenuously while they stood belly to belly, until he was thrusting at her to get into her *kuft*. But Darlene was enjoying herself to much to let him in just yet. She squatted on her haunches and sucked him into her mouth. His legs shook as overpowering sensations rolled through him and he leaned against the wall at his back.

'Take care . . . or I shall do it in your mouth,' he sighed.

In the delirium of his pleasure he forgot to speak English and Darlene was herself too far gone to comprehend the French. But she knew what was heralded by a leaping *zimbriq* and she stood up quickly and tried to feed it into her wet *kuft*. He bent his knees to help her, but matters were too far advanced and he sprayed his hot excitement over her belly. Completely undeterred, she stood on tip-toe and got his spurting *zimbriq* into her *kuft* and pushed her belly at him to help it slide in.

'Oh, that feels fantastic,' she gasped. 'You're so big that you fill me full. . . .'

Her loins heaved rhythmically to slide him in and out of her and though by then Marcel's passion had discharged itself, he bumped his belly back at hers, until with a long gurgling cry she reached her crucial moments and shook against him in frenzy. When she regained as much coherency as her condition of intoxication allowed, she wanted him to stay with her, but he said he must return to the box and led her back to the ball-room, where she wandered away in search of another man.

Marcel thought it sensible to give himself half an hour to recover before inviting Lisette to dance and then step outside with him. Before the time was up, Lucreza swept into the box to exchange greetings with the Ambassador and Jacqueline. She had pushed her mask up, so that she could be recognised, and she was devastatingly desirable, Marcel considered, in a long and backless balloon of shiny black satin. The Ambassador was of the same mind, for he asked her to dance. When they returned, Lucreza sat between him

and Lisette and accepted a glass of champagne, and Marcel believed he detected a faint pink blush on Lisette's neck, her cat-mask concealing her pretty face.

After an inaudible conversation, the two women departed for the powder-room together. With great though secret amusement, Marcel noted the time on his wristwatch. Twenty minutes passed before they came back, Lucreza all smiles and charm and Lisette decidedly flushed. He asked Lucreza for the pleasure of a dance and they half-orbited the floor once before she tugged at his sleeve and led him through an inconspicuous side door and along an empty passage.

'Where are we going?' Marcel enquired. His question was answered when Lucreza opened another door and switched on the light, to reveal a small office. There was a key in the lock inside, and Marcel turned it before taking her in his arms. She had lowered her leopard-mask when they left the box and he pushed it up her forehead again, and raised his own, so that he could kiss her. 'We mustn't be long,' she murmured, 'Salvador will be wondering where I am by now.' She already had his trousers undone and her hand inside to feel his *zimbriq*, which was wet and sticky, limp and small.

'Ah, you've had Lisette!' she said with a laugh.

'And so have you, *cherie,'* Marcel replied suavely, seeing no point in correcting her.

'No milk-skinned foreign girl is going to defeat me,' said Lucreza, her warm tongue touching his lips.

She massaged him skilfully to make him hard again. Not much was necessary to achieve her aim; he was aroused by her warm body pressed against him, and by her delicately erotic perfume, and by the feel of her bare back under his hands. Slowly he traced down her long and sinuous spine, and then felt inside her frock, to find the enchanting little hollow where the smooth cheeks flared out roundly. And all the time her fingers were flickered lightly over the sensitive head of his *zimbriq*, making it rise to its full height and strength.

He walked her carefully backwards until she was against

the small desk so that she could lean on it and raise her long balloon for him to put his hand up between her legs. She gave him a charming little smile when he touched the silk of her knickers and moved her feet apart to let him feel her. His hand found its way into her flimsy underwear and stroked the warm lips between her thighs.

'You are wet!' Marcel gasped. 'This is from Lisette!'

'A quarter of an hour ago her fingers were where yours are – now,' Lucreza murmured, rubbing her *kuft* against his hand.

'But she had nothing else to put inside you,' he answered.

He pulled her knickers down her thighs, in preparation for getting into her. Down her silk-clad legs they slid, down below her knees, and he knelt to pull them over her shoes and off. He was at the right height then to lean forward and kiss her belly and caress the smooth-skinned cheeks of her bottom.

'I want you now,' she said urgently.

Marcel stood up, his stiff *zimbriq* in his hand, to guide it into her, and pressed his belly close to hers.

'Not standing up,' she said, 'Lisette and I played together like that. I want to ride you our way, my little mule!' She turned him round until they changed positions and he was sitting on the edge of the desk. 'Lie back!' she said quickly, and he let himself fall backwards until he lay on the desk with his legs dangling over the edge and his legs spread. Lucreza hitched up her ballgown and got up on the desk to kneel over his loins, her face an exquisite study in concentration. When she let go of her frock, it lay on his belly in shiny black folds and concealed what she was doing.

A tiny gasp of excitement was forced from Marcel as he felt the wet lips of her *kuft* touch the head of his *zimbriq*, and she smiled down a him and pouted her mouth to blow kisses at him. 'Oh Lucreza . . .' he sighed, on the very verge of ecstasy as he felt himself driven deep into her belly by her sudden descent on him. This warm wetness that held him was the excitement Lisette's fingers had caused; it was almost as if Lisette's hand was clasping him and sliding up

and down in a smooth motion that was driving him insane with delight.

But it was Lucreza's *kuft* that held him in its light and yet inescapable embrace of love, though her frock concealed it from him. Light-headed with sensation, he felt for a moment that both women were pleasuring him at the same time and he felt his critical moment hurtling towards him fast and hard and he knew that when it hit him he would be destroyed. His frantic arousal communicated itself to Lucreza and she gasped 'Now I'm mounted on my little mule! Gallop hard for me, little mule – gallop till you fall down exhausted under me!' and she jolted up an down across his loins with unrestrained violence.

The vigour of her movements threw her mask forward from her lustrous black hair to slide down and cover her face. Staring up at her in the intensity of his pleasure, Marcel dreamed that he was being devoured by a beautiful snarling leopard. 'Yes, yes, yes!' he gasped, and bucked upwards sharply and loosed his hot load into her. Lucreza cried out and savaged him even more fiercely, until the spasms of her own climax gripped her.

When they were tranquil again, they sat side by side on the edge of the desk and smiled at each other in satisfaction.

'Phone me tomorrow – but not before midday,' Lucreza said. 'I must run – Salvador will be angry if I am away too long.'

'There is good news you can carry to him,' said Marcel. 'I think he will be very pleased. Tell him that de Murville has left the country and will not be back.'

'But the arrangement they had about commission?' she asked, a puzzled frown on her face. 'What of that?'

'The Minister may keep what he was given – no one will ever ask for its return. And if he makes it known to the Americans and others that a contract is available to supply buses, they will compete against each other to offer the best commission.'

'Oh!' she exclaimed, her dark eyes shining as she grasped the implications. 'Two commissions for one contract! You

are clever, Marcel – Salvador will be very grateful to you. And I absolutely adore you!'

Marcel put his arms round her and kissed her tenderly.

'And I adore you, Lucreza,' he said softly and with great sincerity, 'and more than that, I love you.'

'Yes?' she said, looking at him with tender affection. 'You want to love me again?' She pulled her splendid ballgown up to her waist, took his hand and pushed it down the front of her knickers, to rub his fingers against her wet *kuft*. 'I enjoy being loved by you, *cheri.* ' she said. 'More than by anyone else I know. Lie down and I will ride you.'

This was not the time to attempt an explanation of what he meant, Marcel decided. That must be left for another day, and in the meantime, small blessings were not to be despised. He kissed her and, sitting alongside her on the desk, played with her delicately until her beautiful eyes rolled up in her head and she gasped out her release. Inspired by that, she took off her knickers and mounted him again, and this time he had his hands under her long ballgown to feel the wet lips of her *kuft* while it swallowed his stiffness and drew his desire from him in racking ecstasy.

Sometime after one in the morning he was able to persuade Lisette that a stroll in the open would be refreshing. But once outside the Theatre des Beaux Arts, she made straight for the line of carriages waiting for hire by drunken revellers. They were the open four-wheelers the locals called a *barossa*, and as horses were excessively expensive animals in Santa Sabina, they were drawn by mules. Before Marcel knew what was happening, he and Lisette were sitting in one and the grinning coachman had it on the move.

'The ballroom is so hot and crowded,' said Lisette, 'I had to get out of it for a while.'

One of Marcel's arms slipped around her waist. He saw her red-painted mouth smiling at him below her cat-mask and guessed that she had drunk enough champagne to make her well-disposed.

'You're not a bit like Olivier,' she said, confirming that his guess was accurate. 'If he'd taken me for this ride, his

hand would be up my clothes by now. He took what he wanted, and now he's gone.'

'He will be waiting for you in Paris when you arrive,' said Marcel quickly, to forestall any mood of depression.

'No,' Lisette said simply, 'he's gone for good. He'd have taken me with him if he wanted me.'

'I want you,' said Marcel.

'You've had plenty of chances,' she said, 'but you've never taken me. That's why I said you're not like Olivier.'

Marcel was staggered to realise that he could have had her at any time if he had pressed matters to the ultimate. His head reeled and he put his hand up her short dance-frock and at once she spread her thighs. The cat-mask was turned towards him, but he could not guess what her expression was under it.

'Where to, Monsieur?' the driver asked over his shoulder, careful not to look round at them.

'Anywhere,' Marcel answered.

Lisette was in his arms and his fingers were in her close-fitting knickers far enough to stroke silky curls. The *barossa* rolled at a walking-pace down Esposito Street and into the long Avenue of the Constitution. Crowds drifted singing and laughing along the pavements and loud music played from the open windows the carriage passed. What Marcel and Lisette were doing to each other in the low-sided *barossa* was evident to anyone who looked at them, but they were wearing masks to disguise their identity and it was Festival-time; and every doorway and entrance along the Avenue was occupied by a couple locked in close embrace.

Just as Marcel had been furiously aroused by the thought that the wetness of Lucreza's *kuft* had been due to Lisette's caresses, he was aroused now by the thought that Lisette's wet *kuft* had been caressed only a short time ago by Lucreza. This little bud under his finger-tip – Lucreza's finger-tip had done exactly the same to it and sent Lisette spinning into ecstasy!

'Hold me,' Marcel muttered urgently, and placed her hand on the hard bulge in his trousers.

She unzipped him and slipped her hand inside to take hold

of his trembling *zimbriq*. He sighed in pleasure at her touch and again when she pulled it out of his trousers and slid sideways on the seat until she could put her cheek against his bare belly and kiss him, sending a jolts of sensation through him. The back of her head was presented to him, her silvery-blonde hair gleaming in the light of the street lamps. Marcel stroked it, the fineness of the strands thrilling to his fingers.

Her sideways manoeuvre had taken her *kuft* of reach, and his hand was held flat between the warm flesh of her thighs. 'Take your knickers off,' he whispered and she sat up, raised her knees and sipped them off. He wanted to see her face when she handed the warm little silk garment to him, as if it were a gift, but as with identity, the mask also concealed emotion. He stuffed her knickers into a trouser pocket and pulled her to him, and up and over, until she sat astride his knees, and his hands were up her frock, fondling her bottom.

She put her arms round his neck and tried to kiss him, but their masks made it difficult. 'Marcel, Marcel, why does nothing go easily with you?' she murmured and pressed her pointed breasts against his shirt-front. Down between them, she held his *zimbriq* flat against her bare belly. Marcel put both arms round her, squeezing her close and moving his loins to rub his jerking *zimbriq* against her flesh, almost as if he meant to spatter his sap on her belly. But since he had learned that there was no need to accept lesser pleasures if he insisted on her submission, he said urgently, 'Lisette – put me inside you!'

'No,' she said,'I want to but I can't' – that dreadful mask makes you look like a devil trying to possess me . . . let's go back to the hotel and make love in your room.'

But at this time of triumph, matters had gone too far with Marcel to contemplate a postponement. 'Turn round,' he gasped, 'turn round and face forward!' Lisette stared at him through the eye-holes of her mask and without losing another moment, she raised her knees to her chin and wriggled her bottom round on his lap, until her back was towards him. His fingers clenched on the soft flesh of her

bottom to lift her up, and she reached back between her thighs to take hold of his *zimbriq* and touch the head to the moist lips of her *kuft*.

'Ah, my God,' he exclaimed in rapture as she sat down slowly across his lap, forcing him up into her. He gripped her tightly by the waist while he jerked beneath her, to slide in and out, his *zimbriq* shaking and throbbing and churning her wet flesh into feverish desire. The coachman, hunched on his seat with his back to them, was evidently a connoisseur of love-making in a *barossa,* for he flicked his whip at the mule to make it break into a trot and the springing bounced Marcel up and down in a rhythm that suited his thrusting very well.

This at last was the moment he had been waiting for ever since he first laid eyes on Lisette – this was the exquisite moment when she surrendered herself to him completely! He was jabbing his consuming desire into her soft and beautiful flesh, sighing continuously at the incredible delight that was his! All his manoeuvres, his stratagems, false starts, thwarted attempts and diversions had led finally to this supreme instant!

His heart was pounding and there was a roaring in his ears. Deep inside his belly his diffused pleasure concentrated itself into a point of concentrated bliss and then exploded into a star-burst of ecstasy. He cried out repeatedly as he gushed his triumph into Lisette and she whimpered and shook against him.

As soon as it was over and his senses returned, he was compelled in all honesty to admit that, nice as it had been, he could repeat the pleasure with any pretty young woman picked up at random in the street. This beautiful Lisette, sitting bare-bottomed astride his thighs with his softening *zimbriq* inside her had given him, if the truth were told, no more than Darlene had behind the statue of King Henry. While he pondered this, the coachman slowed his mule to a walk and asked if Monsieur wished to turn back now. Marcel told him to take them back to the Theatre. He lifted Lisette on to the seat beside him and helped her put her little white knickers on.

The party continued until Jacqueline decreed that it should end and it was after three in the morning before Marcel reached his bed in the Grand Hotel Orient. He had drunk more champagne than he intended, and fell immediately into a deep sleep. He thought he was dreaming when he saw Concepcion Costa standing beside his bed in the half-dark, swaying unsteadily as she slid a sheath-like frock over her head. She half-fell naked on the bed with him, pushed him on his back and squatted over him to grasp his sleeping *zimbriq* and stroke it.

When that failed to make it stand, she lay over him to rub it with her soft breasts until she felt a stir, where upon she licked it hotly to bring it to full stretch. By now Marcel knew this was no dream. Concepcion was truly kneeling over him to spike herself on his *zimbriq*. The dark fur between her open thighs was wet and the lips of her *kuft* were slack – who could say how many times she had been *zeqqed* that day? But she had drunk too much *araq* to complete the act of love, even with the stimulus of his stiffness inside her.

She slid off him unconscious, and Marcel caught her in his arms and laid her beside him. She had aroused his desire and it was reasonable that she should satisfy him, awake or asleep. He lacked the energy to have her on her back and lie on her belly to *zeqq* her, and so he arranged her on her side, with her knees drawn up. With his ready *zimbriq* he probed the slippery folds between her legs and a long steady push took him into her. He put his arms loosely round her to feel her breasts while he thrust lightly back and forth against the bare cheeks of her bottom. Concepcion lay still, totally unconscious of how her body was being used, even at the moment when Marcel gasped and flicked his last few drops into her *kuft*.

He fell asleep before he had time to withdraw from and when he woke up it was broad daylight. He was alone and naked, and he asked himself if it had been a dream after all, *zeqqing* pretty little Concepcion. His wristwatch indicated that it was after two in the afternoon, which meant that Lisette and her mother had departed for good. He lay thinking about Lisette for a while, and decided that the

reward had hardly compensated for the effort of the chase. But experience was always valuable – it was by experience alone that a man recognised his mistakes when he made them for the second or third time.

No more nonsense, he decided. He would shower and have lunch on the hotel terrace and then telephone beautiful Lucreza and arrange to meet her. After all, he was in love with Lucreza!